YOUR LOVE IS BREAKING THE LAW 2

Epic and Harley

CAPRICE J

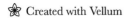 Created with Vellum

Prologue

"*Oh, shit baby this is the best dick ever,*" *I said as I rode Epic's dick. He put one of my breasts in his mouth and I started riding him faster. I started winding my hips tightening my pussy muscles. "Yeah baby do that shit again," he said grabbing my face, giving me a sloppy kiss.*

Epic set up and rolled me on my back and started fucking me rough. "Fuck your pussy is so fucking tight," he said hitting my G-spot. I couldn't take it anymore. I screamed his name and he pulled out of me and started eating my pussy. I didn't think I could cum anymore. He started sucking on my clit and I came in his mouth again. I thought I was going to lose my mind.

Thank God his phone started ringing back to back just as he told me to turn over, so he could hit it from the back. I leaned over and grabbed his phone off the night stand passing it to him.

"Hello," he said out of breath. "What the fuck you just say? When? Fuck alright, I'm on my way," he said jumping up out the bed. I could see on his face whatever happened was not good.

"I have to shower really quick, some shit happened and it's not good," he said walking into the bathroom turning on the shower. I laid there praying everything was going to be okay with whatever problem he had going on and I prayed for Epic's safety.

I started thinking about my dad. It had been over a month now and he was

1

still in the hospital. He was making little progress, but some is better than none. He was supposed to undergo surgery soon, so we were praying for a miracle.

Epic came out of the bathroom and quickly got dressed. I put my tee shirt on and went into my closet to grab some clothes to wear for the day. I was meeting the girls for lunch and I was nervous. I had not seen them in weeks, but we texted most days. I was a little standoffish because I felt like they were keeping something from me, but I was going to find out today.

"Baby, I'm going to get up out of here alright?" Epic said breaking my train of thought. He walked over and kissed my lips. "Be careful okay? I don't know what I will do if anything happens to you." I looked into his eyes.

"You don't have to worry about that. I'm good. A nigga will have to really catch me slipping," he smiled. I looked into those beautiful hazel eyes and yes, I kissed his lips again. "I love you Epic," I confessed.

He just looked at me for a second not saying anything. Then finally he spoke, "I'll call you later okay?" He kissed me again and left my room. I felt so damn stupid! I meant what I said even though he didn't express his love for me. I shouldn't have been disappointed because I know he has a hard time expressing himself.

Later that day

I pulled up to the Relish Restaurant and turned my car off. I was dreading this lunch with the girls. I was already feeling sick and I was nervous about how this was going to end. I was still curious as to why Nena showed up at the hospital that night with Quan. I had my suspicions, but I needed answers. Quan and I only saw each other in passing. We took turns looking after my parents. My mom was so out of it some days, we were afraid something would happen to her.

I grabbed my wallet and cell phone and got out the car. When I walked into the restaurant I spotted the girls and headed over to the table. "Hey ladies," I said taking my seat. They both gave me warm smiles and asked how I was holding up. I told them I was okay as the waitress came over to take our drink orders.

"How are things going with you and Epic?" Nena smiled. Her ass was so fake. I wasn't here to be fake. I wanted to get to the reason I agreed to meet up with them. The waitress came back with our drinks and when she walked away I asked, "So, Nena, how long have you been fucking my brother?" looking at her.

Sundae's eyes almost popped out of her head. "Harley calm down Sis, let

Nena explain," she suggested. I instantly got mad. I could tell by Sundae's reaction that she knew so I gave her a dirty look.

"It just happened Harley. Trust me neither one of us were expecting it to happen," she admitted. I cut her off as she talked, "So, the baby you're crying belongs to my brother? I asked. She shook her head yes.

Nena was foul and if she wasn't pregnant I would have jumped over this table and beat her ass. "That's just nasty Nena! Quan is like a brother to you and you're sneaking around having sex with him. Like what the hell?" I put my hands up in defeat.

She put her hand up to stop me, "First of all Harley, let's get some shit straight. Quan is not like a brother to me okay? That's Sundae," she said looking at Sundae then back at me. "Yawl have always been closer than the two of us and that's cool, it never really bothered me. I visited your house in Houston maybe three times. I never got invited on vacations and that's fine too, so I didn't grow up with Quan thinking he was my family.

"So, what? It's still nasty no matter how you look at it so miss me with what you're talking about. You know what? You're not going to ruin my brother's life trapping him with a baby. We all know you make bad choices in men and now that you found one that has money and a career suddenly you're pregnant."

"Harley calm down, they're not even together like that. Damn you're way out of line right now!" Sundae was trying to defuse the situation, but she was making me madder. I looked over at Nena and said, "Damn really Nena? You're out here giving up free pussy?" I shook my head, leaned back in my chair and folded my arms.

Nena looked hurt. She got up to leave but Sundae grabbed her arm. "Oh little Ms. Perfect Harley, your ass is no better than anybody, last time I checked." Nena squinted her eyes pointing to her head like she was thinking about something, "you couldn't keep a man either. Not too long ago you were running around sleeping with someone else's man," she said looking at me like she wanted to step in the ring.

"Okay, that's enough. This is not that serious," Sundae said

"Oh, shut the fuck up Sundae, you can't even stop your nigga from fucking other bitches and the messed-up part about it is Eric basically broke up with you and he is the one that cheated. If he wouldn't have left you, you would still be sitting there crying every night while he slangs dick all around the city. The fucked-up part is I know in the back of your mind you're contemplating taking his no-good ass back. Both of you are pathetic and insecure."

Sundae jumped out of her seat this time. "Who the hell are you talking to? If we are insecure then what does that make you? Last time I checked your man had a baby on you and you took him back so don't be trying to play me. I'm not pregnant, I'll jump over this table and knock your ass out!" she screamed.

The waitress came over and told us we must keep it down or leave. I grabbed my stuff and told them to lose my phone number and I made my way to my car. I got in my car and started crying. I couldn't believe what had just happened. I felt so betrayed.

I called Epic's phone. I had no one else to talk to. I felt alone. "Hey baby you good? How was lunch?" he asked.

I told him that lunch was a disaster and that Nena was pregnant by Quan and nobody told me. She was damn near ready to pop and held her secret from me for so long.

"I'm not surprised, I figured something was going on with them that night at Eric's party. I saw them arguing but I didn't know what it was about. I don't see what the problem is Harley. Nena is your best friend, why is it a problem if she is messing around with Quan? You do know he is a grown man. Stop acting like he is a kid."

I took the phone from my ear and looked at it in disbelief like he could see me. I couldn't believe he was defending her. I decided to change the subject. I didn't ask for his advice anyway.

"So how is your cousin?" I asked

"I'll tell you about that when I see you. I was actually about to call you, I have some business to handle so I might be gone for about three days. I'll try to call you but just know you can call or text me at any time. I'll make sure I answer okay?" he told me.

I was a little sad because with Epic here it was easier for me to deal with what was going on with my dad. We had been together every day since he came to my house. He would handle his business like usual, but he made sure to sleep next to me at night.

I told him I understood and that I would check in with him and we hung up. I drove down the highway with no destination in mind. I didn't want to go to the hospital because I just wanted a break from everything.

I decided to go to the mall, so I headed to Philadelphia Mills which wasn't *too far from my house. I walked around the mall for about an hour picking up a few things. I felt my phone vibrate so I looked to see a text message from Epic.*

Epic: Hey baby what are you doing at the hospital?

Me: Hey boo, no Philadelphia Mills. Heading home in a second not feeling too well.

Epic: Text me when you get home. Go take a nap let me know how you're feeling when you wake up alright?

I sent him the kissing emoji and put my phone in my bag. I was still a little tight that I told him I loved him and he didn't say it back. But just because I felt that way about him doesn't mean he was there yet. That didn't stop me from feeling stupid.

When I got outside it was getting dark and I was tired. I put my bags in the trunk and closed it. I walked to the driver's side door and just as I was about grab the handle someone grabbed me from behind putting their arm around my neck. I felt a gun pushing up against my side. "Scream and I will kill you right now. Did you think I was going to let you walk out of my life Harley?"

I couldn't believe Jay was here holding a damn gun on me. I guess I underestimated him and now I was wishing I had taken Epic up on his offer to kill him.

Chapter One "Epic"

"Keshia, don't worry. We going to kill that nigga," I said grabbing Rock's wife's hand as she set across from me at the kitchen island. I was fucked up in the head right now. I'm feeling like Rock getting killed was on me.

Instead of killing that nigga when shit got out of control I gave Jamal the option to go to rehab or try to kick his habit on his own. What the fuck was I thinking?

Rock wanted him dead but because I'm a loyal nigga, I wanted to give him a chance to get clean and get back in the game without having to be around the product.

My dad always told me that loyalty will sometimes be your downfall and he couldn't be more right. Rock was my blood and even though I'm not the one who pulled the trigger his blood is on me.

My dad had been calling my phone since yesterday afternoon but that wasn't anything unusual. Sometimes if he couldn't get Rock he would reach out to me if it was about business.

I've been forwarding him to voicemail but now my phone was dead, so I know he knew something was wrong. I don't know how the hell I'm going to tell him his first cousin is dead because I didn't kill Jamal.

Keshia gave me a weak smile and excused herself to go clean up her face. This had been her routine since we showed up last night to tell her we found Rock at the house in King of Prussia shot and killed.

I was fucked up when she fell in my arms screaming at the top of her lungs. They had been together since I was a little shorty.

Keshia was a ride or die chick. She held Rock down, even moving weight when he needed her to. She even took a bullet for him. When he first got in the game, she had gotten shot by some young niggas that were trying to rob him.

They only had two kids together, both were under the age of eight. Rock had a total of nine children.

When bitches came knocking about a love child they shared with him Keshia stayed with him accepting all his kids. She would let all his baby mommas know that she was the queen, and no one was taking her off her throne.

"Man, this shit is like a dream," Eric said as he poured another cup of coffee. It had been over twenty-four hours since we'd had any sleep. We were running off fumes, but it was all good. I just wanted to find Jamal and make this nigga suffer. He was going to pay for this shit.

I started thinking about when Rock's body guard called me yesterday while I was with Harley. He told me to come by the house, that Rock had been shot I couldn't believe it.

When I got there, I wasn't expecting to see big homie laid out with a bullet in his back and head. When I saw Mouse laying across the room dead I knew Jamal had done this shit.

Mouse was a smart little nigga from the hood that wasn't about this life so how Mal convinced him to roll with him on this was beyond me.

Rock's bodyguard claimed Rock gave him the night off because he was cool and wasn't going anywhere. He said he was going to layup with the shorty that he brought home, but I didn't give a fuck. The shit sounded fishy to me, so I killed that nigga.

I had the cleanup crew come and throw his ass in the water with the fishes just like I did Mouse and Rock's little bitch.

"Yeah, I can't believe this shit, but we have to get ready to get going. Keshia looks like she will be okay for a little bit. I want her to get some rest. Her mom should be here any minute, so we can get the fuck out of here and see if we can find this nigga," I said checking my watch.

Ten minutes later she came back in the kitchen. "Guys you've been here all night. My mom and sister just texted me they are about twenty minutes away. I'll be fine until they get here. I'm going to shower, they should be here by the time I get out the bathroom. Go home and get some rest. Jamal will get handled, I know you'll make this right." She looked between Eric and me.

"Alright Keshia if you're sure you'll be cool, we are going to get out your way," I said getting up and giving her a hug.

She gave us both hugs and thanked us for staying. I told her I'd be by later to check on her and give her an update. I was about to start killing every-fucking-body that shared a last name with Jamal. I was going to start with his hoe ass mom. That bitch had to go. I needed to send a message to this nigga that I'm not playing.

I got in Eric's car and put my head back against the headrest as we drove off heading back to Philly. My head was all fucked up. "Yo, where is your charger? I need to charge my phone. I just realized I haven't heard from Harley since yesterday." I looked around for his car charger.

"Damn it's in the other car. I'm at thirty-five percent, just use my phone for now," he said handing it to me. As soon as I took the phone it rang displaying Sundae's name on the screen. "Oh shit, Sundae is calling," I looked over at him smiling. He snatched the phone and hit the talk button. I could see how anxious he was that she was calling. I shook my head and laughed.

"Hello, you good baby?" he said sounding all happy and shit.

"Are you with Epic by any chance?" she said ignoring the fact that he asked if she was okay.

"Yeah, why are you looking for Epic, where is EJ?" he asked

"Eric, EJ is fine. It's Harley. It's almost four in the afternoon and her mom has not heard from her since yesterday. Quan asked me to come check on her and when I got here the house was empty. It don't even look like she slept here."

I could hear the worry in her voice. I felt a lump form in my throat when she said Harley never made it home. I snatched the phone from Eric.

"Sundae, what you mean it looks like she was never there? You didn't talk to her last night after yawl had lunch?"

She told me that they had a huge fight and Harley had stormed out. I had forgotten she told me how she blew up after Nena told her she was having a baby with Quan.

I told Sundae to stay at the house and that we were on our way. We weren't that far out of the city at this point and Eric had started driving fast as hell when Sundae said Harley was missing. I said a silent prayer as he sped down the highway.

Harley and I were finally on the right track. If something happens to her, I'm not sure what the hell I would do. *The devil is working overtime today,* I thought.

When we pulled up to Harley's house Sundae was standing on the porch pacing back and forth with her cellphone in her hand. I could see she had been crying. Eric and I walked up on the porch and Eric went over to give her a hug then we walked in the house.

I grilled Sundae for about an hour about where she could be. We called all the hospitals we could think of, shit even the mortuary, but they didn't have anyone that fit her description.

Harley didn't go many places; our circle was small as hell. I tried to track her phone but didn't have any luck. I didn't want to think that Jamal had gotten to her and to my knowledge he didn't even know she was my girl, but I wasn't putting anything past anyone at this point.

"The last time I talked to her she said she was going to Philadelphia Mills. Let's head over there," I said jumping up. We got in Eric's car and headed to the mall, I was praying my baby was okay. With so much shit going on last night at Rock's, I forgot to call and check on her. Now I was feeling like shit.

When we got to the mall we circled the huge ass parking lot a few times. Philadelphia Mills was big as shit so looking for her car was going to be like looking for a needle in the haystack.

"Right there, is that it?" Sundae screamed. I was jumping out the car before Eric could stop with Sundae on my heels.

Sundae immediately started crying when we got close to the car because it was obvious this was Harley's car by her license plate that she had customized a few weeks ago.

I went to the driver's side and pulled the handle, the door opened. Eric opened the trunk. "It's shopping bags back here!" he yelled. Sundae sat on the passenger side shaking her leg, she was about to lose it.

We stood there trying to figure out what was going on. I was so fucking mad. I called one of my drivers to come and tow her car to her parent's crib. We sat in Eric's car while we waited for the tow truck. He rubbed Sundae's back while she cried in silence.

"It has to be that nigga Jay that has her. I'm thinking this bitch ass nigga came here to make good on his threats," I said looking out the window praying so hard that she was safe. I wasn't one hundred percent sure it was him, but it had to be.

This nigga must have been following her for a few weeks now waiting for the right time to approach her because ever since her dad has been in the hospital she has been with me. Yesterday was the first day she was alone.

"It has to be him. Harley hasn't been here that long for anyone to have beef with her," Sundae said breaking my train of thought.

She burst out crying. I had to get out the car and clear my head for a minute. I love Sundae and I know Harley is more like a sister to her, but I needed time to think. I didn't know this nigga. He wasn't from here so getting at him was going to be a little harder than normal. I needed a phone number or something to try and track his location. I didn't even have that. I was working with absolutely nothing. I heard Sundae calling my name, so I came back over to the car.

"Quan is on the phone," she said, passing me the phone through the window. I took it and walked away from Sundae's crying ass.

I told Quan I was going to come to him, so we could talk. He said he had just gotten in from the hospital and his mom wanted to know where Harley was. I didn't like talking on the phone, so I agreed to come to his house. He gave me the address and we hung up. I called my tow truck driver telling him where the car was, and her license plate information and we left.

We dropped Sundae off at her car, so she could go pick little man up from daycare. I heard Eric tell her he was going to come past the house after we figured some shit out.

I thought about my baby as we drove to her brother's house and how I was going to kill this nigga when we find him.

Chapter Two "Quan"

"*D*o you want me to make you anything to eat Quan? I know you haven't eaten all day baby," Ebony said coming out of my bedroom. She had been really supportive ever since this shit happened with my dad and I appreciated her for it.

It was crazy, but Nena had been supportive also. There was no competition because Nena and I had come to an agreement that we were just going to co-parent our baby girl and nothing more.

We said that shit, but I was still fucking her every chance I got. It was crazy. "No, baby I'm good. I'm waiting for Epic to come by. I don't know what the fuck is going on. I haven't heard from Harley, this shit is not making any sense," I said running my hand over my face.

Soon after Epic texted me and said he was at the door, I got up to let him in. I dapped him and Eric up and we went and sat on the couch. Ebony brought out some water and beer and went into the room.

"What's good yawl? Something happen to Harley?" I saw the stress on Epic's face.

"I'm going to keep it one hundred with you, I don't know where she is. I talked to her yesterday after she left Sundae and Nena. She said she was going to the mall, but I haven't talked to her since some shit jumped off with my peoples. I didn't know she was missing until Sundae called saying you sent her to the house. We found her car at Philadelphia Mills but no trace of her."

I set there in disbelief. Epic's mouth was moving but I don't know what this nigga was saying. The only thing I heard was *missing.* This shit couldn't be happening right now.

"Come on, please don't be telling me no shit like this," I looked back and forth between them.

"You have any information about her ex Jay? He has to be the one behind this. The nigga been calling her and sending her threatening text messages. She told me that when we started fucking with each other," Epic asked.

I was mad now, Harley had never told me Jay was fucking with her. I didn't know much about him except he was a clown ass nigga that thought he was tough. I never liked his ass and the few times he came to the city after we left Houston he didn't really come around because he had beef with my dad. Everything was making sense now.

"I told Harley I was going to take care of him, but she asked me not to. She said he was just fucking with her because she moved back home. Damn I wish I would have just pressed her for some information and got at this nigga. She kept getting defensive when I asked her about him, so I left it alone."

"Don't blame yourself for this shit. I know you got love for my sister. She was telling the truth when she said Jay is a bitch, so she wouldn't have seen this coming."

"I'm going to call some of my homies in Houston and see if they can get me any info on this nigga and we will go from there," I told him.

"Yeah get something. I just need anything, and we can get our peoples on it. I'll check the phone records and get his number and then have my homie trace his cellphone. Fuck I just hope where ever he got her that she's safe," Epic got up and started pacing the floor.

"Come on E don't think like that. Harley is good. We're going to get her back and kill that nigga," Eric said getting up putting his hand on his shoulder.

We sat and talked for a little while. I gave them the status on my dad which wasn't much to give, he was still touch and go. I was just praying he made it through. I can't imagine life without him. My mom was trying her best to hold it together.

I let them know that we had to get on this shit fast and find my sister. My mom will go crazy if something happens to Harley and I wasn't trying to bury any of my family.

"Alright we are going to get out of here. Call me as soon as you have any info on this nigga and we go from there. Call me if you need anything alright?" Epic said as we shook hands.

I walked them to the door and told Epic I would hit him up as soon as I heard something. I wanted to get in my car and go find my sister, but I didn't know where to start. I was trying not to panic, I was hoping this nigga wasn't doing anything to hurt her.

As I stood by the door leaning on the wall with my eyes closed I could feel my heart rate going up. Ebony walked up wrapping her arms around my waist hugging me. I opened my eyes and put my arms around her neck.

"Harley will be okay and your dad too," she said wiping the lone tear that fell down my face.

"I feel like a bitch," I chuckled.

"Stop. You're human that's all. Your family is going through a lot, but everything will work out," she smiled up at me. I was about to say something, but the ringing of my phone interrupted me. I looked down and saw Nena calling, I told her I would call her after I talked to Epic about Harley.

Ebony sucked her teeth and let me go. She stood in front of me mad as hell. "Quan you need to tell me something. why does she always call? I know your sister said she is like a sister to you but come on, I'm not stupid," she said looking at me, waiting for an explanation.

I rejected Nena's call and put my phone back in my pocket. I didn't feel like this shit right now, but I know I had to tell Ebony I was going to be a father. I had been meaning to tell her but between working, getting the new shop in order and making sure Nena was good I had forgotten.

I looked over at her. It wasn't no easy way to tell her what was really going on and I wasn't about to deny my seed.

"Alright, Ebony I'm going to keep it real with you. I was fucking around with her and now she is pregnant, and the baby is mine." I wasn't about to go into detail about our relationship because it was before her and it wasn't any of her business.

Her eyes got wide. She stood there for a minute not saying anything then she walked out the hallway and into my bedroom. I guess she was about to go get all her shit so she could leave, so I went after her. When I got to my room she was throwing her clothes in her overnight bag. "Ma, where are you going?" I asked

"The fact that you have to ask where I'm going is crazy Quan. You just told me you have a kid on the way, and the way you broke it down was like you don't even care about my feelings," she started wiping the tears from her eyes.

"Okay and I made the baby before you and I became official so why the hell are you being all dramatic?" I had so much shit going on in my life right now I didn't need her acting like I cheated on her. If she wanted to leave I was ready to walk her ass to the door she could either accept my seed or keep it moving.

Ebony sat on the bed and looked at me. "I hear what you are saying and all but that means you were sleeping with her when you were sleeping with me. You and I have been dealing with each other for a while. When is she due to have the baby?" she asked.

"A little over two months and like I said, we were not in a relationship Ebony so none of that matters," I said

"Now it makes sense, why she was asking so many questions at the party that night and why she was looking at me like she had a problem. Yup it all makes sense," she was talking more to herself then she was talking to me. "Are you still fucking her Quan?"

I wasn't about to tell her the truth. I hated when women asked this question like I really was going to tell on myself. "No, I'm not fucking her. That's been dead for a long time. We are sharing a child, that's it. The only thing that matters is my daughter, I know I should have told you sooner, but I got a lot of shit going on right now," I explained.

She sat there for a few minutes then grabbed her bag. "I'm going to go home tonight, I'll call you tomorrow," she walked past me, and I followed her to the door.

I wasn't about to sit here and beg her to stay. My daughter was coming whether she liked it or not. I stood on my top step and waited until she was in her car safe. Once she drove off I went back in and grabbed my phone, so I could call some of the homies in Houston to find out what I could about this nigga Jay.

———

"*D*idn't I tell you I didn't want anything to eat Quan?" Nena whined rolling her eyes. "I'm not trying to hear that shit. When I called earlier you said you hadn't eaten and that was three hours ago. Now eat this shit and stop trying to starve my daughter man," I said moving Nena's notepad and eye glasses from in front of her computer.

I loved the fact that she was a hard worker, that was something we both had in common. Ever since she landed that contract for one of the Philadelphia Eagles she has been going hard working extra hours and sometimes forgetting to get in her three meals a day.

"You know how sexy you look when you're on your grind," I kissed her lips as she picked up a piece of asparagus and bit it with a weak smile.

I had just left from meeting up with Epic. I was fucked up because there was still no word on Harley. I had the homies back in Houston getting information on Jay. Epic and I didn't want to take a chance going to Houston and he not be there. I had a feeling this nigga had my sister somewhere in the city tucked away.

I had been up all-night thinking about her, hoping she's safe. My mom called this morning asking if I talked to her, so I know she is getting worried.

I was planning on taking my mom to get something to eat when

I got to the hospital and telling her about Harley. I didn't want to worry her, but I know if I don't keep it real with her she is going to beat my ass when the truth comes out.

I decided to come check on Nena on my way to the hospital. I hadn't planned on coming by today, because when I talked to her earlier she said she was working on something that had to get done today,when I called back hours later she still hadn't eaten, talking about she ate yogurt.

Nena had me fucked up if she thought she was going to starve my baby. I made a U turn to get her some food and to make sure she was okay. I'm not going to lie, I did want to see her pretty face. She was even more beautiful carrying my baby.

"Have you talked to Harley yet? She was pissed when she left the restaurant yesterday. I can't believe the shit she said to me. I'm not going to lie Quan she hurt my damn feelings," she said shaking her head, taking a bite of her sandwich.

Nena didn't know Harley was missing. When she asked if I talked to her yesterday I told her no, she figured Harley was mad at me also and I was going to keep it that way for now.

I told Sundae not to tell her. I want her to stay stress free for the baby. It was bad enough that she was working crazy hours which I'm going to make sure to talk to the doctor about. I want her doctor to convince her to sit her ass down and chill.

"Don't worry about it, she will come around she has no choice. Let me worry about Harley okay, you worry about keeping my baby fed? I swear Nena, if my baby comes out all skinny and shit we are going to have a problem," I said biting her cheek.

"Ouch! Stop Quan," she moved my face and slapped me upside my head. I laughed and kissed her cheek. "I'm going to head over to the hospital to check on my mom, then I have a few clients later in the day. I'll call and check on you." I leaned down and kissed her belly before kissing her lips. I grabbed my cell phone off her computer desk and left.

When I got to the hospital my mom was sitting in the chair next to my dad's bed with her feet up reading him the Daily News off her phone. When she saw me, she forced a smile as I went over to her and we embraced. She held on tight and it fucked me up on the inside. My dad had to pull through because my mom was helpless without him.

"How are you today pretty lady?" I said walking to the chair on the opposite side of his bed where my mom sat. I kissed him on the forehead and said a silent prayer that he would pull through. "I'll be better if my daughter calls me," she said looking stressed.

"She said she was going to call you when she gets out of class later. She overslept this morning," I hated to lie to my mom, but I wasn't about to tell her Harley was missing.

I convinced her to walk down to the cafeteria with me to get some food. I tried to get her to leave the hospital to get some real food, but she refused to be that far away from my dad.

The ride down to the cafeteria was silent. I held her hand as we walked through the hallway telling her everything was going to be okay.

My mom and I got our food and took a seat at one of the tables. I watched as she picked at her sandwich and barely touched her soup. I was nervous about what I was about to say to her, but it was now or never. I had been putting it off because of my dad's condition but Nena was having the baby soon.

"Baby thank you for the food, but I need to get back upstairs. I don't feel comfortable being down here so far away from your father," she said getting up to throw her food in the trash. I didn't argue with her, I just got up and we headed back to the room.

When we got upstairs my mom went over to the bed to check on him. I took a seat and got comfortable, so I can keep her company for a while.

My mind shifted to Harley. Epic had his crew looking everywhere for her, he even had his connects at the airport on the lookout just in case Jay tried booking a flight out of here. I was praying hard that my sister was okay.

"Mom I have to talk to you about something," I was nervous.

She stopped reading her Kindle and looked at me. "Yeah, baby what's wrong?"

Before I could get the first sentence out, the sound of my father's machine going off scared us both as we jumped out of our seats moving closer to the bed. The nurses and the doctor came running in. I heard the doctor call a code, but I didn't know what the hell he was talking about. I don't think I've ever been this scared in my life.

"I need you guys to step out the room!" the nurse said leading us out to the hallway. My mom was crying once we were out the room and when the door closed she fell to the floor. I pulled her up and held her while she cried. I whispered in her ear telling her that my dad was going to pull through, but I wasn't sure at this point.

Suddenly the door opened, and the doctor looked at us with a sad expression on his face, I held my breath hoping this nigga wasn't about to say what I thought he was about to say.

I looked past him and at my dad. My heart got heavy. I put my head down and looked at the ground. My mom didn't give the doctor a chance to say anything she ran past him and ran over to my father.

I walked in the room. As soon as I stepped in my mom let out a gut-wrenching scream. Sliding down the wall, I let the tears fall from my eyes. My dad was gone.

Chapter Three "Sundae"

I was giving EJ a bath when I heard the front door shut. I heard Eric's feet walk across the hard wood floor as he went into the kitchen. Soon after, he came upstairs and stood in the doorway of EJ's bathroom.

"Daddy!" EJ screamed. I smiled, he loved his daddy and that just made me madder that Eric had fucked up our family by sleeping with these hoes.

Eric came over to the bathtub and kissed EJ on his head. "If you want to take a break I'll get him ready for bed," he said. I didn't respond. I just got up and left the bathroom.

I went into EJ's room to get his clothes out for bed. I was hoping Eric had an update on Harley. I was sick to my stomach that my girl went missing and I know Jay was behind this. I'm just praying he is not using her as a punching bag.

Thirty minutes later, Eric came downstairs and took a seat next to me as I laid on the couch watching the nightly news. He grabbed my feet and put them on his lap and started massaging them. His ass wasn't slick, he knew I loved when he massaged my feet, but the shit wasn't going to work this time.

"What are you doing Eric?" I said taking my feet out of his lap and sitting up.

"I'm not doing anything. I'm trying to help you relax. I know you're stressing about Harley," he said.

I sucked my teeth and rolled my eyes. He was full of shit. "Yeah, I am but I'll get through this on my own. I don't need you here all in my personal space. Remember you moved out, so I'm going to need you to leave now." I got up off the couch and stood over him with my hands folded. I meant what I said to him. When we had that big blow-up, I was done.

"I hear what you're saying but I ain't going no damn where. Jamal killed Rock and he is coming for us. Until we kill that nigga I need to be here with you and EJ," he said taking off his shoes, getting really comfortable.

I was sorry to hear about Rock. I know Epic had to be going through it right now along with trying to find Harley. I made a mental note to call and check on him before the night was over.

"Okay, well I ain't do shit to Jamal so what the fuck would he be coming after me for?" I put my hands up in defeat. "What you need to do if you think we need protection, is get some of your hitters to sit outside the house Eric. Get out!" I stomped my feet while he looked at me smiling, undressing me with his eyes. I ignored the tingling sensation between my legs. I was going to remain strong.

"Fuck all that, you're my family and I want to protect you so sit your ass down and finish watching TV," he said pulling his shirt over his head. I rolled my eyes and sat down. I didn't have the energy to fight with him tonight. I was tired as hell and I had to go to the shop in the morning to check inventory.

I zoned out and thought about the fight Nena and I had with Harley. I was still fucked up about it and the shit she said to me. I looked over at Eric and he had his eyes closed. I could hear the light snore from where I sat. He was tired.

I wanted so badly to take him back. I was missing him like crazy, but Harley was right. Eric was a dog and if I take him back it will only be a matter of time before he fucks me over again.

I shared my blanket with him as I got comfortable as the Jimmy

Kimmel show started. I felt my eyes getting tired then my phone rang.

"Hey boo, what's up?" I said to Nena. She wasn't aware that Harley was missing, it was killing me not to tell her that it may be a possibility that Jay has taken Harley, but I was going to respect Quan's wishes for now. He said he don't want Nena to stress because of the baby.

Just thinking about Quan and how concerned he is with Nena's well being made me smile. "I have some bad news to tell you," I could hear her sniffing. She sounded sad.

"What's going on?" I asked.

"Mr. Rob just passed away, Quan just called me. I'm headed to the hospital now. I tried calling Harley, but her phone is going to voicemail and Epic is not answering his phone either," she cried.

I was at a loss for words. This had to be a dream. I can't imagine life without Mr. Rob, he was one of the most generous men on the planet and now he was gone.

"No, please Nena don't say that!" I cried. Eric jumped up out of his sleep asking me what was wrong. I was hysterical. I couldn't tell him what was going on.

He grabbed the phone from me asking Nena what was going on. She was able to tell him that Harley's dad passed away.

Eric told Nena we were on our way and told her to drive safe and if she couldn't then we would pick her up. I heard him say he would text her when we got to the hospital then he hung up.

I went into the closet and grabbed my sneakers and leather jacket. I searched around for my car keys but couldn't find them.

"Sun baby what are you doing?" Eric said standing in the middle of the floor looking at me like I was crazy.

"I need my keys. I have to go see about Mrs. Savannah," I said looking in the couch for my keys.

"Baby the keys are in your hand," he said walking over to me taking them.

"Let me go wake EJ up, you are not driving to Philly by yourself."

"No, it's late, I don't want him out this late. Eric I'm fine."

"Say what you want but I'm not letting you leave here. It's almost midnight so let me go get EJ. We can drop him off to my mom and head over to the hospital," he said before taking his hand running it down his face.

I could tell he was sad about Mr. Rob. Eric got along great with him, not to mention the love he had for EJ. I walked over to Eric and wrapped my arms around his waist and he hugged me. I closed my eyes and prayed for Mr. Rob's soul, Mrs. Savannah, Quan, and Harley's safe return. This news was going to break my girl.

———

*T*he ride to the hospital seemed like it took forever. When we pulled up I jumped out of the car leaving Eric to find a parking spot. As I rode the elevator up to the fourth floor where Mr. Rob's room was I felt my heart rate speed up. I wish I was dreaming.

When I entered the room, I saw Mrs. Savannah and her four sisters standing near the bed. Mrs. Savannah was rubbing his cheek, he looked so peaceful.

When she looked up and saw me tears started falling from her eyes. I walked over and gave her a hug and together we stood there crying.

Quan walked in along with Eric. They stood off to the side. I walked over and hugged Quan, we stood there holding each other for a minute.

I know Quan is hurting right now, he loved his dad and the fact that Harley is missing is weighing on my little brother's heart.

Quan, Eric and I walked into the waiting room, I could tell Quan was about to lose his mind.

"Any word on Harley man? My mom keeps asking for her and I don't know what the fuck to tell her," he asked Eric.

"Epic has our crew on it, but I'm going to be honest Quan, we don't have much to go on. We tracked that phone that he used to text and call Harley but came up empty. I think he got rid of that phone number. I'm asking you to just sit tight. We will find her. That nigga got everybody on it," Eric tried to reassure Quan of Harley's safe return. I was praying like hell he was right.

Chapter Four "Harley"

he Next Day
"Jay, you can't hold me hostage in this fucking room forever. I need to call my mom, so I can check on my dad. It's been two days. You proved your point, now let me go home," I kicked my feet as I sat on the edge of the bed.

We were in a rundown efficiency somewhere in North Philly. This nigga had the nerve to blindfold me after he forced me into his rental car at gunpoint. I have been sick as a dog since we got here, and I didn't know what the hell was wrong with me.

I was also worried sick about my dad. I was hoping he was okay, I was praying to God that when I did get out of here and see him he will be awake and building his strength to go home.

"You are going home back to Houston. I mean what the hell I said Harley, the only way you're leaving me is in a body bag. You know I love you," he said rubbing my leg. I swiped his hand off my thigh and sucked my teeth.

I felt my stomach do a dance, so I got up and ran to the bathroom. I barely made it before the dinner I ate an hour ago came right back up. I didn't know what the hell was going on with me. I had thrown up a few times since I've been here.

When I walked out the bathroom Jay was sitting on the bed looking at me like he was about to whip my ass. I was praying I'd get out of here soon because between him trying to have sex with me and me getting sick he was tired of my ass.

I was trying not to show any fear, but I was scared out of my mind. This nigga is so unpredictable and I'm just not up for a fight.

I lay in bed at night crying, praying to God that he gets me out of this. The only time I was alone was when he went to get food and most times he did that in the middle of the night when I'm sleep or in the afternoon when everyone was at work.

"Why the fuck you keep throwing up Harley? Every time your ass eat the shit comes back up. You have something you need to tell?" he said looking at me with a hostile stare.

I hadn't even put that much thought into me throwing up, I just thought I had a stomach bug.

"Did you fuck that nigga and let him knock you the fuck up?" he asked standing up getting in my face. I backed up a little because he was making me uncomfortable and I was weak. I didn't have the energy to go toe to toe with him.

"Jay I'm not pregnant alright? It has to be a stomach bug. Maybe you need to take me to the hospital," I suggested.

We stood there staring at each other then he grabbed my neck and pinned me up against the wall. "You think it's a fucking game? So, let me tell you what's about to happen. I'm going to go to the drug store and get your ass a pregnancy test and if the shit comes back positive I'm killing you and that fucking baby!" he mugged me in my head.

I watched as he put his sneakers on and grabbed his leather jacket. "Get the fuck over here and put your hands behind your back," he said gesturing for me to come across the room where he was standing.

Every time he would leave he put handcuffs on my feet and hands. He would also put a sock in my mouth with tape, so I wouldn't scream.

As he picked me up and laid me on the bed I felt the tears

stream down my face. I wanted to kill this nigga for disrespecting me.

"I'll be back in a few minutes, it's a store at the corner," he said walking out and locking the door.

As I laid on my side my mind drifted to Epic and how I was missing him so much right now. I know he must be going crazy wondering where I am.

I closed my eyes and thought about the other day when we were in my bed making love. Just thinking about those hazel eyes made my heart skip a beat and although he didn't express his love for me, I still love him.

The thought of carrying Epic's baby made me so warm inside but I was sure hoping the test will show a negative result. I believe Jay when he says he will kill me and my unborn child if the test comes back positive.

Jay has always wanted me to carry his baby, but I knew that would never happen. I could never see myself tied to him for the rest of my life and carrying his demon child was never an option.

As I drifted off into a peaceful sleep I heard the front door open and Jay walked in. He was wet which confirmed the sounds I was hearing against the window. It sounded like it was pouring down rain outside and as he closed the door I heard thunder.

He walked over to the little kitchen table and threw the test on it. I watched as he took his jacket off and set his gun beside the pregnancy test. I was so nervous.

He untied my hands and feet and took the sock out my mouth. "Sorry baby, I just didn't want you hollering and screaming drawing attention and all." He kissed my cheek and I wiped it.

I swear this nigga has a mental illness. I was mad at myself for never noticing it years ago. I wished I would have looked the other way the night I met him.

"Alright this is the moment of truth, get the fuck up and go pee on this stick," he handed me the test.

"Fuck no Jay! I'm not peeing on nothing! I'm not having his baby okay? Matter fact we have not even had sex yet so stop," I tried handing the test back to him.

"Harley I'm about two seconds from beating your ass. Get up and pee on this fucking stick!" he put the stick in my hand and helped me up from the bed.

I walked into the bathroom and tried to shut the door, but he stopped me. "Hell no, leave that shit open," he said leaning up against the door. I shook my head and sat on the toilet.

After I peed on the stick I walked out and sat on the bed. "Okay, the paper says five minutes," he said as he took a seat in the kitchen area setting the timer on his phone.

I was so scared. *What the fuck am I going to do if this test comes back positive? I think this nigga is going to kill me, so I have to do something. Please God don't let me die! Please get me home safe,* I prayed silently to myself.

I watched Jay stand up and walk into the bathroom, when he came out he stood there looking at me shaking his head.

"You're a dead bitch tonight!" he said rushing over to me, before I could run he punched the shit out of me. I instantly felt my eye swell up as I screamed for him to get off me.

He hit me repeatedly, the only thing I could think of was my unborn baby. "Jay stop! Please stop! The test is wrong!" I yelled trying to block his hits. Clearly, he had blacked out and was trying to make good on his threats.

I took a deep breath and with all my strength I took my thumbs and pushed them into his eyes he screamed and stopped hitting me for a moment. I took my knee and hit him as hard as I could in his nuts.

"Agh, you bitch!" he hollered as he fell back on the bed I got up and ran towards the kitchen. I could barely see because my left eye was swollen shut.

I grabbed the gun, before I could turn around he grabbed my hair I could feel my hair detaching from my scalp.

"Get off me!" I cried. I started moving wildly hoping to get him off me. I was in survival mode, I was fighting for my baby.

I managed to get loose I backed up and pointed the gun at him. "Oh, so you're going to shoot me Harley?" he said

"Get back!" I screamed. When I saw him move a little closer I let off two shots. Jay hit the floor. I jumped up and unlocked the door screaming for help. Of course, no one opened their door. I ran as fast as I could down the steps and out the door.

When I got outside it was raining so hard I looked up and saw the lightening followed by thunder.

I ran down the street screaming for help before I knew it I turned on Girard Avenue. I saw a car coming towards me, so I ran in the street screaming for help. Two guys jumped out the car rushing over to me.

"You okay shorty? Somebody hurt you?" the guy said. His friend took his gun out his holster and looked around.

"My ex-boyfriend tried to kill me! We have to go now!" I screamed trying to pull the guy that was in front of me by the arm.

"You good shorty calm down," I kept screaming trying to pull him, so he picked me up and put me in the car as I cried so hard my throat hurt.

Once the three of us were in the car he pulled into traffic. I heard him tell his friend they were going to take me to the hospital before I passed out.

Chapter Five "Epic"

I drove down Lehigh Ave listening to *Percocet & Stripper Joint* by Future. I was on one. My life was fucked up right now.

Dealing with the fact that Rock was gone was fucking with me. This shit was all my fault. My dad had been calling me, word had gotten back to him that Jamal killed Rock and he wanted to see me, but he had to wait.

Harley was weighing heavy on my heart. I needed to find my baby, I wasn't sure before but just the thought of not seeing her ever again had me all fucked up. I can admit, I love her ass.

I parked my car down the street from Jamal's mom house and got out. I put my hood over my head. It was pouring down raining, but I didn't give a fuck. I was here to send a message. Jamal knows the type of nigga I am. I guess tonight I was going to have to remind him.

I dabbed one of my hitters up as he pointed to the couch, I walked in she was wiping her eyes, but I didn't give a fuck about her tears right now. She looked up and saw me coming in the house. I took a seat in the chair that was in front of her.

"Where the fuck is Jamal?" I said cutting to the chase. She shook her head no.

"Epic I don't know. I haven't talked to him in weeks. What is this all about? Why you have these men in my house with guns?" she cried.

"Don't act fucking stupid Ms. Alice, you know what the fuck this is. Jamal killed my fucking cousin and if you don't tell me where he is, prepare to meet your maker tonight," I told her leaning back in my seat.

Ms. Alice was a cool mom, growing up I loved spending the night over here because she didn't care what we did.

She was the one who taught us how to roll and inhale weed. Shit I even got my first piece of ass in this crib, but right now I didn't give a fuck about any of that. If Jamal wanted to come for blood I was all in.

"Call him," I said taking her cellphone from one of my hitters. She snatched the phone and dialed his phone number. She was shaking, I could tell she was scared.

"Jamal!" she yelled when he said hello, I snatched the phone from her.

"My nigga what's up? You think it's a game?" I said. He was silent for a minute

"Let my mom go nigga!" he said.

I leaned back in the chair. Jamal was a fucking punk and I'm mad I ever ran with his bitch ass. Obviously, he was high. He was slurring his words. I couldn't wait to put him out of his misery.

"Since you want to be a bitch and hide out let's see how you respond to this," I pulled my gun out and took the safety off.

Ms. Alice's eyes got big and she started screaming I pulled the trigger and shot her ass in the head her body fell over and hit the floor.

Jamal started screaming calling me all types of bitches. I was going to torture his ass when I got my hands on him.

"That was for Rock my nigga. I'm warning you Mal, you better run nigga you know how I get down pussy. Now come get me!" I said hanging up.

"Clean this shit up," I said grabbing my phone out my pocket after realizing it was ringing.

"Yo?" I said to my worker Pee Wee. It was late as hell, so I'm wondering what the fuck had happened now.

"Epic, I think we found your girl," he said. I stopped in my tracks. I know I wasn't hearing this nigga right.

"What the fuck you say?" I had to make sure I was hearing him right.

"Yeah me and Drew were riding down Girard Ave and a shorty jumped in front of the car with no shoes on, she was beat the fuck up yelling that her ex-boyfriend was trying to kill her or some shit like that," he slurred.

I could tell this nigga was high, taking forever to explain what happened. As bad as it sounded I was praying this girl was Harley.

"Where is she?" I asked cutting him off.

"We took her to Temple and dropped her off, one of the nurses recognized her. She told me she knew her parent's, so we bounced.

"Good looks!" I said hanging up. I rushed out of the house and sped all the way to the hospital.

When I got to the hospital I ran up to the receptionist desk and gave her Harley's name. She told me which room she was in and gave me a visitor pass.

I don't think I'd ever been as nervous as I was right now riding the elevator to the floor where Harley was. A nigga was happy as shit right now. I was just hoping everything was okay with her.

When I got off the floor and headed to her room I saw Sundae and Quan outside the door sitting in a chair. They both got up when they saw me. I will admit I was a little pissed at their asses for not calling me and telling me she was here.

"Hey Epic, I was going to call you but so much shit has been going on I forgot," Sundae confessed. She must have noticed the look on my face.

"Look E, Harley is doing okay but my dad passed yesterday, and she don't know yet. My mom is in there with her, but she doesn't know how to tell her," Quan said. I hung my head low for a second wiping my hand across my face. Shit couldn't get any worst.

"Before you go in there, he beat her up pretty bad. The doctor said she will recover just fine, but I want you to know her face looks bad," Sundae said. I could tell she had been crying.

The three of us walked in the room. I waved to their mom. She looked like the world had beat her down. Harley had her back to her mom, so I went around the bed to face her, so she could see me.

"Hey baby," I said standing in front of her. Harley looked up and when I saw her face it fucked me up. Her eye was black, her lip was busted, and her cheek was swollen. I could tell she was fighting for her life.

She leaned up off the bed and threw her arms around me and cried her heart out. I stroked her hair letting her know she was safe. I looked at her mom and she put her hands over her face and cried silently.

Once she calmed down, I looked over at Quan and Sundae. I could tell he had the weight of the world on his shoulders. The doctor came in to give us an update on Harley.

"Ms. Smith how are you feeling right now?" he asked Harley

"My mouth still hurts. The medicine is not really helping me, it hurts so bad and so does my eye. Can I have a little more pain medicine?" she asked. I took a seat in the chair next to the bed and rubbed her leg while she spoke.

"Well Harley, I have to watch how much medicine I give you because of the baby you're carrying. We have to be careful with your medicine intake," he said.

I had to make sure I was hearing him right. I know this man didn't say Harley was having my baby. She looked at me with a weak smile. I looked around the room and could tell everyone else knew.

"Are you mad?" she asked me.

I shook my head no. "Hell no I'm not mad shocked yes, but I'm not mad," I said kissing her forehead. I was happy. If any woman was going to carry my baby I wanted it to be Harley, but this only complicated things because I know the news of her father was going to fuck her up.

"We are going to keep you under observation for the next twenty-four hours, once we confirm that you and the baby are doing well you'll be free to go home and get well," he said turning to walk away.

"Oh, and before I go, I want to send my condolences to you and the family Mrs. Smith. Your husband was a great man," the doctor said.

Harley turned around and looked around the room then she looked at her Mom. "Mom what is he talking about? Where is Daddy? I need to see him," she said with tears falling from her eyes.

"Sweetie get some rest. We will talk about Daddy tomorrow," her Mom said looking at me for help.

I grabbed Harley's hand. She turned and looked at me. "Baby look get some sleep. You've been through a lot. Let's talk about your dad tomorrow okay?" I said. She shook her head no.

"Epic baby please take me to see my dad. How was his surgery? Quan how did daddy do with his surgery huh?" she pleaded with him with her eyes to give her an update.

She pulled the cover back to get up. I looked over at Quan. He had his head down to the floor, Sundae was wiping her eyes.

I looked at Mrs. Savannah. She shook her head up and down giving me permission to break the news to her. This was going to be the hardest thing I ever had to do.

"Baby your dad passed away last night," I said to her. She looked up at me in shock then started screaming *no* as she punched me in the chest repeatedly.

I didn't know what to do. The doctor ran in the room calling a code, the nurses came in holding Harley down.

She was screaming at the top of her lungs, kicking and screaming. I looked up and saw Quan holding his mom as she cried. I didn't know what the fuck was going on. The nurse pulled out a big ass needle sticking it in Harley's arm. She instantly stopped fighting and slowly closed her eyes as they laid her on the bed.

"What the fuck you do to my girl? Don't make me shoot this fucking hospital up! You know she pregnant right?" I was about to pop both these bitches and this stupid ass doctor.

"Harley and the baby are fine, we just needed to calm her down. She is early in her pregnancy and stress causes miscarriages. This will just calm her down, when she wakes up she should be much calmer.

I took a seat and just stared at my baby. I didn't know if this nigga was dead but if he wasn't I was going to kill him. I needed Harley to get herself together enough to tell me what the hell happened.

"I'm sorry to put that on you Epic, I just couldn't tell her," Mrs. Savannah said stroking Harley's hair as she slept. "He really hurt my baby, I can't believe this," she said crying.

"I'm going to take care of it, don't worry about Harley. I promise I got her," I gave her an assuring look.

———

I was on my way back to the hospital. I had to run to the mall to get Harley something to wear because she was being discharged today.

As I got closer to the hospital I thought about last night's events. I was happy as shit my workers had found her. I was beginning to think I was never going to see her again. Walking into that hospital and seeing her face all beat up made me want to kill that nigga.

Harley told me this morning that she shot him. She vaguely remembered where she was, so I sent my people to the apartments in that area. They were able to narrow it down and find the location but when they got there they found the apartment empty, blood was on the floor, but the nigga got away. The bullet Harley put in him was enough for her to get away and I was thankful.

I asked her about the baby and how long she knew she was pregnant. She said she didn't know and Jay suspected it getting a test and making her pee on the stick.

She said that's when things got crazy because of the positive result of the test. I cringed thinking about how she said he told her he was going to kill her and our baby. But I was going to take care of this nigga.

I couldn't believe I was going to be a dad. I never thought I would have kids because I couldn't see myself trusting a bitch that much, but Harley changed that side of me in the short time we've been together.

I didn't think it was possible to love any women besides my mom and Nana, but Harley had my heart and the fact that she fought for her life to save our unborn child made me love her even more.

When I got to the hospital Harley was laying on her side looking at the wall. She was in the same spot she was when I left. I could only tell she took a shower because she had on her robe. I was wondering if she even ate the breakfast I got her before I left.

"Epic," she softly said my name. I could hear the hurt in her voice. "I didn't even get a chance to say goodbye," she started crying. I walked over to the bed and sat down pulling her into me, hugging her.

"I know baby, but your dad knows that you love him," I assured her rubbing her back.

"He took that away from me. I just wish I had a chance to say goodbye," she cried harder.

"I know baby, I'm going to make that nigga pay for all this shit, I promise," I told her meaning every word I spoke.

I waited until she got herself together, then I got up and grabbed the bag of clothes taking the sweat suit out, so I could help her dress.

I opened her robe and helped her out of it. I looked at her face, the swelling had gone down a little but her black eye was going to take a few more days to heal before her eye would completely open. I rubbed her stomach before helping her into her shirt.

"Baby I know you're in pain right now because of your dad and trust me I wish he was still here, but you know you're not that far along in this pregnancy. The doctor said this is the most critical time, so if you don't get your depression and stress under control you might lose the baby," I looked at her hoping I was getting through to her. The last thing I wanted was for her to miscarry.

She shook her head up and down like she understood. I grabbed the sweat pants and helped her put them on, grabbing the box of sneakers and taking them out. "Jordan's Epic? Really? Why didn't you just get me slippers?" she cracked a smile.

"I can't have you stepping out the hospital with slippers," I laughed.

Harley shook her head as she took them out the box and put them on her feet.

She stood up and I gave her a hug, telling her it was going to be okay. When we pulled away we stood there staring at each other. Even with her bruises she was still the most beautiful woman I'd ever seen in my life. I got caught slipping this time, but I was never letting anything else happen to her and I put that on my mom.

"Stop staring at me, I know my face is a mess," she put her hair behind her ear and looked away.

"Stop that shit. You're still beautiful alright?" I said picking her chin up, making her look at me.

"I love you," I said meaning every word I spoke. She looked up at me as some tears fell from her eyes.

"You're not just saying that because I got kidnapped? Or because I'm having your baby and my daddy passed, are you?" she asked.

"Fuck no, don't say no shit like that. I can't lie, you being kidnapped made me realize that I do love you. I'm not saying I didn't know before, but I wasn't being real with myself. With this happening it made me be true to myself. I was fucked up not knowing where you were. It made me realize that I don't want to ever lose you and that's on some real shit Ma." I kissed her forehead. She hugged me again.

"I love you too," she said

"I know you do," I smiled pulling away and smacking her on her ass. She laughed.

I went to the door and told the nurse we were ready. She called an escort to bring a wheel chair to walk us out. Harley told them she was okay to walk but the doctor refused to let her leave without it. Their asses just didn't want to catch a case if she fell on this hard ass floor.

The ride home was quite until Harley realized we weren't heading in the direction of my condo. "Where are we going boo?" she asked.

"To my house in Delaware, the one I told you about." I looked over at her. I could tell she was confused.

"I can't Epic, take me home. I need to be with my mom," she said shaking her head from side to side.

"Your mom is fine baby. She is with your aunts right now making arrangements for your dad. I have a car waiting for her when she is done handling business and my driver is going to bring her to you," I said grabbing her hand and kissing it. "I need you to trust me," I told her.

I didn't want to tell her I had to keep her close because I didn't know what Jamal had planned next. I was trying to get at this nigga before he got at us.

"I got some business to handle so I'm going to be gone until tomorrow afternoon. I promise it won't be longer than that. Some of my workers are posted up outside my house for protection," she just shook her head and looked out the window.

"I need to call my mom and Quan."

"I know but can't it wait until we get to the house? I just want you to relax and enjoy the ride. Sundae is coming to the house to keep an eye on you until your Mom gets there, she should be at the house when we pull up." I heard Harley suck her teeth.

"I don't need a babysitter, stop treating me like I need one. I'm fine and did you forget I had a big fight with Sundae and Nena so why would you invite her to look after me?" she rolled her eyes.

"Sundae don't give a fuck about that shit and neither does Nena. Cut that shit out man, she is coming whether you like it or not." I turned the music up letting her know I was done with the conversation.

An hour later we pulled up to my house in Delaware. It was off by itself surrounded by land. I loved the peace I had when I came up here mostly to clear my head. I laughed to myself because I didn't come here often and now it was going to be a place where Harley and I raise our family.

I entered the security code at the gate and it opened. "It's beautiful baby," Harley said looking around at the land. Her smile faded when she spotted Sundae's car parked in the driveway.

I parked my car in the driveway and turned the car off. I went around to the passenger side and opened her door. When she got out the car she said, "I know she don't have a key." She gave me the side eye.

"How else was she supposed to get in to cook lunch for your mean ass? These niggas ain't getting a key," I pointed to my workers. I kissed her check and grabbed her hand, so we could go inside.

When we walked in the smell of fried chicken filled the air. It smelled good as fuck. Sundae came out the kitchen smiling, walking over to Harley hugging her.

"Hey boo, I'm glad you are feeling a little better. I made your favorite, so you can feed my god child in there," she said rubbing Harley's belly while she stood there emotionless.

"Where is the bedroom baby? I have a headache and want to lie down," Harley said turning her head towards me ignoring everything Sundae said.

I gave her a strange look and shook my head, then pointed to the steps leading the way. I told Sundae to give us a minute and we went upstairs.

I was debating if I wanted to take this trip out of town leaving Harley alone. It was now or never, the connect cut me off at the request of my dad. He got word to me that I would continue to be cutoff if I didn't come see him and tell him what happened.

That nigga was tripping. I was going to go see him but on my own time. My main priority is Harley right now. I don't take orders from no nigga, not even my dad now because he wants to play with my money. I will just find another connect.

At first, I didn't know what I was going to do because I needed my dad to stay in business, but my homie Truth reached out to me after word got out about Rock being dead. He called to give his condolences.

He told me if I needed anything to hit him up. When my dad cut me off I called Truth and asked if he could call a meeting between me and his connect, he didn't hesitate to say he would help me out.

Truth and I had been homies for a long time, we used to ball together in the summer league. He was older than me but because I was one of the best players in the city I got to ball with the older players.

When he got the opportunity years ago to make some money in Baltimore he did and now he ran Baltimore and DC. His connect had the best cocaine and heroin in Baltimore. Now that the meeting was setup I had to take this trip.

I shut the door after Harley walked in. She went over to my bed and took her shoes off. "Baby stop being mean to Sundae alright? She is here to help. You know I have to go away on this business trip, trust me I feel bad leaving you with all this going on but like I said this is the only day I can go with my cousin's funeral being this Saturday."

"I know, I'm sorry," she let out a heavy sigh.

"Don't be sorry, just take care of our baby and make up with your friends. They love you and they're worried about you, that's all." I kissed her lips.

I went into the bathroom to get a shower, I had to focus on this meeting. Everything I've ever worked for depended on it.

Chapter Six "Sundae"

*a*s I stirred the cabbage I thought of Harley and how she just ignored me. I can't lie, my feelings were a little hurt when she dismissed me and went upstairs. I wasn't going to cry about it because my girl is going through a lot right now and no matter what type of mood she is in I will always be there for her.

I was still messed up in the head about Mr. Rob. It's so hard to believe that he passed away. I couldn't bring myself to tell EJ that his grandpa was in heaven.

I was starting to get emotional thinking about the other day when EJ asked for both Mr. Rob and Mrs. Savannah. It had been a while since he saw either of them, the last time he was with them was the night Harley brought him to my beauty shop after he spent the day with them.

I was also worried about Quan because he was walking around like nothing happened. That was a sure sign that my boy was in so much pain but trying to console him was something he didn't want.

Nena was trying to be there for him, but it was hard. He just worked all day at the tattoo shop avoiding everyone. I know he was so mad at himself for not being able to protect Harley from Jay, but no one knew Jay was crazy enough to bring his bipolar ass to Philly and kidnap my girl. I swear he was on some Lifetime movie shit.

I heard a knock at the door and turned the stove off before walking to the front door to answer it. I was hoping it was okay for me to. Epic did have security at the gate and niggas posted up all around the house, so I guess it was okay.

When I opened the door I froze, I couldn't believe who was standing before me. I was wondering if this nigga was a stalker.

"Am I at the right house?" he stepped back and looked around making sure he was at the correct address.

"I'm sorry but are you following me?" I said with a smile.

"Nah baby I'm not stalking your pretty ass, I thought this was my homie Epic's house," he said still looking confused.

"Truth, right?" I pointed my finger, squinting my eyes asking him his name, but I knew who the hell he was.

"Yeah, that's me beautiful, Sundae, right?" he asked I shook my head up and down then we just stood there staring at each other.

I was wondering how he knew Epic because, I had never seen them together before but something in me wanted to know who this mystery man was. I could tell he was older than Epic, I was thinking he was in his early thirty's.

"So, are you going to let me in or are you going to stand there starring at a nigga like you want to fuck me?" he smiled. I sucked my teeth and opened the door wider, so he could come in.

He followed me to the kitchen. I know he was watching my fat ass, so I made sure to give him a show.

He took a seat at the kitchen island. I went into the refrigerator and handed him a water as I checked on the biscuits.

"It smells good in here, damn I can't wait until you cook for me," he told me.

I laughed and shook my head. "Cook for you? Why would I do that? Didn't I tell you I have a man?" I put my hand on my hip looking at him.

"Whatever shorty, the way you looked at me when you opened that door, I can't tell you got a man." He sipped his water and waited for me to answer. I paid him no mind as I took a plate out the cabinet to fix Harley's food.

"So, what are you doing here? How do you know Epic?" he inquired.

"If you must know, Harley, his girlfriend, is my best friend. I'm here taking care of her while he goes and handles his business. Would you like a plate of food?" I offered.

"No, I don't have time to eat. We have to hit the road as soon as this nigga comes down, but I'd rather wait anyway for when you cook for me at my house," he winked at me.

I wanted to fuck his fine ass right in this kitchen. His chocolate skin was so smooth, I could smell his cologne from where I stood and the way his loc's sat on top of his head was so sexy.

"You're really confident Mr. Truth," I smiled at him.

"I know I am and I noticed you didn't disagree with me, so stop playing and give me your cell phone number." He slid his phone across the table, so I could put it in his phone.

I slid that shit right back to him, I wasn't giving him nothing. I was trying to figure out my life especially since Eric's ass was weaseling his way back in the house.

He was about to speak when Epic walked into the kitchen.

"What up Truth? My bad homie, I had to make sure my girl was settled in. She straight now, so we get up out of here," Epic said grabbing a biscuit.

He told me to call him if I needed him and hugged me, thanking me for staying with Harley until Mrs. Savannah got here.

I waved to them both. Truth winked at me and followed Epic out the kitchen. I was hoping this nigga went back to where ever he came from, because if he didn't I know some drama was going to pop off. If he knew Epic, then that meant he knew Eric and I don't want any problems.

———

I knocked on the door to Harley and Epic's bedroom. I wasn't surprised when she didn't yell for me to come in.

I opened the door to see Harley laying on the bed playing with her new cell phone that Epic asked me to pick up on my way over because Jay destroyed her other phone.

"Bitch stop playing with me. I know you heard me knocking on the door," I walked in and stood in front of the bed. When she didn't respond I sat her food on the nightstand and sat beside her.

I watched her play with her phone until she got tired of me staring. "Stop looking at me," she demanded.

I leaned over and started hugging her, careful not to be so rough or touch her face.

"Get off me," she laughed. I sat up and we both laughed.

"Damn bitch about time, I miss you best friend," I hugged her again.

Harley started crying, I just held her and let her cry. I know she was missing her dad, anyone who knows Harley knows how she is with her dad. Harley was a true daddy's girl and I know it's going to take a long time for her heart to heal.

"I'm sorry Sun," she said leaning up, grabbing a tissue and gently whipping her face. I let her know it was okay and she could cry all night if she needed to.

"You don't know how thankful I am to be alive. I really think he was going to kill me," she shook her head.

"He is going to get his as soon as they find him. Do you want to talk about it?" I asked.

"No, I'm sorry I don't. I just want to forget about that shit," she said grabbing her food.

We made small talk while she ate. I was told by Epic to take a video of her eating and to send a picture of her plate when she was done. She laughed as I recorded her but didn't protest, she didn't want any problems with Epic.

"So how is Nena?" she asked drinking her orange juice.

"Worried about you," I gave her a sympatric look.

Nena wanted to come to the hospital when we finally told her about Harley. She cursed Quan and I out for hours.

She didn't want to upset Harley anymore then she was, so she decided to stay away but made sure she was at the hospital to console Mrs. Savannah when we got word the Mr. Rob passed away.

"Harley she is really sorry about how things went down with Quan," I said.

"It's not about her sleeping with Quan if that's what they want to do then oh well. I'm mad that she felt the need to lie to me instead of being straight up. Painting this picture of a deadbeat dad when all along she was talking about my damn brother."

"Okay, Harley I get it boo I really do but she knows how you are about Quan. You would have flipped your lid no matter what so stop it. You need to talk to her. She is due to have your niece in two months bitch, so you need to get over it."

Harley smiled. I know she was excited at the thought of her niece being born no matter how mad she tried to seem. "She's having a girl?" she gave me a warm smile.

I shook my head yes. "You didn't know that?" she told me she hasn't spoken to Quan about it and she was sure her mom didn't know either.

"Sundae, I'm sorry for the things I said at lunch that day. I didn't mean that shit, I was just mad because I felt like yawl were keeping secrets and I was hurt that Nena had been pregnant by Quan all this time and nobody knew."

"No need to say sorry, boo. I mean you read my ass," I rolled my eyes, "and for your information I'm not taking Eric back!" we both cracked up laughing.

I stayed with Harley until Mrs. Savannah showed up. The three of us laid across Epic's big ass bed and just talked about everything, sharing stories about Mr. Rob. We laughed and cried.

When I noticed Harley dozing off, I got ready to leave. I got my things together and told Mrs. Savannah that I would call them tomorrow and gave her a hug. I told one of Eric and Epic's workers I was ready to leave, and he got in his car following me home.

———

*W*hen I got home I went straight into the house and up to my baby's bedroom to check on him.

Eric came up about ten minutes later after talking to his worker. I rolled my eyes when I passed him heading to my bedroom with him on my heels. "Why are you following me?" I asked as I took off my shoes.

"What you mean? It's time to go to bed." This nigga must have lost his mind while he was out there cheating on me.

"Eric, nothing has changed. You are not sleeping in the bed with me. Go to the guest room, damn!" I was so annoyed with him.

"Stop playing with me Sundae! Keep fucking with me and I'm really going to leave your ass," he pointed his finger at me.

"Leave me nigga! We are not together, I meant that shit when I said I was done. Now I wish you would get out of my house!" I threw a pillow across the room at him and it hit the floor.

"I'm not going anywhere. We're going to grow old in this moth-erfucker together, now let's go to sleep," he walked across the room and took off his shirt getting in bed.

"Fine you can have the bed, I'll go to the guess bedroom. Nigga got me fucked up thinking he is going to keep playing me with his side hoes!" I said talking out loud to myself as I left the room slam-ming the door.

When I got to the guest bedroom I made sure I locked the door then I took off my clothes and got under the covers.

Eric called my phone, but I forwarded him to voicemail turning my phone off and the lamp on the nightstand.

I thought about Truth as I got comfortable. I wish he didn't know Eric because I can't lie I was attracted to him, but it would never work. Eric would kill me before he let me be with another man.

Chapter Seven "Eric"

*D*ays Later

"Sundae come on, we can't be late!" I hollered upstairs. Today was Rock's funeral and I was still fucked up about it. I still can't believe my nigga was gone. We had a bounty out on Jamal's head. I wasn't too worried about not catching that nigga because he couldn't hide forever.

I knew he was going to strike but I didn't know when. I know Jamal and he knows us so if I had to guess he was tucked away at a bitch crib.

His family didn't really fuck with him, but he did have a cousin in Pittsburg.

Epic had sent some hitters up there to see if he was there but there was no trace of him. His cousin wasn't from the streets so him getting help from him wasn't an option.

He was a young nigga on his way to college. He would have to be dumb as fuck to get involved with grown man business but only time will tell.

I looked up and saw Sundae coming down the steps holding EJ's hand. She looked good in some black pants and a black top. She was carrying her blazer in her hand. When she got to the bottom of the steps and started walking towards the kitchen, I watched her ass bounce and my dick immediately got hard.

I walked up behind her and wrapped my arms around her waist pushing my hard dick on her ass. I can't remember the last time we had sex and I was horny as hell.

"What are you doing Eric? Get off me," she tried pushing me away.

"Man stop playing Sundae you know you miss daddy's dick," I licked the back of her neck.

"Boy, please don't flatter yourself. Now get the hell off me, call one of your hoes to handle that because I'm not," I let her go and stood there staring at her. She ignored me and grabbed a muffin off the table. She looked down at my hard on as she walked past me and snickered.

"Keep talking shit Sundae, I'm really going to stop fucking with you" I warned.

"Good, you'd be doing me a favor if you left me alone," she said walking past me headed for the living room.

I grabbed everything I needed and went to the car. I rolled a blunt and took a few pulls as I waited for her slow ass to come out the house. Sundae had pissed me off, so I had to leave before I said some shit that I couldn't take back.

I was going to let her play the angry black women role, but she wasn't going to leave me. We've been together to long. That was my pussy and she knew it.

I watched as she finally came walking out the house holding EJ with one hand and a box in the other. If she wasn't being so mean I would have gotten out to help her but since she wanted to act like she didn't need me, I was going to stay in this warm car.

"Umm excuse me Eric, stop playing and help me," she said standing next to the passenger side door. I chuckled as I got out to put EJ in the car. She put her things in the trunk and got in. Once we were all settled in the car I drove off.

———

*W*e made it to Frankford in record time after we dropped EJ off at daycare. I sped to the church making sure we got here on time.

When we pulled up in the parking lot at the church it was packed. It looked like everyone in Philly came out to show my nigga love. The funeral was being held at Keshia's home church. I was surprised she was able to put everything in order because she was going through it but Keshia was loyal to Rock, riding with him to the very end.

"Damn this look like the let out at the club," Sundae said grabbing her purse and getting out the car. "Nena just texted me, she is near the entrance," she let me know as we walked towards the church. I spoke to everyone as we walked past. I saw Nena and Epic standing together, so Sundae and I headed over.

"You good?" I asked Epic as we approached. He shook his head yeah. I know my nigga was hurting on the inside. He was blaming himself for Rock's death. I can admit we played a part but how were we to know Jamal was going to go against the family and kill him?

We were some loyal niggas and Jamal played on that, but his ass was going to pay. Now shit was fucked up between Epic and his dad. This nigga was tripping having the connect cut us off, but he wasn't going to stop shit, we were still going to make money.

"There go that nigga Truth," I said pointing his way as he walked in our direction. Truth wasn't my favorite person, but he was about that money. He was closer to Epic because they used to play in the summer leagues back in the day.

He had beef with me because I tried to get at one of his bitches a few years back. Yeah, I knew she was with him, but I didn't give a fuck, he wasn't my homie. So, he didn't really fuck with me but if he stayed out my way it didn't matter.

I looked over at Sundae who was standing next to me. I wrapped my arms around her. I knew her ass was cold. I never knew why women wore little ass jackets in the winter trying to look sexy. She tried to pull away, but I held her tighter.

"What's up?" he said shaking hands with Epic and giving me the head nod. "I came over to make sure yawl were holding up okay. The hood came out today for Rock," he said scanning the parking lot as the people walked into the church.

"Man, I just want to find this nigga and kill him, that's the only thing on my mind right now," Epic told him.

"How yawl ladies doing today?" he looked between Sundae and Nena. They both smiled I introduced him to them both.

"My bad, this is Nena, and this is my girl Sundae, ladies this is Truth," I saw Sundae look at me with the side eye. I was the only one that caught it, but I just ignored her.

"We're going to go inside and take our seats," Sundae said moving out of my arms, they both waved bye and walked into the church. We stood there talking a little business before it was time for the family to line up to walk into the church.

I sat there zoned out while the preacher spoke. It was a sad sight to see, Keshia went off when it was time to close Rock's casket. I was wondering why the hell she had the casket open. He looked really fucked up. His head was extra big and swollen from catching that bullet in the head. I shook my head just thinking about it. Rock would be mad at how Keshia got him on display.

All his baby mommas were sitting together crying on the opposite side of the church. It looked awkward to me but hey, who was I to judge? I did notice that none of them spoke a word to Keshia. I laughed because Keshia was a boss bitch.

———

$\mathscr{K}$eshia rented out a big hall not too far from where the church was for the repast. Sundae and Nena didn't want to go so Nena agreed to take Sundae to her hair salon and I would pick her up later when it was time to close the salon.

Epic and I sat in my car smoking a blunt. It was way too many niggas inside the hall, so we decided to dip out. I was fucked up. I popped two Percocet's after the service and had sipped some syrup now the weed was making me high as fuck.

I blame the pastor for me getting so high, I wasn't a religious man and he was talking to much about life after death and changing your life to get right with God. I wasn't trying to hear that shit so to get my mind off that bullshit he was talking,, I had to pop some pills to relax.

"How is Harley man?" I asked Epic. My nigga was zoned out. I could tell he had a lot on his mind.

"She good. The swelling went down a lot, her mom postponed the funeral until next weekend, so she could heal. That nigga beat the shit out of her man. Her eye is just starting to heal," he shook his head. "I was hoping she would skip her Pop's funeral shit. I don't want her losing the baby," he said puffing the blunt.

I felt bad for my nigga right now. It was funny because I never saw Epic this gone over a chick, but I wasn't surprised. He always had his eye on Harley and now this nigga had got her pregnant and was about to be a daddy, I was happy for my homie.

"Don't think like that man, Harley will be good," I assured him taking the blunt as he passed it to me. "Man, the pastor had me ready to change my life my nigga. I'm going to stop fucking around on Sundae. She not fucking with me and it's fucking my head up." Someone beeped their horn and flashed their high beams behind us.

Epic pulled his gun out. "Who the fuck is that?" he said. I turned around to see Venessa waving her hand out the passenger side of the car she was in letting me know she was here.

"That's that bitch Vanessa. Aye I'll be back I'm about to go holla at her. I'll come back through," I told Epic waiting for him to get out the car. I looked in the mirror and saw Vanessa getting out of the car.

"My nigga, I know that's not the jawn that's friends with Nena," Epic had a shocked look on his face. I didn't say anything I just chuckled.

"Yeah that's her man, she kept eyeing me at my party like she wanted the dick and then she slid me her phone number before Sundae and I left the club. She a nasty bitch too," I said.

"Sundae is going to fuck both of yawl up but do you my nigga. I'm about to take my ass home to my girl. Be ready tomorrow, this is our first shipment. I need you to be ready," he said grabbing the handle and getting out the car.

"I stay ready my nigga," I said taking a pull of my blunt.

Vanessa got in the car and I sped off down the block headed to her crib, she texted me after the funeral asking if she could see me. I didn't hesitate to say yeah, Sundae didn't want to give me no pussy.

"I'm glad you agreed to see me," she smiled. I didn't answer I just started unbuckling my pants. I wanted some head. I'm glad I had tinted windows.

"Damn Eric, you not even going to speak? Just right to it huh" she said.

"I mean what the fuck we need to talk about? You going to suck my dick or not?" I looked at her and then back at the road, she didn't say anything she just pushed her hair behind her shoulder and grabbed my dick, wrapping her warm lips around it.

Vanessa was a cute girl and she had some good pussy, but she was a snake bitch. She knew Sundae and had partied with her smiling all up in her face and now she was in my car giving me some head. These bitches were shiesty as fuck. That's why I was glad Sundae's circle was so small. Nena and Harley would never do no shit like this.

I had to pull over because she was sucking my dick so good that I didn't want to get in a car accident. I was already high as shit, I didn't need any problems with the law.

I grabbed the back of her head and pumped harder. She started gagging and that shit made my dick harder. I was fucking the shit out of her mouth. Minutes later I was cumming all down her throat.

Vanessa sat up and took a baby wipe out my glove box to wipe her mouth.

"Where are we going now?" she asked.

"To your house so I can get some pussy then I got some business to handle," I told her tucking my dick in my pants.

I looked over at her because I was waiting for her to start complaining about my relationship with Sundae, or us spending time together, but she didn't. I pulled into traffic headed to her house. I had about an hour before EJ had to be picked up.

Chapter Eight "Nena"

I rode down Broad Street singing along with my girl Jill Scott. Her song *Golden* was on repeat, I was in a good mood. I was finally finished working my huge contract with Jordan Matthews, wide receiver of the Philadelphia Eagles.

I did my thing too, his house was so beautiful, I was so happy with the fabrics, rugs and accessories that I chose. He posted sections of his home on Instagram and Snapchat making sure to tag me. My followers had gone up and now more celebrities were contacting my boss requesting meetings with me.

I can't take on any new clients with the baby coming but I was going to be booked when I got back to work, and I wasn't going to complain. Everything I did was for this little beauty growing inside of me.

I was trying to distance myself from Quan. We hadn't had much interaction since Mr. Rob passed away. I was trying so hard to be there for him, but he just wanted to shut me out. I didn't want to push.

I would text him every day letting him know I was here for him if he needed me. Prior to that, we were still fucking like every other day. It was so bad I was wondering if this nigga was taking pills, because it was no way he had time to fuck Ebony because we were wearing each other out between the sheets.

I just can't play games with Quan. He doesn't know if he wants her or me and I'm not going to sit here and continue to play second to his bitch. I was going to start by going on this date with Orlando who was Jordan Matthews Manager.

I wasn't really attracted to him because he was one of those nerdy guys, but he was nice, and we had come to know each other a little when I was working on the house. He asked to take me out a few times, I always declined because I was pregnant with another man's baby but to hell with Quan. He had a girlfriend.

I wasn't planning on sleeping with Orlando while carrying his baby but hell I needed some attention, so if he was going to give it to me then I didn't mind going to dinner with him.

I thought about Harley as I tuned on my block. I was missing her so much, but I couldn't work up enough courage to call her.

I was so mad when I found out Jay had kidnapped my girl and beat her. I was still a little tight with Sundae and Quan for not telling me even though they had good reason. I'm just happy she is safe.

I was in awe when Sundae said Harley was carrying Epic's baby. I was shocked but super excited that our kids will be so close in age and would grow up together.

I was thinking about calling her before the funeral next week, but for the life of me, I just couldn't find the right words to say when I dialed her phone number, so I would just hang up before I could press send.

After I parked my car I texted Quan to let him know I was praying for God to give him strength. I put my phone in my bag and got out the car. I stopped in my tracks when I reached my steps.

"Mom, what are you doing here?" I said holding back tears. My mom has been on drugs most of my life and every time I saw her it hurt my heart.

"Nena, I need a few dollars baby can you help me out?" she said. I looked away and wiped the tears that fell from my eyes.

My mom was so beautiful back in the day. She still had her wild curly hair, but it was matted and had lint all over it.

Her once beautiful light skin was now full of blemishes and deep scars, she looked like she hadn't had a bath in months.

"Ma are you hungry? Come upstairs and get some food and maybe take a shower," I pleaded with her. She shook her head no and looked down the street at the corner. I saw a guy who looked just as dirty as she was standing by the tree.

"Is he waiting for you?" I asked pointing towards the corner. She sucked her teeth.

"Stop with the questions Nena damn are you going to help me out or what?" she asked scratching her arm.

I opened my purse and handed her sixty dollars in cash. She snatched the money and walked quickly down the block. I watched as she showed the guy the three twenty-dollar bills and rushed down the block. When she turned the corner, I wiped my tears and went in the house.

I set on the couch and called Sundae. I needed to talk to someone. I was in such a good mood and now my mom had ruined my night.

"Hey boo, your pregnant ass better be getting ready for your little date and not thinking about Quan!" she yelled in the phone.

"I don't know if I want to go. I came home, and my mom was sitting on the steps of course begging for money, the sad part is I had my coat open and she didn't even acknowledge my belly," I let out a loud sigh.

"I'm sorry Nena. Baby girl, your mom is sick. You can't help her if she doesn't want the help, you can only keep praying for her. Don't cancel your date, you need to get out and have some fun," I could hear the sincerity in her voice.

"I know but I'm not even attracted to him," I laughed.

Sundae sucked her teeth. "Oh well but your ass is hungry so go and get that free meal bitch," we laughed again.

I was happy I called her, Sundae was right I needed to get out the house. She stayed on the phone with me while I picked out something to wear. I asked about Harley and how she was holding up, she said she was holding up as best she could but still didn't want to talk about that night.

Once my clothes were picked out, I told Sundae I would call her tomorrow to fill her in on my date and then we hung up. I went to the bathroom to shower, I was not ready for this date.

———

*O*rlando and I were at Maggiano's Little Italy in down town Philly. This was one of my favorite places to eat and ever since I got pregnant I came here more often. I would always make Quan bring me here at least twice a week.

Orlando sat across from me looking good in his blazer and button up shirt. He was about six feet tall with brown skin. He wore glasses with a low haircut. He dresses like Carlton from the Fresh Prince of Bel Air. I thought it was cute, he had his own style. He was a nice guy and I wasn't sure why the hell he wanted to date me.

"So, Orlando why did you want to ask me out on a date? I mean I know you're not used to dating an around the way girl," I smiled eating a bread stick.

He laughed pushing his glasses up on his face. "I think you're beautiful Nena. Your personality is out of this world and don't let the looks fool you, I've dated an around the way girl before," he said using air quotes. "But let me ask you a question, am I not your type?"

I shrugged my shoulders. "I mean I'm used to dating thug niggas to be honest so are you my type? No," I shook my head, "but you're a great guy, very respectful so I don't mind getting to know you." I was being honest.

I was about to ask Orlando about his family when I saw Quan walking up to the table with the meanest look on his handsome face. He looked so good I was mad that my panties were getting wet. *Just my luck*, I thought.

"What the fuck is this?" he pointed between the two of us.

"Well hi Quan, this is my date Orlando," I smiled at him. He was tripping right now, and I was loving it.

Orlando put his hand out to shake Quan's, of course he ignored him.

"This nigga knows you're pregnant?" he asked pointing to Orlando.

I looked at him like he was crazy. I was seven months pregnant and my belly was big as hell. "What, is that a trick question? Everyone in this damn restaurant can see that I'm having a baby. Can you leave so I can continue my date please?" I said grabbing another bread stick. Quan looked like he wanted to knock me out of the chair.

I saw Ebony walking towards our table and I put my fork down.

"Quan what is going on? Our food is at the table," she told him looking between the three of us.

"Chill Ebony go sit down I'm coming." She folded her arms and looked at him like he was crazy.

"Are you kidding me? I know you're not tripping because your baby momma is out on a date?" she squinted her eyes at him.

"Bitch, you know my name and it's not baby momma. Quan take your girl and get away from my table, damn!" I was getting frustrated.

"Fuck you!" she yelled. I smiled and said, "No boo your man is doing a good job fucking me, so no thank you." I winked at her.

"Really Nena?" Quan said. "Yo, get the fuck up it's time for you to go home. My nigga this date is over. I don't need you to be feeding my baby," Quan said gesturing for Orlando to get up. Orlando just looked at him, he was about to speak until Ebony's ass started going off on Quan.

"Nigga you lost your mind? You're my man but over here worrying about this bitch? Quan take me home! I'm so done, take me home now!" she yelled while everyone looked at our table trying to see what was going to happen next.

"Quan if you don't get her away from me I'm going to start swinging pregnant and all," I warned.

Ebony turned and walked out. Quan looked at me and said, "I swear on my daddy Nena you better be home in the next hour or

I'm fucking this nigga up!" he said looking at Orlando then he walked off to go after Ebony.

Orlando sat there shaking his head. I apologized for Quan's rude ass, but Orlando wasn't feeling it. He asked for the check and to go boxes.

I knew I shouldn't have listened to Sundae's ass.

Chapter Nine "Quan"

"*I* can't believe you just played me like that! I can't believe this shit!" Ebony said talking to herself.

I wasn't really listening to her. She's been yelling since we got in the car as I headed to her house.

I just wanted to get her home and then drive across town to make sure Nena made it home.

I can't believe she was really sitting in a restaurant with a square ass nigga smiling all up in is face like she wasn't having my baby.

Nena thought shit was sweet over here but if she keeps playing with me she is going to find out.

I got too much shit on my plate right now. My dad just died, and I catch her on a date while she pregnant with my daughter? Oh yeah, I couldn't wait to get to her house.

"Are you listening to me? I don't know how much longer I can do this with you Quan. I asked you after the party if something was going on with you and her, she was interrogating me in the bathroom and your fake ass sister was talking about Nena was like your sister, now you tell me this bitch is having your baby!" she yelled.

"It's not like that with me and Nena, she just carrying my baby that's it. Chill the fuck out!" I gave her the side eye.

She put her hands up in the air. "I'm starting to think that you believe I'm stupid. If you expect me to believe there is nothing more then what meets the eye, then you need to seek help. She just sat there and said, the two of you are fucking so don't lie to me"

I didn't say anything, I just kept driving. I was glad when I turned down her block. I wasn't admitting shit. It was her call, I've never been that nigga to beg a shorty to stay with me.

"So, you're not going to answer the question huh?" she shook her head. I put my car in park and looked over at her, I don't know what the hell she wanted me to say.

"Man, I got some business to handle, I'll call you later," I said looking at her.

Grabbing the handle, she said, "You know what? Don't bother calling me, because I know you're on your way to her house, I'm not stupid," she looked hurt.

"Did I say I was going over there to see her? I told you I had some shit to take care of so if you don't believe me that's on you," I was getting tired of her. She didn't say anything, she grabbed her purse and slammed my door. I waited until she got in then I sped off.

———

*W*hen I pulled up to Nena's house I could see the light on in the living room letting me know she was there. I parked my car and walked up the steps using my key to get in the apartment.

She must have just gotten in because when I walked into her bedroom she was changing into her night clothes. I stood in the doorway admiring how beautiful she was carrying my baby. Her belly was getting bigger.

"What the fuck was that all about Nena?" I leaned up against the doorway. She was making me mad acting like she didn't see me standing here.

"I don't know what you're talking about. I was on a date just like you were," she gave me the side eye grabbing her hair and putting it into a ponytail.

"Why are you playing with me? You know what the fuck I'm talking about. Who was that nigga? You're having my baby, what were you thinking going on a date? Did you fuck him?" I was heated.

"Quan get out of my house!" she said coming over, trying to push me to the living room, so I could leave. "You are so disrespect-ful. If I was fucking him that's my business," she said still trying to push me towards the door.

I stopped and looked at her. She backed up a little knowing she crossed the line. "So, what are you trying to say? That nigga fucked you while my baby in there?" I cocked my head to the side.

Nena shook her head and headed to the kitchen to heat up her food from dinner. "No, I did not fuck him, I would never do no shit like that to you okay? But I have a right to have a life. You got a whole girlfriend so why do you care?" she looked at me with her hands on the kitchen table.

"I care because you're carrying my baby, that's why the fuck I care!" I told her. She was talking a bunch of bullshit right now. "I just lost my dad and you out here entertaining that man!" I shook my head.

Nena stopped what she was doing and looked at me, walking over to me she said, "Wow, okay that's how you feel? I've tried to be there for you Quan, but you just continue to push me away. That's so not fair. I've been calling you every day to check on you and you answer whenever you feel like it, and on top of that you have a girl-friend so why the hell do you care if I'm there for you? I loved your dad. I'm hurt to that he is gone, and I can't even be there for Harley because she hates me right now," she stopped talking and put her hand up shaking her head. "You know what? Just get out my house. I'm done. I just want to eat my food and go to bed," she said walking away.

I just stood there looking at her as she moved around in the kitchen. "So, you're going to feed my daughter that shit another nigga paid for?" I asked.

"Get out!" she screamed.

I was about to say something but decided against it. I just turned and walked away. I didn't want to upset her anymore, so I was going to wait until she calmed down.

As I drove home, I thought about my relationship with Nena and how this situation was all fucked up. I was fighting with myself when it came to my feelings for her. Not that I didn't have strong feelings for her, but I wasn't sure I wanted to deal with her drama and besides that I had Ebony but the more I think about it I'm not even sure I want to deal with Ebony. Her main concern was what I got going on and that was a turnoff.

I know Nena love a nigga, I don't need her to say it. I see how she looks at me and how she wants to ride for me, but she always hit me with that young boy shit and that was the main reason I was curving her ass.

Until she learns I'm a fucking man, shit will remain the same between us. My phone started vibrating, when I looked I saw Ebony had text me.

Ebony: I like you a lot Quan and I can see a future between us, but I'm not competing with your baby momma!

I put my phone back in the cup holder. I wasn't dealing with this shit tonight. I was going to go home, take me a shower and try to get some sleep, something I haven't had since my dad died. I was dealing with the fact that he was no longer here and now I had to step up for my mom and sister.

I was already mad as fuck that Jay had beat Harley up, but that nigga was going to get his sooner than later. My homies said they hadn't seen him back in Houston yet, but he had to show up at some point. I knew Epic had his crew on it and he was willing to take care of it, but Harley is my sister, so I was trying to get to him first. I don't claim to be a thug or nothing like that but when it comes to my family I'll do what I have to do.

———

$\mathcal{T}$**he next day**

I knocked on Epic's door waiting for someone to answer. Harley and my mom had been staying at his house in Delaware ever since my dad passed away. My mom was refusing to step foot in the house so now I had to talk to a realtor about selling it. I couldn't even get Harley's help with this because she was still in a state of depression, not to mention she was trying to deal with getting kidnapped.

"Hey baby," my mom said opening the door. I leaned down and gave her a hug. "Come on in. Harley and I were just making sure everything's in order for the funeral tomorrow."

Epic had a big house. He was only one person, so I couldn't understand why this nigga had this big ass crib. He told me yesterday Harley was moving in. That didn't shock me because she was pregnant, and Harley has been liking this nigga since I was a kid.

When I walked in his family room Harley was laying on the couch looking like she ain't have a bath in a few weeks. "Hey Sis," I said leaning down to hug her, I noticed her eyes were puffy and her hair was all over the place. I wanted to talk to her about Nena and how she needs to squash that shit but now wasn't the time.

"Hey Bro, how are you?" she said sitting up.

"I should be asking you that. Are you good?" I asked.

She shrugged her shoulders. "I'm getting by and I can't keep anything down. This baby is taking me through it. Thank god for mommy," she chuckled.

I shook my head. "Speaking of babies, mom I have to tell you something," I took a seat on the couch opposite Harley.

"What do you need to tell me Quan? Don't come over here telling me you have a baby on the way. We have too much going on right now and so do you with your business," she gave me the side eye.

Fuck it, it's now or never, I thought. "Yeah I do have a baby on the way and it's a girl actually." She didn't say anything, she just shook her head and folded her arms. I could tell she was a little upset, but my mom could never stay mad at me.

"I don't believe you Quan. What have your father and I been telling you? These girls are just waiting to get knocked up by your young ass, always sniffing around you," she threw her hands in the air.

"Ma calm down Nena is having his baby," Harley said sitting up looking like a smoker from around the way.

My mom looked between the both of us. "Lord Jesus! Nena well how did that happen?" she wanted to know.

"I don't feel comfortable telling you that," I smiled at her.

"Boy you know what I mean," she laughed, it felt good to see her smile.

"I'm just shocked that's all. I didn't even know you were into Nena, and I'm going to get her for not telling me. Isn't she about to deliver the baby soon and we're just finding out?" she asked shaking her head.

I knew my mom wasn't going to trip out too much especially when she found out Nena was my baby's mother. Nena was a lot of things, but I know she will never be petty when it comes to our baby.

"Well how do you feel about this Harley?" my mom asked. Harley just shrugged her shoulders she was on her bullshit right now, but she can't stay mad forever.

"I was pissed off in the beginning not going to lie, and I don't feel like getting into all that now but Quan I'm happy for you. I know your daughter is going to be so beautiful and I can't wait to meet her," she smiled at me.

"Well when is the baby coming? Nena is carrying big and I guess that explains why she is always up at the hospital with you?" my mom asked.

"Two more months, but I'm not sure she is going to make it," we all laughed.

"Well, I'll call her later and check on her. God took your daddy and is now sending us two precious gifts!" she wiped her eyes. "But anyway, I'm glad you're here," she got up and went into her purse and handed both Harley and I envelopes.

"What's this?" I inquired holding it up. She told me to just open it. When I did there were two checks, one for five hundred thousand dollars and the second one for two hundred and fifty thousand dollars. I looked up at her in shock.

"That's the insurance policy daddy had for the both of you the two hundred and fifty thousand is what he had set aside in the bank for your business. That money was already there. He also has stocks and bonds for you guys but now that we will be having new editions, I'll keep those in my name until the babies are born then I'll put them in their names. I'm going to sell the house and figure out my next move depending on what Harley is going to do because I need to be near her with her being a new mom. I'm sure both Harley and Nena will need me," she looked between Harley and me.

Harley just stared at her check while my mom talked and then put it back in the envelope, she looked towards the muted television not saying a word.

I shook my head letting her know I understand. I was a little fucked up. My dad always said if he died we would be okay. "Thanks mom, but if this is what we have how much did dad leave you?" I chuckled.

"Enough for me to be okay forever," she laughed.

I sat and talked to them for a few more hours. We ordered pizza and just enjoyed each other's company. Tomorrow was going to be hard for us because my dad was being laid to rest. I told my mom I would see them in the morning at the church and I left.

When I got in the car I stared down at the checks before I pulled off. A single tear fell from my eye. I quickly wiped it. I was going to miss my old dude and even in death he was taking care of his family.

Chapter Ten "Harley"

I was laying in the bed letting the tears fall freely from my eyes. It was four a.m. and I couldn't sleep. My daddy was being laid to rest in a few hours and I just couldn't wrap my head around the fact that he was gone.

I was so depressed and trying to keep myself from falling into a deeper depression. I tried to focus on my pregnancy, but it was hard. It seems like every time I closed my eyes I saw his face and the memories of the last time I saw him filled my mind.

We were having so much fun that day, I enjoyed car shopping with him and eating dinner. I remembered reassuring him that Jay was out of my life for good. He was so relieved to know that I wasn't going back to him. We were finally getting back to where we were before he left Texas and now he was gone forever.

I heard Epic come in the room and shut the door. He had been coming in the house later and later every night and although I knew this was all a part of the game, I wasn't sure if I was built for this shit.

I always imagined being with a man who worked a regular nine to five, but I had fallen in love with the total opposite, Epic was a thug, a hustler that was married to the streets. I wanted a life with him, so I was going to get used to this lifestyle.

We recently had a conversation about our life and how things were about to change. Epic didn't tell me a lot about the business, but he told me what I needed to know. He shared with me that Truth's connect was excited to work with him.

He gave me a crash course on the business and how he had to operate. After we talked I understood there would be nights that he came home late or not at all depending on what was going on.

My baby schooled me on watching my surroundings, checking my mirrors when driving and just being on alert. The hardest part I'm dealing with is the nights I sleep alone.

Epic was stressed out and I could see it on his face this morning when he left. He was still dealing with the loss of Rock and trying to find Jay and the biggest problem is Jamal. He not only lost a friend, but he looked at Jamal like a brother and I know it hurt him so much that he was betrayed by someone he trusted with his life.

I knew Jamal was going to be a problem before any of this happened. Now Epic's cousin was dead, and he was on the hunt for Jamal. I was just praying that after he got rid of Jamal and Jay that we would go back to spending time together. I just wanted some normality in my life.

"Baby you sleep?" he said leaning over on the bed and rubbing my thigh. I turned around to face him.

"No, I can't sleep. Maybe I will when this is over," I said wiping my tears.

"I know. How is the baby?" he said rubbing my flat stomach.

Epic was already obsessed with our baby and I thought it was the cutest thing. I felt bad I was trying to be happy about this pregnancy but right now I was just faking it for his sake.

If my dad wasn't on my mind, then Jay was. I had thoughts of torturing that nigga for what he did to me and the fact that I didn't get a chance to say bye to my dad was haunting me.

"The baby is great boo," I forced a smile. "Any word on Jay? I want him dead." I looked him in the face. I never wished death on anyone, but Jay had to die. I was never going to be the same because my Dad was gone but if he was gone just maybe it will bring me a little peace.

"I'm on it Harley, I promise baby," Epic assured me. He got up off the bed and went to take a shower.

I laid in the dark thinking about what he just said. I heard him, but I was running out of patience and if he didn't hurry up and catch this nigga I was going to handle it myself.

———

$\mathcal{I}$ woke up a few hour later to Epic poking me in the ass with his dick as he slept. I laughed and eased out of bed. I looked down at him. I was so in love with this man it was crazy. I know he was sexually frustrated, but I had to much shit on my mind right now.

When I walked in the bathroom I looked at myself in the mirror. I looked a fucking mess. My hair was all over the place. "Get yourself together Harley," I said as I got in the shower. I let the hot water run down my face. Today was going to be the hardest day of my life.

When I got out the shower Epic was at the sink brushing his teeth. I kissed his back and went into the room to get dressed. I laughed to myself because the Epic I knew would have been in the shower and fucking me crazy against the shower wall, but my baby was being respectful because I lost my dad. I was promising myself to make it up to him.

I blow dried my hair and put it in a bun. I put on some black slacks a black body suit black red bottoms and brown blazer.

"You look good baby," Epic said walking up behind me kissing my neck. He pressed his dick on my ass. I turned around and kissed his lips. "I promise soon baby, I'm sorry," I said kissing him again. We stood there hugging, not saying a word and I needed that.

"It's cool but there are other things you can do. You know that right? And you do it well," he said referring to me giving him a blow job. I laughed and hit him on his chest and left the room to check on my mom.

When I got downstairs my Mom was sitting in the kitchen drinking tea, listening to Tamela Mann's gospel song *I Can Only Imagine*. She was staring off in space. I kissed her cheek and she jumped.

"Hey baby. How long have you been standing there?" she asked.

"Not long, Epic will be down in a minute, so we can get going," I stared at her for a second. She looked so sad. "We are going to get through this mom don't worry," I assured her as I grabbed a banana out of the fruit bowl.

I was telling her that, but I was unsure how we were going to make it without my dad. I had learned over the last few days how to hold it together in front of her, but I was dying inside.

Epic came downstairs fifteen minutes later. He walked over and hugged my mom and I smiled. Epic and my mom had gotten close this week.

The two of them had stayed up a few nights talking when he came in late. She couldn't sleep so having Epic around to talk to helped her a lot. I loved it because they got a chance to get to know each other.

I was so grateful for him letting my mom stay here with us. He tried to convince her to move in because it was plenty of room, but she wanted her own space.

She kept saying she wanted to live by herself but I'm not sure if she was trying to convince Quan and I or herself. I didn't think it was a good idea right now, but I wasn't going to push because I know once the baby gets here she is going to fall in love and never want to leave.

I was going to help her find a condo or something when she figured out where she wanted to live but of course I was going to try and hold off until the baby got here. My mom had so much money thanks to my dad, so she was going to be fine.

I had no plans for the five-hundred thousand dollars he left me, so I put it in the bank. My Mom had paid off my car that my Dad purchased with her insurance money so that was not an issue and besides Epic paid for everything, so money was not an issue.

We grabbed our things and headed for the front door. Epic had a driver come pick us up. We climbed in the car and he took my hand kissing it. I looked up at him and smiled as we pulled out of the driveway.

The ride to Philly was quiet, my mom stared out the window the whole time in her own thoughts. I laid my head on Epic and closed my eyes as he rubbed my arm. I eventually dozed off.

When we got to the church I watched as people got out of their cars and headed for the entrance. My dad didn't have much family, it was always him and my Grandma and when she passed away he had us.

My mom had the big family and my dad was close to all of them. He had a lot of work family also. Some of his co-workers from Texas had flew in yesterday to come pay their respect.

I saw Quan walking up the street towards the car we were sitting in. I know he was coming to get my mom, he was so worried about her. He wanted her to stay with him at his apartment, so he could keep an eye on her. Quan was a momma's boy, he hated seeing her hurt.

Ebony was walking beside him holding his hand. I wondered if she knew he had a baby on the way with Nena.

Epic asked my mom and I if we were ready. We both said yes, he kissed my cheek got out the car and came around to open the door for us.

I turned around and Nena, Eric, and Sundae were walking up. I couldn't believe how big Nena's stomach had gotten since the last time I saw her. We hadn't been in touch since the blow up at the restaurant and I was missing my girl.

"How are you feeling?" she came over and give me a hug.

"I'm just taking it one day at a time, how are the both of you?" I gave her a smile and rubbed her belly. I was so excited that I would soon have a niece, I wondered if she was going to look like Quan.

I heard Ebony suck her teeth and when I looked over she rolled her eyes. I didn't have a problem with this girl, so I don't know what her issue was, but today was not the day.

The usher came out to greet my mom and let her know it was time. When my mom's family saw us, they came out and got in line after we all greeted each other then we walked into the church.

The pews were full. I was kind of surprised because we were only expecting my mom's family some co-workers from here and of course his Texas friends. His circle was small. He spends most of his free time with my mom, but I was happy it was such a big turnout.

As we sat in the pew the reverend preached about life and making the best of it while we're here.

He preached about how God had used my dad to save lives and now his mission was complete. I just sat there staring at the casket. I couldn't believe my father was gone. It was unreal to me that he would not see Quan and I raise our kids or grow old with my Mom.

I looked over at Mom, the tears were running down her face as she rocked slowly from side to side. I don't know how she is going to live without my dad.

Epic gave my hand a squeeze and I looked up at him. "The service is about to be over baby, you good? We are about to go up and carry the casket out," he said

I must have zoned out because the only thing I remember was walking into the church sitting down and a little of what the pastor preached. I shook my head up and down letting him know I was going to be okay.

I stood next to my mom holding her hand tight as the men carried his casket out of the church. I felt her body stiffen up. I kept telling her to take deep breaths as I coached her on breathing.

When it was our turn to get up both of my girls were there. Nena grabbed my hand and Sundae grabbed the other as we followed my mom and uncle out to get into the cars. I watched them slide my Dad's casket in the hearse. I said a silent prayer, I was going to miss him.

"Did you hear some of the guys that spoke?" Sundae asked, I shook my head no. "Girl like four niggas that had gotten all shot up came up to thank your Daddy for saving their lives," we laughed.

"Yawl ready?" Quan walked over asking us he cut his eye at Nena and looked at me asking if I was okay. I told him yes. Nena rolled her eyes and headed to her car. I didn't know what that was about but I'm sure Sundae would give me the details later.

After the cemetery we went back to the church for the repast, it was hard for my Mom, but she got through it. People kept coming up to her telling her stories about my Dad, but she took it like a Gee and didn't break.

When the repast was over my Mom wanted to stay in Philly, so she went home with Quan while Epic and I went to the house in Delaware. I couldn't wait to get home and get a good night's sleep. I was so tired, and I felt a little comfort because now my Daddy was laid to rest. But no matter what he will always be in my heart.

———

A **few days later**
"Everything looks perfect Harley. The baby is fine, keep taking your vitamins and remember no stress. You're in the first trimester, so you have to be careful," my doctor said as she helped me sit up.

"You don't have to worry about that doc, I got her. My baby is good in there," Epic told her, I just shook my head. The doctor told me she would see me in a month and left the room, so I could get dressed.

I got up to grab my sweatpants off the chair, but Epic stopped me. "What are you doing?" I said as he pulled me in between his legs.

"Baby feel how hard my dick is right now," he said rubbing my hand against it. "It's been like a whole month since I touched your pussy, so you got two choices. You can sit on my dick or bend that ass over and let me hit it from the back," he said taking off my hospital gown. I laughed.

I bent over and kissed his lips letting the gown fall to the floor, he hit the lock on the door and I leaned over on the hospital bed like he suggested. He jumped up and started unbuckling his belt. I smiled at him.

Epic lightly rubbed my back and reached around to grab my

breast, he kissed my back then gripped my hips, pulling me closer to him and rubbing his dick down the crack of my ass then he entered me.

We both let out a sigh. It had been a long time since I felt him inside of me and it felt so good. Epic had some good dick. He started out slow enjoying the feeling of his dick inside of me. "Damn baby you missed this dick, didn't you?" he said moving a little faster.

"Yesssss! I said holding my head back letting my eyes roll in the back of my head. "Oh, baby it feels so good, go faster!" I said throwing my ass back at him.

Epic grabbed my hips a little tighter as he moved faster. He was hitting my G-spot and I couldn't help but scream.

"Oh my God! Baby don't stop! Yessssss!" I said as I creamed all over his dick. There was a knock at the door, but Epic ass didn't care, he kept pumping inside of me.

"Is everything alright in there?" one of the nurses screamed.

"We good, we will be out in a minute," he said sounding out of breath. He continued to abuse my middle. Moments later he was cumming inside of me then he bent down and kissed the back of my neck.

We both laughed as we tried to catch our breath. He let me go and I turned around kissing him hungrily. This was my nigga.

"Here baby," he said handing me some wet towels. We cleaned ourselves up and he helped me get dressed.

"Oh my God, baby I don't want to walk out there. What if they know we were in here fucking? I cannot believe you had me in here having sex," I said holding my hand over my mouth shaking my head.

"Man fuck them, they probably be getting fucked in these rooms too," he grabbed my hand and opened the door.

A few nurses looked at us as we walked towards the exit. Epic waved goodbye to them and I burst out laughing.

When we got in the car he asked if I wanted to grab a bite to eat before he dropped me off at his condo. He had business to take care of, so we were going to stay in Philly for a few days. He had some of his crew members that would post outside his condo just in case Jamal showed his face.

Epic told me this morning that after my doctor's appointment he had some business to attend to. I was okay with it when he first told me but as we drove home, I was feeling a little sad that I wasn't going to see him until late.

I wasn't going to complain, I was just going to enjoy our moment. I don't want to come off as the needy girlfriend, Kayla has done that, and we were nothing alike.

I had a taste for Pizza, so we stopped at City View on Cecil B. Moore. As soon as our pizza was ready we sat down, and I dug right in. Epic laughed at me and shook his head.

"What I'm so hungry? It's been a few hours since I've eaten anything," I said taking another bite of my pizza.

"It's all good, just feed my son and we're good," he said then took a sip of his water.

"Babe who told you it's a boy?" I shook my head.

"I just know," he smiled at me with those hazel eyes. I was hoping my baby inherited his eyes.

We sat there in silence, both of us eating and in our own thoughts. I decided to tell Epic what had been on my mind for a few weeks now.

"I want to talk to you about my plans boo. I'm ready to go back to school, sitting in that big ole house all day is driving me crazy. I just think about my dad and it drives me insane. I think I'm ready to get back to my life," I said.

Epic leaned back in his chair and didn't say anything for a second. I was afraid of what he would say because he wanted me to stay in Delaware and I didn't want to be that far away from the city.

"I mean the last thing I want to do is hold you back from making yourself better and I know you want your degree and to become a nurse and I'm all for it. I'll have my boys follow you to school and back until I get at this nigga."

He was tripping if he thought I was going to travel from Delaware to Philly every day in traffic. "Well now, I was thinking we can just stay at the condo since my parents' house is being sold.

Epic shook his head no. I knew it sounded too good to be true. "We can stay at the condo for now but when you have the baby it's a no go. Delaware will be our main home," he said.

I slumped down in my seat. I didn't want to live in Delaware. "Why? I want to work, and the best hospitals are in Philly," I whined.

"You can find a job in Delaware," he said leaning up in his seat. "Come on Harley don't fight me on this. I don't want you and our baby in Philly. This is where I work. I need you to always be protected. Niggas will try and get at me and you will be the main target," he was serious. I knew he was only trying to protect me.

"I know, well can we at least move to Jersey?" I raised my eyebrow.

He laughed, "I'll think about it and if you keep letting me fuck you in public, I'll buy you whatever you want," he laughed.

"Deal," I said putting my hand out, we shook on it and continued eating our food.

When we finished, we stopped at the grocery store, so we could get some food for the condo because we would be here for a few days. My mom was going to come over later to spend some time with me. She was still staying at Quan's apartment.

Epic dropped me off and after I put the groceries away I started a bath. I just wanted to relax and take a nap before my mom came over to visit with me. I laid my head back in the tub and thought about my future with Epic. I wish my dad had gotten a chance to meet him.

Chapter Eleven "Epic"

$\mathcal{I}$ was sitting at the prison waiting for my dad to come out, I was tired of this nigga blowing my phone up. He thought just because he was the plug he could cut me off and stop my money, but he was mistaken.

Thanks to my nigga Truth, we were back in business and the shit was better than Rock's pussy ass connect. I shook my head as I thought about my dad and how he thought he had some type of control over me. I knew in my heart this was going to be the last time I visited him.

I could tell he blames me for Rock's murder and I will admit some of that was my fault, but Rock knew better then to get caught slipping in this line of business. If it was true that he let his body-guard leave that night and it wasn't a setup, then I'm not sure what he was thinking letting his bodyguard leave.

I saw my dad come in and search the room. When he spotted me, he walked over and sat down. He didn't come over to hug me like he did on our visits and his face was serious, so I already knew what it was.

"You wanted to see me?" I asked.

"What took you so long to come here? I summoned your ass

weeks ago. Rock has been dead for over a month and you're just getting around to having a sit down with me?" he was stern with his words, but that shit didn't affect me.

"I had shit to handle, you know my girl's Dad died and I had to make sure she was straight. She carrying my shorty so making sure she is good comes before anything," I told him.

He sat up in his seat and put his elbows on the table, "I don't give a fuck if that bitch got ran over by a truck. When I tell your ass, I need to see you that's what the fuck I mean. This is nothing new you know the rules."

"Call my girl another bitch old man and see how long you live. I just told you my girl is carrying your grandchild and that's all you have to say?" I couldn't believe this nigga.

"I don't give a fuck about none of that shit. Why the fuck you let Jamal kill Rock? I told you to handle that nigga, now my fucking cousin is dead, and that shit is on you!" he pointed to me waiting for my response.

I shook my head up and down. "I'll give you that, I can admit I fucked up but so did Rock. He knew Jamal was coming for us and he got caught slipping. That's not on me, but you don't have to worry, I'm going to get at Jamal," I waved him off.

"You better get at him and blow his fucking brains out when you see him. I don't give a fuck who is around," he pointed at me calling himself scolding me like I was a damn child.

"Don't worry about how I take care of it just know that I will. Listen I'm not you. I'm not shooting niggas in broad daylight getting caught up with these pigs out here. I have a family to look after and you remember your mom, right? I'm all she's got so don't tell me how to run my shit alright?"

We just sat there staring at each other for a few minutes. I gave respect where respect was due but him calling Harley a bitch and dismissing my seed had me feeling some type of way. He sat back in his seat just looking at me.

I got up. "Well I guess we're done here so I'm going to see if I can get up out of here," I pointed to the exit.

"No, you are going to sit the fuck down. This conversation isn't over," he demanded.

I stood there staring at him before taking my seat, he was testing my patience. I sat down so I could hear what he had to say, but something was telling me to just leave and never look back.

"Let me ask you something," I said putting my elbows on the table looking him in the eyes. "You got a whole lot to say telling me how to make moves and you in here for life. You're sitting here telling me to and kill someone in broad daylight, and I just sat here telling you my girl his pregnant with your grandchild. Do you ever think about what the hell you did and how it affected me growing up? It's like you only think about yourself nigga."

"It's all a part of the game, and why the hell you over here complaining? I had to do what I had to do. You still turned out okay. I will never let anyone play me for a fool, family or no family, when a nigga crosses me he has to go," he let me know.

I shook my head up and down finally understanding how selfish he really is. "Man fuck you! You never gave a fuck about me because if you did, you wouldn't have done that shit. You killing that man in front of me fucked me up as a kid. You never asked how I felt after everything went down, the nightmares, the times I was scared out of my sleep from seeing that bullet go through his brain, waking up in a bed full of piss because the dreams scared the shit out of me. As I got older I kept having them fucking nightmares. Rock told me I would probably continue to have them until I caught my first body." He sat there looking at me taking in every word I said but my father was emotionless.

I looked around the room at all the families that were visiting and looked at the little boys having conversations with their fathers, reminding me of when I used to come here as a kid. I used to pray every night to God asking him to free my pop and let him come home to me, so we could go to basketball games. I remember praying hard for things to go back to the way there where before he lost his freedom that day.

I turned back to him and said, "The only thing I ever wanted was a father," I sighed.

He chuckled. "What the fuck are you talking about Epic? Shut the fuck up and man up! That shit was so long ago, it is what it is," he shrugged his shoulders. "All that shit is in the past, and I ain't raise no bitch, do you hear me? I'm talking about my cousin and until you make this shit right you're cut off from the connect," he said.

"Fuck you nigga and I am a man! I'm more man than you will ever be. You're a dumb motherfucker. Call me another bitch and I don't need you or your fucking connect. I'm the one who makes sure you get what you need in here so what are you saying? I'll have your throat slit in this motherfucker. I got little niggas in here doing life bids and would love for me to keep their books stacked and their families taking care of. Fuck with me," I warned.

When I said that he jumped up and came across the table, he hit me grabbing my collared shirt. The guards ran over and tried to get him off me, he snuck a hit in before they pulled him off me. I laughed and wiped the blood from my lip as they fought with him to get him out of the visitation room.

"You're dead to me! And you're going to pay for this shit! Watch your back motherfucker! You're not my son anymore!" he yelled.

The guards escorted me out the visiting room and let me know I was suspended from visiting. That was okay with me because I wasn't coming back. Just like he said I was dead to him, he was dead to me.

My dad had niggas out here that would move if he told them to. Now I had to watch my back. I knew he meant what he said. One thing about Trip was he never made promises he didn't keep but I would be ready for this nigga whenever he came my way.

———

I drove back to Philly in silence. No music just me and my thoughts. Shit was getting crazy and I was getting mad as fuck that nobody was able to find Jamal's ass. I knew he was still in Philly, but I was going to find that nigga if my life depended on it.

My phone rung and when I looked I saw Truth calling, I hit the phone button on my Bluetooth and said hello. "What's good my nigga?" I asked.

"Epic what's good? I was just calling to check on you. Everything is straight you're on your own now. The only thing left to do is that exit interview and you're straight," he assured me.

Truth was talking in code letting me know I passed the test with the connect and he liked how I ran my business. Truth was no longer going to be the middle man. I was going to work directly with the connect. All our hard work had paid off. I couldn't wait to meet with Eric.

"But umm I called to ask you a question now that we got that etched in stone. What's up with Eric and the shorty Sundae my nigga?"

I laughed. "What you mean what's up with them? I'm saying they been fucking around since we were in high school. She got his son. They been together forever," I said as I switched lanes.

"Oh word, shorty didn't seem like she was into him at Rock's funeral. I just wanted to know what's up," he chuckled.

"Why the fuck is you asking nigga? I know you are not trying to get at Sundae are you?" I questioned.

"I mean shorty is bad as hell. I took my daughter to her salon to get her hair done when we were in town. I didn't know who the hell she was, but I was feeling her then I saw her at your house and I was like damn. I didn't know she was Eric's girl until he was all hugged up on her at the funeral, you know I'm not in town much, so I had no idea, but I like what I see," he said.

"Yeah, that's all Eric," I made sure I said that. I didn't want any bad blood between the two of them. Eric and Truth didn't really get along, but business was business and with the two of them that's all it really was. I was staying out of this shit because I wasn't into playing doctor Phil, but when it all came down to it Eric was like my brother and Truth was one of my closest friends. I wasn't choosing sides if they started fighting over Sundae.

"I hear you, but okay I'll be in the city in a few weeks, so we can link up. I'll let you know the details of the next step soon," he told me, and we hung up.

When I pulled up to my condo I parked my car and got out. I walked past my Denali and noticed all four of my tires were slashed. *What the fuck?* I said to myself as I got close. I shook my head. I owned a body shop so whoever did this shit was dumb as a box of rocks if they thought this was going to upset me. I thought about Kayla. I wondered if it was her, but I didn't have time to think about that, I had business to take care of.

When I got in the house, I went in the room and Harley was knocked out. She had the trash can and bottle of water near the bed. I felt sorry for my baby, but my dick was hard, so she was about to wake up.

My phone rung and I saw Eric calling. I went into the bathroom and answered.

"Yo, Jamal just sent a message. That nigga set his old trap house on fire. I need you to bring your ass here now!" he yelled.

I left out the bathroom and looked at Harley. She was in such a deep sleep she didn't even hear me moving around. I left out the house and jumped in my car to see what the fuck this nigga had done. I'm just glad the new shipment wasn't coming in until tomorrow.

Chapter Twelve "Eric"

I was thinking to myself how this was some bullshit. I was standing outside the trap house while the fire department hosed it down. I was told Jamal rode past and threw a pipe bomb inside sending the house up in flames. There was no one inside, we had switched things up, so the product wasn't coming in until tomorrow.

I saw Epic walking up to me and three of our hitters. We all started walking down the street away from the crowd that was watching the fire fighters put the fire out.

"What the fuck happened? I want that nigga caught or I'm going to start killing niggas on payroll. It seems like everyone is slacking on the job. It can't be that hard to find one nigga, and if motherfuckers can't do their jobs then what are we paying them for?" He kicked the trash can sending it flying in the middle of the street.

"Somebody said they saw him coming out of Onyx with one of those strippers or some shit like that," Dre said.

"Alright now we are getting somewhere, so what I need from you and Cecil is to first, get a name and go sit outside the motherfucking club. As soon as you see that bitch grab her up. She knows where that nigga at. Don't call our fucking phones unless you got some good news. You got that?" I asked.

Once we had that squared away, Epic and I talked for a little longer hanging out until the fire department left. We agreed to meet tomorrow and I headed home.

When I got to the house Sundae was laying across the bed sleep. She had a tee shirt on and no panties, my dick immediately stood at attention. I took my clothes off and got in the bed behind her. I started kissing on her neck and biting on her ear.

She squirmed. "Move Eric go in the other room." She pushed her shoulder against me trying to make me move but I wasn't trying to hear that shit. It had been so long since I fucked Sundae and I was missing her calling my name.

I pulled her panties down and started playing in her pussy, I laughed to myself because she was soaking wet. I knew she still wanted a nigga. She spread her legs giving me full access. I put two fingers inside of her and moved them in and out as she moaned.

She turned on her back and opened her eyes. We stared into each other's eyes. I love this girl with all my heart. I want to grow old with Sundae, I was promising myself as I looked at her pretty ass in the dark that I was never going to cheat on her again. I didn't want to lose her. I was willing to forgive her for killing my seed, I just wanted her.

She leaned up and kissed me. As we kissed I helped her out of her shirt. I got on top of her and eased my dick inside of her, it fit like a glove. Her pussy was made for me and only me. As I stroked her she moaned louder.

"I love you to death Sundae you know that right? I would die for you," I said as I moved a little faster. She started moving her hips with me matching my pace. "Shit," I said. She felt so good.

"I love you too! Ugh, please don't stop baby yes!" she threw her head back. I grabbed her legs and wrapped them around my arms and started beating her pussy up. This was my baby. I was never letting her leave me.

We kissed as I hit her G-spot. The more she screamed the harder I hit it and soon after we were cumming together. While we tried catching our breath, I looked at her and tears were rolling down her face.

"What's wrong Sun?" I asked wiping her tears.

"This is your last chance Eric. If something else happens I'm gone for good," she said. I could tell in her eyes she was serious, but I was going to do right by her as if my life depended on it.

"I promise," I assured her looking into her eyes for a second then kissing her, my dick got hard again. I pulled her on top of me for round two.

The next morning Sundae and I laid in bed. She was lying on my chest. "What do you want for breakfast?" she asked me. I kissed her forehead and told her whatever she wanted to make was good with me.

Our bedroom door opened and EJ came walking in with one of his toy cars in his hand. He climbed up in the bed and kissed Sundae on her cheek. EJ loves his mother. "Mommy, Daddy," he said jumping on the bed.

I leaned over and grabbed my boxers. "Come on man lets go to your bathroom so we can brush our teeth," I said grabbing him up, so I could give Sundae time to get her shower.

I went downstairs to prepare breakfast for all of us after EJ and I took care of our morning hygiene. My phone started vibrating in my sweats, I looked at it and saw Vanessa's phone number. This bitch had been calling me for a few days, but I kept forwarding her calls.

Vanessa was like all the rest, I got tired of her pussy, so I stopped calling her ass. I hated when these bitches didn't get the message. I hit the green button to see what the fuck she wanted. Sundae would be coming down soon and if my phone was ringing off the hook then she was going to fuck me up.

"What the fuck you want?" I said in a low voice while I scrambled the eggs.

"You need to come to my house today, I have to tell you something and I'm not playing Eric," she warned.

This hoe had the game fucked up. I don't know who she thought she was talking to. "Who the fuck is you talking to?" I asked. "You know what? Give me two hours I'll be there. You are getting on my fucking nerves!" I said and hung up. I didn't even wait to hear what the hell she had to say.

As soon as I hung up Sundae came walking into the kitchen tying her hair up. "Are you cooking for little ole me?" she smiled kissing EJ and then coming over to kiss me.

"Hell yeah, I'm trying to get out the dog house," I said, and she laughed.

We sat and ate breakfast, Sundae said she didn't have any clients today and just wanted to hang around the house today. That sounds like a good idea, but I had work to do later when the shipment came in, I told her. I was going to make a run that had to do with business and I would be back, but I was really going to see what the fuck Vanessa wanted.

After I got dressed I headed to the city. I finally made it to Vanessa's house in Nice town and texted her to open the door. When she came to the door I got out and walked up her steps. I went in and sat on the couch.

"What the fuck you want that's so damn important that you're blowing me up?"

She stood near the door with her arms folded. "I have Chlamydia, so I think you need to get checked out. And I'm pregnant," she said being straight forward. I wanted to crack her neck.

I got up and got in her face. "What the hell you mean you have Chlamydia bitch? You gave me a STD!" I jumped up pushing her up against the wall. I had only fucked her raw that day when we left Rock's funeral and that was only because I was high as fuck or I wouldn't have fucked her without a condom.

My mind went to Sundae and the fact that I just had sex with her yesterday. Just the thought that she might have an STD scared me. There was no way around it, I had to tell her.

"I should shoot your ass!" I said grabbing her by the neck. "And don't come telling me you're pregnant because it's not mine so don't even think about telling Sundae."

I pointed my finger in her face. She started crying. All these bitches were the same and I was tired of them crying when I cut them off and told them to lose my number.

"What do you mean? It is a possibility it could be yours," she said confused.

I was done with Vanessa. "I don't give a fuck what you say, that ain't my kid, but I will say this, if I'm burning or my girl burning I'm going to come back and kill your ass and I mean that shit. I don't give a fuck if you're pregnant or not," I warned.

I slammed her door and got in my car. I sat there for a minute gathering my thoughts. It hadn't been a whole day since Sundae and I got back together, now I had to tell her she might have Chlamydia. I was hoping we could get past this shit. I couldn't lose my family.

When I finally made it to Jersey I sat in the car just looking at the house. I had done a lot of shit to Sundae in the past, and yeah, I cheated but I was always careful when I slept with these hoes. I had never given my baby a disease. I didn't know what the fuck she was going to do.

I took a deep breath and walked into the house. When I got in I could smell cookies which meant Sundae was baking my favorite chocolate chip cookies from scratch. My stomach instantly started hurting at the thought of her leaving me again.

EJ saw me. He came running over and gave me a hug then went back to playing with his toys.

I walked in the kitchen. When she saw me she smiled. "Did you handle your business? Now are you ready to chill with me and EJ?" she smiled.

I just stood there staring at her, she was so fucking beautiful. I was mad at myself for what I was about to tell her. I was even more mad that I kept fucking up.

"What's going on Eric, something is wrong," she said as a statement and not a question.

I took a deep breath. "Sun, I have to tell you something, but first I want to apologize for always being a fuck up and making you cry. I don't know why I do the shit I do baby, but my intentions are never to embarrass you or put your life on the line."

She held the baking sheet in her hands and leaned against the sink. "Please just say what you have to say," she pleaded with her eyes.

I was quiet for a few seconds then I said. "I was fucking with this bitch weeks ago and she just told me she has Chlamydia, so we have to get checked out," I held my breath. The look on her face said a lot.

She put the baking sheet down and took off the glove. She stood there for a second not saying anything. I could see the hurt in her eyes and I felt like the biggest asshole in the world, she didn't say anything, she just came over and slapped the shit out of me.

"I'm so fucking done with you nigga! Did you really just come in here and tell me you let a bitch burn your stupid ass?" she poked me in the forehead.

"Baby listen!" I pleaded.

She put her hand up stopping me. "No, you listen nigga, I'm so done with you! I want nothing to do with you! So, what you're saying is, you're out her fucking these hoes raw?" she yelled pushing me in the chest.

EJ came running into the kitchen. I scooped him up and followed her as she walked out the kitchen.

"I was high as fuck that night. I swear it only happened once. I promise you it did," I confessed.

"Shut up, shut up," she said stopping in her tracks and facing me. "I'm done with you forever! You hear me Eric? Forever! Now get your shit and get the fuck out my house!" she yelled walking upstairs as I followed with EJ in my arms.

"No! we need to talk about this! I'm not going anywhere shorty!" I told her.

She threw her hands up in surrender. "Okay fine. You know what? You don't have to leave, this is your house anyway. You paid for the shit, so I will move out. I don't want nothing to do with this house or you! You are a fuck up! I blame your mom and dad for raising your stupid ass! Matter fact, I should slap the shit out of both their asses!" she threatened.

"Okay Sundae you are taking it way to far, leave my momma out of this," I told her.

"Fuck you bitch! You lost your damn mind! You keep doing shit and I'm dumb enough to keep taking you back!" she yelled. Her face was wet from crying.

I watched as she opened a trash bag and started throwing stuff in them. After filling two bags, she dragged them down the steps the whole time talking to herself about how I was a dirty dick nigga.

"Baby where are you going? It's late and EJ needs you. Calm the fuck down we are going to get through this Sundae!" I panicked, I knew if Sundae walked out this door she wasn't coming back.

She wasn't listening to anything I had to say as she loaded the car with clothes. When she was done she came in the house and grabbed her keys. She was yelling all types of shit talking to herself. EJ started crying.

When she had her keys and purse, she put her coat on and walked over trying to take EJ from me.

"Man, you must be crazy if you think I'm going to let you leave all angry with my son and it's cold outside!" I said.

"I don't care what you say. Give me my son Eric!" she whined as the tears rolled down her face.

"I'm so fucking stupid, I was actually thinking this time was going to be different. I figured I let you sweat long enough and it was time for us to work our shit out because I love your ass with everything in me, but I'm tired of this. Chlamydia? Are you fucking serious!" She looked at me hurt.

EJ continued to cry reaching for her, I know he was crying because how upset she was, but I wasn't letting her take him.

"I know and I'm sorry. I didn't mean to hurt you, you have to believe that. I fucked that bitch when we were on a break. I told you I was high as fuck when it happened, so I slipped up. Baby don't do this shit, we can work through this!" I begged.

I wasn't about to tell her the bitch was Vanessa and she was pregnant. I wasn't claiming that baby. Vanessa fucked everybody, for all I know that baby had every niggas DNA in Nice- Town and until she showed some proof and we got a blood test, I wasn't telling anyone shit.

"Just please give me my son please!" she cried.

"Fuck no. You either stay or leave him here," I told her as I pushed her hands away as she reached for EJ. I know Sundae will never turn her back on our son.

"Oh well, I'm leaving call Nena or Harley when you're ready to drop him off to me nigga!" She turned around and walked out the house slamming the door.

I was fucked up right now, this shit couldn't be happening, I wasn't expecting her to walk out on EJ. We stood there as I thought about what just happened. I had gotten my girl back and lost her in less than twenty-four hours. I shook my head and took EJ I n the family room, so I could clam him down this can't be life.

Chapter Thirteen "Nena"

J was sitting in Quan's new tattoo shop going over colors and furniture for the booths. Everything was coming together, and I couldn't wait until it was complete. I had stopped working last week and was officially on maternity leave. Now I was able to focus on his project because Quan was not going through the company I worked for to have his tattoo shop decorated. This was strictly a personal project and I was honored to do it for him.

Quan insisted that he pay me for my services, but I refused to take his money. He wrote me a personal check when I started the job and I had a credit card to use for all expenses. I meant what I said about not charging him, so the money he gave me I put in our daughters savings account.

"How are you making out?" he said walking into the room with a Chic-fil-A bag that I didn't ask for.

"Everything is fine. I need you to go over the colors for the backsplash. I know you're going to draw some art on the walls, but we need to settle on a color. Oh, and the chairs you picked for the stations look like they're in stock. I'm just waiting for the manager to get back to me," I said taking a waffle fry out the bag.

"Cool, that's what's up. Now eat, my daughter is hungry." He handed me the chicken sandwich.

I let out a deep breath. "No, she is not. You think you know everything. I swear every time you look at me you think she is hungry. I'm going to need you to stop, okay?" I rolled my eyes.

"Whatever you haven't eaten since we got here, and we've been here for over three hours in case you forgot," he drank from his cup.

My phone started ringing. Both of us looked down to see Orlando calling. I forwarded him to voicemail, but I knew Quan was about to start his shit.

"Why the fuck is he calling, you still talking to that nigga?" he questioned.

"You still talking to Ebony?" I raised my eyebrow and he didn't say anything.

"Exactly," I said going back to what I was doing.

"Keep playing with me Nena. You can't talk to that nigga while my daughter is in there and I mean that shit," he said with anger.

"Umm, last time I checked you were not my daddy...I'm going to need you to stop. I don't say shit while you're over there still boo loving with Ebony ugly ass." He was getting on my nerves.

"It's different alright? Now calm your ass down," his face was stern.

I was so sick of Quan and what made it worst, was I was still having sex with him. He came over last night, so we would only have to drive one car here today. He claimed he didn't want me to drive because it was supposed to snow but I knew he wanted some booty. We fucked all night and came into work together.

I just sucked my teeth. I didn't know what the hell was going on with us. I never say it out loud, but I think he knows I'm in love with him and I think he has strong feelings for me. I'm not sure if it's love, but I know he cares and for the life of me I can't understand why he doesn't want to just be with me.

I keep telling myself, I'm not going to have sex with him but every time he crossed my doorstep I find myself submitting to him.

He made sure to come by and check on me most days and when

he did, we would always end up in my bed and he would fuck me crazy.

Mrs. Savannah was still staying at his house. I was wondering if she was developing a relationship with Ebony when she was there, and the thought mad me upset.

"My bad, I don't want to upset you alright? I'm just asking that you don't entertain that nigga while you are carrying my baby that's all." I knew he meant what he was saying.

"Please stop trying to tell me what to do," I told him.

He shut me up by bending down and kissing my lips. He slipped his tongue in my mouth. As our tongues did a slow dance, I was thinking how much I loved him.

There was a knock at the door, he backed up and told whomever it was to come in. The electrician stuck his head in asking Quan to come into the other room, so he could show him something.

I watched him walk out the door when he was gone, I closed my eyes Quan was driving me crazy. I shook my head and bit my sandwich.

———

*T*wo hours later Quan and I were on our way back to my house. I couldn't wait to lay down even though I didn't really do much today. I was glad I didn't drive because the weather was getting bad.

"Are you still going to tattoo? The weather is getting nasty," I asked.

I was secretly wishing he would just stay with me tonight, so we could cuddle and watch a movie, but my ass was living in fantasy land and I needed to stop. The reality was Quan and I were in a situation and he had a girl.

"Yeah, my client said he's there but if it gets too bad, I'll cancel the other appointments. He turned down my block and double parked. "Who is that?" He pointed towards my house.

I looked over and saw my mom sitting on the cold concrete. She had on a jacket that was too small even for her small frame.

"What does she want now? That's my mom," I shook my head looking over at her. I really wish she would get it together," I sighed.

"You want me to stay?" he asked.

"No, go and handle your business. I'll text you before I go to bed okay?" I said.

"Alright well it's a little slippery out here so I'm going to help you up the steps," he insisted.

When we got to the steps my mom stood up. She was looking a fucking mess. "Hey mom, this is Quan, Harley's brother." I pointed to Quan and he gave her a head nod. "Mom what are you doing here? It's snowing out and it's freezing," I shivered.

"The guy you saw me with that day he kicked me out and I have nowhere to go. The shelter I normally go to is full tonight. Can I please spend the night?" she pleaded with her eyes.

"Nena it's cold as fuck out here and you don't need to be getting sick with the baby and all," Quan said.

I rolled my eyes at him. He was getting on my damn nerves always telling me what to do. I couldn't wait until the baby got here so he could get off my back. "Alright, I guess you can stay let's go so I can get you warm." I told her.

When we got in the house she told me she had to use the bathroom. After she excused herself, I got her a towel and wash cloth, so she could shower. I knocked on the bathroom door and when she opened it I handed her the stuff. She took it and shut the door.

If she was going to stay here and sleep on my furniture, she had no choice but to get herself clean.

When I came out the room Quan followed me into the kitchen to get some water. Some time had passed, and he was still standing around. I could tell he was a little skeptical of my mom because he acted like he didn't want to leave.

"Yo, I know that's your mom and all, but I don't trust her ass. I got to roll but I'll be back," he said looking me in the eyes with a serious face.

"Quan, that's my mom. I'll be fine. Now go, she will be coming out the bathroom any second." I looked towards the bathroom door.

"Man okay, if something happens to you, mom or not I'm fucking her up. Matter of fact here, take my gun," he pulled it from his waist and I jumped back.

"Oh, now see get out. I don't need you to come back, I'll text you tomorrow," I pushed him to the door.

"I said I'm coming back. I'm not leaving you in here with her," he said when we got to the door. I pushed him out and shut it shaking my head.

I heard the bathroom door open and went into the hallway. My mom was just standing there. I looked her over, she was so skinny. I saw marks all over her arms and neck making me shiver inside.

"Harley's brother is fine. That's your man?" she asked.

"Nope, it's complicated but this is his baby I'm carrying," I pointed to my big ass belly.

She smiled and walked over. "Oh, wow Nena, congratulations! I take it you will be delivering soon huh?" she looked at me for confirmation. I shook my head yes.

"Let me get you something to sleep in," I said walking into my room. She followed, and I gave her some old clothes I couldn't fit.

I asked if she was hungry, she said yes so, we went into the living room and she took a seat. I made her some soup and a turkey sandwich.

We made small talk while she ate, I don't even think she blew the soup and it was hot.

"Mom I don't mind you saying here for a little bit, but you have to go to rehab. Don't you want to see Nia? She really misses you and asks about you all the time?" she looked away.

"I do miss her baby. I promise I will get myself together but until I can get a bed in a rehab it's okay that I stay here?" she was more so telling me then asking me.

I agreed to let her stay with me, but I knew I was going to have to keep a close eye on her ass, she was sick. I worked hard as hell for everything I have, and I'd be damned if I let her take my shit. I was glad I was on maternity leave, so I could focus on getting her clean.

Chapter Fourteen "Kayla"

"Yeah girl I'm at his house now. I don't see any of his cars," I laughed talking to one of my friends.

"But I'm about to go knock on the door and see if he's home. I'll call you back," I said hanging up.

I had just pulled up to Epic's condo. I was still feeling some type of way that he ended things between us. I tired reaching out to him after my car was delivered back to me after I caused that flat tire, but he blocked me. I was livid and because of that, I was going to make his life a living hell.

I came by the other night and slashed his tires. It made me feel good in the moment but when I woke up the next morning I still felt like shit.

I got out the car and walked into his building. I knew the code to get inside, so I took the elevator to his floor. When I got to his door I took a deep breath and knocked. Minutes later I heard the lock turn and the door open.

I was surprised to see this bitch Harley. She was standing in front of me looking pretty which made me mad as hell. She looked like she was napping. She had on a wife beater, Epic's boxers and some faux locks in her hair. I wanted to beat her ass.

"Can I help you?" she said with an attitude.

"Where the hell is Epic?" I asked with one hand on my hip.

"He's not home and why are you showing up here? Epic is not your man anymore." She squinted her eyes like she was confused.

"You're right he is not my man anymore thanks to you. That's really low that you would sleep with a guy who already had a girl-friend. I thought you had a little class but clearly, I was mistaken. You're nothing but a hood rat like your friends," I told her matter of fact.

"Kayla, I'm not doing this with you today okay? I'm just trying relax and get some sleep before I have to get up and cook dinner for my man, so I can have his food waiting for him when he gets home. You do know what a kitchen is used for right? Did you want to come in and watch me prepare the food, so I can give you some pointers for the next man you fuck with?" she had a wicked smile on her face and I just wanted to punch her in it.

Now I was heated because that clearly meant Epic told her I couldn't cook, and that was something he always complained about. He would say all I did was bitch and complain but couldn't make him a decent meal after a long day of work. I wanted to cry but I wasn't going to let this bitch know she was getting to me.

I just shook my head up and down. "You know what? I just want you to enjoy this little thing yawl have going on," I pointed my finger in the air and made a circle. "Epic will never be faithful to you. It's all fun in the beginning but this nigga just got promoted and the bitches are going to come even harder, you will lose him the same why I did… to another bitch." I shook my head in disgust.

She kept her game face on, but I know her ass was listening to me and thinking hard about what I was saying. I was laughing on the inside. I was hoping I was right about what I was saying.

"You got two seconds to tell me why you're here and then I'm slamming this door in your face. Why the hell are you here?" she dismissed my lasted comment.

"I actually came by to tell him thank you for getting my car fixed. I just wanted to say it to him in person," I lied.

"Your car fixed?" she looked confused.

"Yes, see? What you don't understand is that Epic will always be a part of my life. My car caught a flat and he rushed right over to help me out taking care of the expenses and making sure I got home safe." I crossed my arms over my chest waiting for her reply.

"Okay, I'll be sure to tell him but don't bring your ass back over here. The next time you knock on this damn door I'm fucking you up okay? Oh, and just to let you know I live up in here now, not that it's any of your business so try me if you want," she warned.

Before I could reply she slammed the door in my face. I was standing here with steam coming out of my ears. I was going to fuck Epic up when I saw him.

I ran to my car, so I could ride around to the places I knew he could be. I was hoping to catch him coming out of the barbershop or something because I was pissed at his ass. I asked him time and time again to move in with me and he told me no, and put that shit to rest because he said it would never happen, and now he has the nerve to move her in and they haven't even been together long. He was an ignorant ass motherfucker and I hate him.

I rushed back to Philly, when I pulled up to the barbershop it must have been my lucky day because he was walking out. I jumped out of my car making sure not to bust my ass on the ice.

"Epic!" I yelled, he looked up and when he saw me a frown crept up on his faced hurting my feelings.

"What the hell are you doing here Kayla?" he asked as I approached.

"You moved her into your condo nigga? I've been asking for months for a damn key to your house when we were together, and you moved her right in. Is that how you do me?" I cried.

"Man, I'm not doing this shit with you alright? I have somewhere to be. And how the fuck you know Harley is at my house? I know you didn't go to my crib." I could see the darkness in his eyes and I was regretting ever approaching him in the first place.

He came closer, he was so close I could smell the mint on is breath. "You are going to keep fucking with me and I'm going to kill your ass. Stay the fuck away from my house and my girl. I'm begging you to stop. I don't want your brother to have to bury your dumb ass over something so stupid now walk away," he ordered.

I wanted to protest but I hated this side of him, so I decided against it. When I got to my car he was still standing in the same spot staring at me until I drove off. As I pulled into traffic I started crying. He was defending his relationship and that was fucking me up inside.

Chapter Fifteen "Sundae"

I was currently sitting in my office with my elbows on the table and my hands covering my face. It had been two weeks since my blowup with Eric and I couldn't get over this shit. The doctor said I didn't have any STD, but I was still given a shot. I was so embarrassed.

I had never been in this type of situation. I know he had stepped out on me on countless occasions but to stand in my face and tell me I may have Chlamydia was unforgiveable. As bad as I was missing him, I couldn't get past this shit.

I deserved better then what he was given me. Just thinking about last night, and that I slept with him made tears fall from my eyes because I thought this time was going to be different. I figured I let him sweat long enough so when he got in the bed and cuddled up behind me it just felt so right this time.

I knew something was wrong when he came into the kitchen. The look on his face let me know whatever he was about to expose was not good. I was proud of myself for only giving him a hard slap across his face and nothing more.

I heard a knock at the door and I yelled come in. Jade walked in with his happy ass smiling from ear to ear. I could only imagine what the hell he wanted.

"Hey boo, you have a visitor and he is tall, dark and handsome yesssss!" he snapped his finger.

"Okay, who is it? I'm really busy right now Jade. Can you handle it for me please?" I wiped the tears as they fell.

"Awe sweetie stop crying. You keep giving Eric way too much power over you baby. Let me get a wet cloth for your face and I need you to come take care of this client. He doesn't want to talk to me only you. Okay?" he said shaking his head up and down.

I told him okay and waited while he went to get the cloth for me. When he came back he started wiping my face, it took everything in me to hold the tears back.

"Deep breaths baby. Take a deep breath," he said as I took his advice. "Yes, just like that. Okay let me put a little makeup on your face really quick," he said going into my basket and taking out the councealer to put it under my eyes.

"Is all of this necessary Jade? Let me go get rid of this client," I said pushing his hand away as he tried to apply the makeup. I moved his hand and walked out my office and onto the salon floor.

When I walked out I saw Truth sitting in the waiting area texting on his phone. A lump instantly formed in my throat and my heart skipped a beat.

This nigga was so damn fine. He had on a black hoodie, black jeans and black Timberland boots. His white shirt hung below his hoodie and his dreads sat on top of his head in a bun.

"Good afternoon, Truth. How can I help you?" I said approaching him. I was trying to play it cool, but I was excited to see him.

He looked me up and down undressing me with his eyes like he'd done the last two times I've seen him.

"I came to see if you wanted to go have lunch with me. I was in the neighborhood, so I figured I'd stop by," he said standing up.

"How sweet... but I have an appointment in two hours, so I can't but thank you for thinking about me," I smiled.

"I only need an hour. I'll have you back in time." He chuckled

"I mean you do owe me since you stood my daughter up for her appointment," he looked down at me with a smirk on his face. He thought he was funny.

I looked around the salon and everyone was staring at us. I was about to respond but of course Jade had to put his two cents in.

"Yep Sis you did stand that little pretty girl up, so I think you should go have lunch with sexy chocolate, I mean Mr. Truth, so yawl can call it even," Jade said leaning against the receptionist desk.

I squinted my eyes at him and turned back to Truth. After a few seconds of thinking about it I said, "Okay. So, I apologize for that. It wasn't professional of me. I have a feeling that if I say no you will not leave so let me grab my purse and I'll be right out."

I went into my office and grabbed my purse. I put my leather jacket on, locked my office door, took a deep breath and headed to the front. He kept his eyes on me as I walked towards him making me feel so uncomfortable. I tried not to make eye contact with Jade as we headed out, I was hoping he would just keep his mouth shut.

"Enjoy boo and take your time. I'll prep all of your clients for you. I'll have them ready when you get back. Have a good time, Truth take care of my girl!" he yelled.

"Yo, dude be tripping. Is he always like that?" he shook his head as we walked to his car.

"Who Jade? Yeah, he means well, don't pay him any mind," I laughed.

Truth opened my door and closed it once I was seated. I watched him as he walked to the other side and got in, once he was seated he started the car and pulled off.

I was laughing to myself because I was far from shy but for some reason he had me feeling like a little school girl. "Where do you want to eat at? I know you're pressed for time," he looked over at me.

"We can go to one of the diners close by, you know how to get to Port Richmond right?" I asked.

"Yeah, I know how, just because I don't live in Philly anymore don't mean I don't still know my way around," he smiled showing his pretty white teeth.

We both laughed as we pulled into traffic. We made small talk as we drove down Frankford avenue. My nervousness was going away.

When we made it to the diner, we took our seats and the waitress took our drink orders. She gave us a few minutes to look over the menu before we placed our order.

"Order whatever you want. I hope you're not one of those shy girls that's afraid to eat in front of a nigga," he chuckled.

"I'm far from shy okay, so don't worry about that," I smiled at him.

The waitress came back and took our orders, when she walked away Truth asked if I was okay.

"I'm fine, why wouldn't I be?" I was confused.

"Your eyes are a little puffy that's all," he said.

I was kicking myself for not letting Jade put the concealer on my face. "Oh, it's nothing just some personal shit I'm dealing with, but I'll be okay," I smiled.

"So why are you so persistent with me? Didn't I tell you I have a man?" I looked at him with a raised eyebrow and there he was again with that smile.

"I mean I'm not going to sit here and act like I don't know who your man is. Epic is my boy and I saw you and Eric all hugged up at Rock's funeral, but I can tell you're not happy, so I don't see anything wrong with me pursuing you," he shrugged his shoulders.

I didn't say anything at first, I just sat there. I wasn't sure if I wanted to share with him that my relationship with Eric was over. I wasn't even sure if I wanted to deal with him on any level. He was friends with Eric so that just seems so shady to me.

"I mean I get what you're saying and all, but you and Eric are friends and although I think you are a handsome guy it ends with this lunch because I don't want to create problems with you two," I confessed.

He shook his head in agreement. "So, I just want to tell you something about me. I'm going to start by saying I'm a grown man. I can tell you're not used to dealing with niggas like me, I'm a loyal ass nigga before anything. So, if me and Eric were cool then no matter how beautiful I think you are we would not be sitting here. I'm friends with Epic from way back. Eric and I have never really clicked. I deal with him because he is Epic's right hand and nothing more," he stated.

I was stuck at this point. I can't lie. I do want to see where this could go but Eric would kill me if he knew I was seeing Truth, so I had to really think about this. I needed a meeting with my girls before I decided to entertain him.

The waitress came over with our food and we started eating. We were quiet for a little bit, both of us enjoying our lunch.

"So, Truth I know you're from Philly but where do you live?" I took a sip of my drink.

"Baltimore is where I rest my head, but my sister and mom are still here in the city, so I come home to visit but not as often as I'd like. I'm helping Epic and your boy get back on track I've visiting more often than normal."

I was a little bummed because even if I wanted to see where things could go I was not into long distance relationships, so I could scratch him off my list.

"I'm saying if I had a reason to be in Philly then I would. I'm a boss, so I don't have to live in B-more," he winked at me and I smiled.

"So, does your daughter live in the city?" I asked.

"No, she lives in D.C. with her mom. She was visiting my mom when I came by to get her hair done, but I'm thinking about taking her from her mom. That bitch, I mean woman, wants to run the streets and pass my daughter around to her family while she goes out and shake her ass and I'm not for the dumb shit. So, we're beefing right now," he ate the last piece of his steak.

I just admired how handsome and sexy he was. Truth was the shit. He had a nice build to him; his chocolate skin was so smooth, and his dreads were so neat as they sat on top of his head. I had to calm my girl down between my legs because she was begging for his attention.

"I thought I had a lot going on, but I see we have some things in common," we both laughed.

We continued to make small talk after we ate. Truth paid the bill and we left the diner.

When we got in the car he turned on his music and pulled off. *What's Beef* by Biggie Smalls played as we rode back to my salon. I snuck looks at him out the corner of my eyes as he bobbed his head to the music. I was in trouble, I thought.

When we pulled up to the shop I was down because I was not ready to leave him. I looked over and gave him a warm smile. "Well Truth, thanks for lunch the next one is on me," I said.

"Oh, so there is going to be a next time?" he said shaking his head. "So now that you're feeling a nigga I can get your phone number this time, right?" He handed me his phone.

I took it and put my phone number in it. I purposely didn't take his, I wanted to see just how much he was feeling me. I handed him his phone back and grabbed the handle to get out.

"Damn, a nigga can't get a kiss or a hug" he laughed.

"I gave you my phone number, didn't I?" I quizzed.

He shook his head yes. I told him goodbye and got out the car. When I got to the door I turned around and waved to him, he honked the horn and pulled off.

I turned around Jade was standing there smiling, he was always in somebody business.

"Umm I see you miss thang, smiling. I knew you liked that sexy chocolate so tell me what happened.?" Jade followed me into my office.

"There is nothing really to tell it was only lunch and I have my first client, so I'll fill you in later," I smiled.

I went back onto the floor and called my first client to my chair. I thought about Truth as I parted her hair. I was glad he came by to see me because my depression had eased up a little and surprisingly, I wasn't even thinking about Eric.

"*I* see you over their smiling friend. I'm actually happy for you. I've met Truth, he seems like great guy," Harley smiled.

We were sitting in her parents living room. I was currently staying here since the house was empty and Mrs. Savannah refused to step foot in the house. Quan had recently spoke with a realtor, so the house was going up for sell very soon but I had some time to figure out my next plan. Right now, EJ and I were sleeping in the guest bedroom.

"Yeah, he is alright, but I know that nigga is a player and I don't have time for that. Eric has taken me to hell and back. I need me a nigga on wall street or something. A nerd because these hood niggas ain't nothing but trouble," we both started laughing.

There was a knock on the door. Harley looked at the door and back at me. "Are you expecting anyone?" she said standing up to answer it.

Before I could say anything, she was opening the door and Nena was standing there with her big ole belly. Harley stood to the side letting her in. It was so awkward, and I couldn't take it anymore.

Nena took her shoes and jacket off and came and set down. Harley set on the other side of the sectional. I loved these girls with everything in me and I just wanted everything to go back to normal.

Chapter Sixteen "Harley"

*W*hen I opened the door and saw Nena standing in my parent's doorway with her big ole belly looking like she was about to burst I wanted to grab her and hug her. I missed my girl and I didn't want to fight with her anymore.

I hadn't seen her since my dad's funeral, but Sundae kept me up to date with her health and my niece. I didn't know how to approach her and tell her I was sorry because I had said some fucked up things to her and I felt like shit.

"Okay ladies, I love you both and I miss us hanging out as a trio, so I will admit I'm a sneaky bitch because I had to get both of you here, so we can clear the air. Say whatever we have to say and move past this because Thanksgiving is coming up bitches and we all need to be there to eat Mrs. Savannah's good cooking," Sundae said, and we all started laughing. Then it was an awkward silence.

"Listen Harley, I apologize for not telling you about Quan and me when it happened. I thought it was going to be a onetime thing with us, but you know how that goes. Yeah, I slipped up and got pregnant, but I was not trying to trap him. We were just being irresponsible.

I put my hand up because she was telling me too much. "You

don't have to explain yourself Nena. I'm sorry I blew it up at the restaurant, I just had so much going on at that time. My daddy's health was questionable and to know that you, Sundae and Quan were hiding this from me," I pointed to her stomach, "made me angry. I thought we were closer than that, but that is no excuse. I'm sorry for what I said," I told her.

"Bitch we know how you are about Quan. That's why nobody said anything so just stop Harley!" Sundae yelled we laughed.

"I know I can be overprotective of Quan. You're right I just wish you guys would have told me. But for me to question it when my dad got admitted into the hospital seeing you rub his back and make sure he was holding it together had me say what the hell," I said

"Trust me Harley, how Quan and I got here is still a mystery to me. I saw him in the club and he took me home. I promise I never had a crush on him or thought about getting with him until I saw him in the club that night when I was with Vanessa. Something just sparked between us and it just never stopped," she told us.

"Huh, you were horny that's what happened," Sundae looked at her with the side eye.

"I mean I was but what I'm saying is I wasn't checking for Quan or trying to get pregnant by him on purpose. That was not my intent," Nena said with a serious expression on her face. I instantly felt bad for saying she was trying to trap Quan.

"I'm sorry for saying you were trying to trap him Nena. I really am. I was mad and trying to hurt you because I was hurting. I know you and I know you would never try to intentionally trap Quan, and now look, you have a winner after all the fuck boys you've been with," I laughed. She shook her head no. "Girl I don't know what Quan and I have going on. I mean the feelings are there and I will admit I'm so in love with your brother, but he sends me so many mixed messages. We're still sleeping together like dogs in heat. I'm saying he's at my house so much but I'm not sure if it's for me or the baby. It's like when we are together it's him and I but when he leaves man, it's so different. I have to keep reminding myself that he's in a relationship with Ms. Ebony," Nena shook her head.

I felt bad for her. I had no idea she was going through this emotional rollercoaster with my brother. I could tell when she talked that she loved Quan. I didn't need for her to admit it.

"Well I know it's easier said than done boo, but you are going to have to cut ties with Quan on that level and let him come to you. Don't let him have his cake and eat it too. Fuck that, he needs to know what he is missing," I snapped my fingers.

"I missed you so much," she said. Getting up Nena walked over to me and I got up. We stood there hugging, both of us crying.

"Yawl two pregnant bitches making me cry too," Sundae got up and joined us.

After our little crying session, we sat back down and chatted like old times. My phone beeped letting me know I had a text message. I unlocked my phone to see who it was.

Unknown: I'm sorry about that shit that happened Harley. I don't know where my head was. I miss you baby, I don't give a fuck that you shot me."

I stared at my phone for a second. I was in shock that Jay was really texting me. I heard Sundae calling my name. I closed my phone and looked up.

"Bitch who is texting you? I called your name three times?" she asked.

"Epic he is a little mad at me because I cursed him out about Kayla's thirsty ass. Do you know she showed up at the house talking about Epic is basically with me for the season and she wanted to thank him for coming to her rescue when she caught a flat tire? I cursed that nigga out so bad when he got home," I confessed.

Sundae shook her head. "Harley leave my brother alone, he does not want that thirst bucket," she sucked her teeth.

"Yeah, I felt like an ass when he told me that happened before we got back together. I can't wait to see that bitch, I'm going to beat her ass." I was so serious. Pregnant or not she was going to get it and I wasn't playing.

"It's alright girl, I'll beat her ass for you," Sundae waved me off.

I laughed, "Sun, do you know Eric is walking around our condo like every day? He has spent the night more times than I care to remember." We all laughed.

"I'm not thinking about Eric to tell you the truth. That nigga put my health on the line. I'm done." I knew she was serious this time.

"Good bitch because that nigga Truth sounds like the one," Nena told her.

Sundae smiled from ear to ear. She was feeling that man, I could tell. I was hoping she gave him a chance. He wasn't necessarily Eric's friend, so I don't see what the issue was, but I do know my girl is scared to deal with another man. She had been with Eric for so long he is all she knows.

We sat and talked for a few more hours, ordering food. It felt good to be with them, I missed my sisters and now we were back. There was a lot to look forward to even though my dad was not here. We were about to have two new additions to the family, Sundae had freed herself from Eric, I had Epic and Thanksgiving was coming. The addition of Epic and his Nana for Thanksgiving was going to be a treat and I was looking forward to it.

Thanksgiving

"Yes, baby right there! Oh my gosh!" I was currently sitting on Epic's face while he ate my pussy.

"Right there yesssss!" I yelled. I worked my hips as I held onto the headboard. He was feasting like it was his last meal and I was loving it.

My clit was swelling up as he sucked on it. I held my head back letting my eyes roll in the back of my head. I closed my eyes. "No, okay wait, wait! Baby stop! Wait!" I cried as my eyes popped back open.

The more I begged him to stop the harder he sucked and before I knew it I was cumming all in his face.

Epic laughed as he moved from under me and got up. I sat on my knees still facing the headboard. I was trying to get myself together, my pussy was still throbbing.

I laid down on the bed and looked over at him as he checked his cell phone. We had been having sex all damn morning and I was tired.

"What are you looking at?" he said leaning over and kissing my lips.

"I'm guessing you're not mad at me anymore," I looked at him. I was referring to how I blew up at him about Kayla coming to the house. I tried to act like everything she said to me wasn't bothering me, but it was.

The thought of him running to Kayla's rescue had me so mad and as soon as he came home I blew up at him cursing him out, accusing him of wanting to be with her.

When he broke it down and told me what really went down I felt so stupid and what made it worst was that Kayla got what she wanted and that was to start a fight between us. But Epic wasn't having it. He was being petty, ignoring me when he came home, and it was killing me. He had eased up a few days ago and that was only because I had been having a lot of morning sickness and he felt sorry for me.

"No, we're good but don't let it happen again alright? I'm your man and you need to remember that alright?" I shook my head letting him know I understood. "I love your jealous ass," he said smiling and heading for the bathroom, so he could shower.

I laid there smiling. Life was great right now. I thought of my dad and said a silent prayer asking God to bless his soul. I was missing him like crazy, but I had to be strong for my baby.

I got under the cover and closed my eyes I was so tired. Epic had come in around six in the morning and of course he wanted to fuck. So now I was planning on taking a little nap until I had to get up and help my mom with prepping the food.

I was excited because everyone was coming to dinner, this would be Epic's first-time hosting Thanksgiving in this house and I know he was excited even though he acted like he wasn't.

I couldn't wait for my mom to meet his Nana and she was also bringing her boyfriend Mr. Fred. I had warned Nena that Quan side he was bringing Ebony and she said it was okay, she wasn't thinking about Quan and his bitch.

I thought about uninviting her, but Nena insisted that she was not bothered. I was sure hoping this gathering wasn't going to be a disaster. Eric and Sundae were on the outs right now, so I was hoping those two could keep it together and not kill each other.

Of course, Eric was here at the house getting in early this morning with Epic. Eric was so damn lost without Sundae it was crazy. I almost felt sorry for the dog but not enough to convince Sundae to go back to him, that's for sure.

A few hours later

I woke up to the smell of candy yams and collard greens. I heard some chatter downstairs and a bunch of laughter. I looked at the clock and saw that is was noon. I jumped up and headed for the shower. I was going to kill Epic. I couldn't believe he let me sleep so late.

When I got out the shower I got dressed in a pair of black tights and a gray tee shirt. I was feeling a little sluggish because of my pregnancy I was hoping today was going to be a good day.

I picked up my phone and noticed I had two text messages. When I opened my phone, my breath got caught in my throat. Jay was not letting up.

Jay: Harley baby please call me, so I can tell you how sorry I am for what happened when I came to Philly. I love you and I just want you to come home.

Jay: Bitch don't act like you didn't get my last text. I was going to say sorry but fuck that keep ignoring me and I will come back and this time you won't get away!

I stood there reading his text messages repeatedly. My heart started beating fast. All types of things were running through my mind.

The bedroom door opened, and I jumped when I turned around Epic was standing there eating food out of a bowl. I quickly put my phone down and grabbed my slippers, sliding them on my feet.

"Hey baby, I was coming to check on you. Are you good?" he asked.

"Yeah, I was actually on my way down stairs, but umm what is the status on Jay?" I asked.

"I'm on it Harley, stop worrying about it. That nigga hasn't tried to call you has he?"

I shook my head no, grabbed my phone off the bed and walked to the door. He grabbed me.

"Chill stop worrying about that shit. You know I got you. That nigga will be handled real soon," he assured me. I shook my head again and walked out.

When I got downstairs my mom was in the kitchen laughing and talking with Epic's Nana. When she saw me her face lit up. She walked from behind the kitchen counter and came over hugging me.

"Hi baby, how are you? My Beatle told me when I got here that you were having a baby, I'm so excited!" she smiled hugging me again and kissing my cheek.

"Thank you! I'm sorry I wasn't down here when you arrived, I've been so tired lately." I smiled.

"Oh hush, baby it's alright and I got to spend time with your beautiful mom and guess what? I gave her some of my recipes!" She laughed.

I looked up and a man with a walker was walking into the kitchen. I'm guessing this was Mr. Fred, Nana's boo.

I introduced myself to him and helped him take a seat at the kitchen table. He was an old cutie, but I couldn't help but think he looked a little like the old guy from Big Momma's House and as I watched Nana's interaction with him I could tell they were in love.

I walked over to the counter where my mom and Nana were preparing Thanksgiving dinner and asked if I could help. My mom gave me a bunch of vegetables and asked me to start cutting them.

As I started cutting the onion the smell became too much for me, so I ran into the powder room. I threw up my dinner from the night before. This was going to be a long day, I thought.

About an hour later everyone had arrived. Maze and Frankie Beverly's *Back to Basics* was playing in the kitchen as the older women set around talking. My mom's sisters were here and a few of my uncles too. I was glad they had showed up because my mom needed all the support she could get. I noticed she would stare off into space from time to time.

"Why the hell did Nena bring Ms. Barb here? You better watch her, Epic got a lot of nice shit laying around," Sundae whispered in my ear as she looked over at Nena's mom who was on the phone smiling hard. That's when I noticed she had lost her four front teeth.

She looked bad. I could tell the drugs had taken a toll on her. I was wondering when she was going to report to rehab and clean herself up. It would be nice if she was off the drugs before Nena had the baby.

"Girl I don't think she is crazy enough to steal from Epic because if she does he will shoot her ass," we laughed.

"What the hell is so funny?" Nena said walking up to us, eating a piece of ham.

"Nothing girl. What is my God daughter doing in there?" Sundae said.

I looked at her and rolled my eyes. I was a little tight because Nena had picked Sundae to be the baby's God mother, but it was only because the baby was my niece.

"You know I love you girl," Nena said and both girls laughed. I didn't find anything funny.

Chapter Seventeen "Nena"

"*Mom* you've been on the phone ever since we walked in the door. You need to get off the phone." She was sitting on Epic's nice furniture with her legs tucked in the couch like this was her house.

Rolling her eyes, she said, "Girl these people are not thinking about me." She went back to talking to whomever she was on the phone with. She was so happy I purchased her a cricket phone she didn't know how to act.

My mom was doing good. It was a struggle having her with me because she was going through withdrawal without any help. I would give her twenty dollars a day, just so she would have some money.

I wasn't stupid, I knew when she left my house she was out getting high but there was nothing I could do about it. I just hoped I could get her into a rehab she was happy with. We had visited some of the best ones in the Tri-state area, but she found something wrong with each one. I was willing to pay for her to go to a nice facility.

Quan was pissed at me for letting my mom stay with me. He kept saying he didn't trust her but that was his issue.

We had gotten into a huge argument two days ago about my mother and how he wanted me to make her leave because in his mind she was using me, he had some nerve. I didn't tell him what to do with his mom, so he had no rights telling me what to do with mine.

"You want me to fix you a plate of fruit until the food is ready?" he walked up to me asking. I just rolled eyes.

"Quan get away from me, I don't need you to do anything for me. Go over there with Ebony's insecure ass," I said trying to walk away.

"Come on Nena, Harley said she asked you if it was okay for her to come and you said you didn't care. Now you're acting like you have a problem." He grabbed my arm.

"I don't care, now get off me," I yanked my arm way from him and walked off.

I noticed her staring at me as I walked over to the couch and took a seat next to my mom.

After I sat down I started playing on my phone. I looked up and Ebony was still looking at me. I couldn't take it anymore. I said, "Do you have to take a shit or something?" All the guys in the room stopped talking and looked at us.

"Excuse me? What are you talking about?" she rolled her eyes looking at me waiting for a response.

"I'm saying you keep looking at me with your face all balled up, I was wondering if you had to go to the bathroom," I reiterated.

Eric started laughing so hard and stomping his feet. He was such an immature instigator.

"I'm so sick of you, I swear! Bitches always got a lot to say when their carrying a baby but after you drop that load let's see what you have to say!" Ebony rolled her neck.

"Oh no you didn't just threaten my daughter you little hoe. Don't talk to my baby like that. I will drag you all over these nice floors!" my mom warned.

Eric laughed harder. He got up and started stomping his feet holding his stomach like it was that funny.

"Okay, yawl need to chill out. Ms. Barb, you can't be threat-

116

ening to fuck people up, and Eric stop hyping her up man," Epic said trying not to laugh.

"Well Epic, you tell that big forehead slut to leave my baby alone. She just mad because Nena is having a baby by her nigga. Now tell me I'm wrong," she folded her arms waiting for Ebony to respond.

"What is going on in here? I know she is not in here starting trouble with you?" Sundae stood in the center of the room looking around at everyone.

Quan walked in behind Sundae looking at me and then at Ebony. I was really starting to hate this nigga for playing with my emotions. I couldn't take it anymore. "What's the problem Nena?" he asked.

"You're my problem," I tried to push him, but he wouldn't move. "I'm tired of you trying to play me for this ugly big forehead bitch. I think you love seeing my heart break every time you bring her around!" I was screaming so loud everyone came into the room.

"Yo, calm the fuck down before you go into labor. You're drawing attention for nothing. You can't ever just relax without being on some bullshit and you think I'm trying to put up with your shit for the rest of my life? That's why your ass is alone now!" he yelled.

I could have sworn my heart stopped beating when he said that. I was so done with Quan and all his games. I just wanted to get in my car and go home. The entire room got quiet. I looked over and saw Ebony standing there smiling.

"Oh, hell no! What did you just say to my baby?" my mom jumped up asking. Epic grabbed her arm holding her frail body back.

"Oh no, Barb I got this," Mrs. Savannah said holding her hand up to my mom. "Now wait a minute Quan. What the hell is wrong with you, talking to Nena like that? You were not raised like that and for God's sake she is having your baby. That's the mother of your child and you are going to show her some damn respect!" Mrs. Savannah said poking him in the chest.

"Mom, my bad alright, just chill out let me talk to Nena," he said.

"If you want to talk to Nena, you need to do it in privacy. Don't sit in here and embarrass her in front of everyone, Quan. You don't want me to get involved because it will get ugly. If you can't control miss thang over there she needs to leave now," she grabbed some empty cups off the table and walked out the room.

"I'm trying to understand why the fuck you keep smiling," Sundae asked Ebony.

"Sun chill. Stay out of it please," Eric begged.

Sundae cut her eye at him and then back at me. "You good friend? because I will beat this bitch ass in here right now if you give me the word," she asked.

"No, I'm good. I think I'm going to leave, Mom let's go!" I yelled.

I noticed Quan was still standing in front of me, but I acted like he wasn't there.

"Nena, come on man don't leave. You know I didn't mean that shit, I just don't want you to get all hype and go into early labor!" he confessed.

"Well if you don't want me to go into early labor then you wouldn't have brought her here. You know she don't like me and could care less about this baby. You play way too many games and I can't do this with you anymore," I shook my head.

Harley walked over and wiped my tears away. Looking me in the eyes she said, "you're not leaving, I don't care what you say. It's Thanksgiving we're family. If you need to go upstairs and get yourself together then do that but you're not leaving, and you know my mom won't allow you to," she said, and I laughed.

"Quan, we need to talk now!" Ebony demanded.

"Chill, Ebony just sit down give me a minute damn!"

I told my mom to have a seat. I tried not to laugh as she walked back to the sofa where she was sitting, She eye-balled Ebony. "You better watch your back bitch, let me catch you in the streets," my mom warned.

Eric and Epic started laughing. I turned to walk out the room. I

118

decided to take Harley's advice and go get myself together. I wasn't giving Ebony the satisfaction of leaving that's what she wanted, but she better believe when I have my daughter I'm coming for her.

I had been laying in one of the guess bedrooms for about twenty minutes when I heard a tap on the door. I ignored it because I had a feeling it was Quan. Seconds later the door opened I sucked my teeth when he walked through the door.

"Did I tell you to come in? What the hell you want?" I yelled.

"Nena stop yelling for real! I came to check on you," he said

I didn't say anything I just continued to look past him. I just wanted him to leave me alone. He came over and sat on the bed rubbing my stomach. The baby started doing flips. She always did this whenever Quan was around.

"Quan please leave, I can't do this with you anymore. I'm so serious I'm done." I told him.

"Ebony left, Epic had one of his drivers take her back to Philly. I admit I fucked up bringing her here. I'm sorry about that. I didn't think you would care on some real shit," he said.

"I always thought you were smart Quan but I'm second guessing myself. You really don't get it," I shook my head as the tears rolled down my face.

"Why the hell are you crying? I swear my daughter better not be a cry baby or I'm fucking you up," he laughed.

I wasn't laughing, none of this is funny. "Quan you think everything is a game," I told him. I was getting irritated.

"You love me, don't you?" he asked catching me off guard.

I didn't say anything for a second, I was afraid of getting my feelings hurt and the fact remains that he is with Ebony so me confessing my love to him didn't matter.

"No, I don't now leave," I pointed to the door. He shook his head and got up. He put his hand out for me to grab it.

"It's time to feed my daughter, now let's go," he said.

I grabbed his hand and he helped my big ass up. He grabbed me and hugged me. I closed my eyes, it felt so right being in his arms. I wondered if he thought the same thing, but with Quan you never know.

Chapter Eighteen "Sundae"

I was happy when Quan told his little girlfriend to hit the road because I was two seconds off her ass. His big forehead bitch thought it was a game, but I was going to show her the next time I ran into her.

Things had calmed down after Ebony left and now everything was back to normal. Nena looked like she was feeling better to, she was currently sitting in the kitchen with Mrs. Savannah going over baby names. I laughed to myself because for the life of me I still couldn't believe she was having a baby with Quan.

Quan was more relaxed now talking with the guys about football, I didn't understand why he brought her here anyway. I was starting to think he liked getting Nena upset and that wasn't cool.

Before Nena went into the kitchen I caught him stealing glances at her, I just wanted them to get their shit right. I couldn't understand why these two were not together. I was hoping they would figure it out.

Poor Harley was laying on the sofa next to Epic with her legs stretched across him as he rubbed her feet while she watched the game. My girl was over this pregnancy and she was just getting started.

Eric looked up at me and winked his eye, I gave him the finger and rolled my eyes. I had been ignoring him for the past few weeks and I was going to continue to. He laughed and went back to playing cars with EJ while he watched the football game.

I was waiting for my mom to get here, she had texted twenty minutes ago and said she was close. I was hoping she would hurry up because we were waiting for her before we start dinner.

I was shocked when she said she was coming, I found it odd that she couldn't even drive to Jersey to see me but wanted to drive all the way to Delaware for a free meal.

I prewarned her not to start no ghetto shit when she got here. She was jealous of Mrs. Savannah, so I was kind of on edge that she was coming.

When I invited her, I was expecting her to say no, but she surprised my ass this morning when she texted and said she would be here by four. My cell phone beeped, and I looked to see who it was.

A huge smile crept on my face when Truth's name came across the screen. He had been texting me ever since he took me to lunch. He was coming to Philly in a few days and wanted to see me. I didn't know if that was a good idea.

Truth: Hey baby girl just checking on you. Happy Thanksgiving.

Me: Happy Thanksgiving to you! How are you?

Truth: I'm good but I would be better if I could see you!

Me: To bad you're in D.C.

Truth: I'll be in Philly in two days I want to see you.

*T*ruth told me he was spending Thanksgiving with his daughter. I was a little jealous because all I could think about was him being hugged up with his baby momma.

I didn't respond to his text because I didn't know what my plan was. I felt someone staring at me I looked up and Eric was giving me an evil eye. I just ignored him and headed to the kitchen. The doorbell rang, and I walked down the hallway leading to the front door.

"Hey baby!" my mom yelled when I opened the door. She was standing here with this nigga that looked like he was broke and waiting for her to get her paycheck. He had a mini afro, brown corduroys with a button up silk shirt, the four buttons from the top were unbuttoned like it wasn't cold as hell outside. I got an instant attitude.

"Hi Sundae, right?" he put his hand out to shake mine. I liked to die when he smiled displaying his grill on his bottom teeth with his old ass.

"Umm did I say you could bring a guest?" I gave her the side eye I was really regretting inviting her.

"Excuse me! little girl who are you talking to? move out my damn way, it's cold out here," she said pushing pass me to get in the house.

"Hey everybody," I heard her say as I shut the door I said a prayer to God. I know I was going to need it.

I followed them into the family room where everyone was. I watched as she went over to Harley and hugged her followed by Eric. She picked EJ up and started giving him kisses.

Mrs. Savannah and Nena walked in the room to greet her and when EJ saw Mrs. Savannah he fought for my mom to put him down and ran over grabbing Mrs. Savannah's legs and hugging them.

"See this is why I told you I need to see him more Sundae. My grandson doesn't really know me," she put her hands up in defeat.

"Do that look like my fault? Miss *my car is old, I can't make it to Jersey*," I mimicked her.

"Well, hi Joyce how have you been?" Harley's mom asked

"I'm good, what do yawl have to drink in here Epic?" she said dismissing Mrs. Savannah.

Mrs. Savannah shook her head and then turned around to leave the room. "Same old Joyce I see," she said grabbing EJ's hand.

"Stuck up bitch," I heard my mom say under her breath.

My mom was on her bullshit and I was still mad she showed up with this broke down nigga. Her and I were going to have it out if she tried to start trouble.

"The drinks are downstairs at the bar, come on I'll show you," he said to my mom ushering for Quan and Eric to join them.

"I'm so mad I invited her here!" I said to Harley and Nena as I plopped down on the sofa. My mom was going to humiliate both of us.

My phone chimed again. I knew it was Truth.

Truth: Don't make me pop up on you again. I see you ignored what I said, but I'm not sweating that shit just make sure you're ready to cook for me. You said the next meal is on you and I want you to cook me dinner at my condo!

Harley snatched the phone and read it. "Oh, bitch you're so sneaky hiding shit from us!" she laughed handing the phone to Nena, so she could read it.

"Yes, sis I'm so happy for you, you're about to sample some new dick after all these years!" Nena whispered as she high fived Harley.

I rolled my eyes and snatched my phone. I didn't want to admit it, but I think Nena was right. But I wasn't going to tell her that.

19

Chapter Nineteen "Eric"

I was sitting at Epic's bar laughing at Sundae's mom and her boyfriend. I'm not sure where she got this nigga from. He was sitting here drinking all Epic's liquor like he paid for it. *Niggas,* I said to myself as I watched him pour his third shot.

"Old head calm down, the liquor is not going anywhere," Epic told him.

"Alright young blood my bad," he said leaning back in the chair almost falling out of it.

I wasn't surprised that Ms. Joyce was dating him. Sundae's mom was pretty for an old head. I didn't understand why she always dated these guys that didn't have shit to offer her.

"Eric so when are you going to marry my baby? You guys have been together forever, come on now," she tilted her head to the side.

I chuckled. I'm guessing she didn't know about Sundae and I breaking up, and I know she didn't because if she did she would have beat my ass as soon as she walked in the door.

"That's Sundae Ms. Joyce, you have to take that up with her, you know I love her" I said.

"June bug, this is my son in law okay? He always got my back

124

and if you fuck with me he will come after your ass, right Eric?" she said sipping her drink waiting for me to agree with her.

"Joyce be quiet alright? You keep saying that same shit. I said I'm not going to hurt you baby, you're going to be my wife real soon," he smiled showing his gold tooth.

"I hear you baby and I believe you," she smiled then turned her attention back to me. "Yeah well I'll talk to her. You better continue to treat my baby like the queen she is, okay?" she threw her shot back.

My phone was vibrating, I looked to see Vanessa calling. She had been calling me lately talking about her morning sickness was bad. I kept telling her I didn't give a fuck, that wasn't my baby, so she could go ahead with that trying to trap me with someone else's seed.

Harley yelled down the steps that dinner was ready. We all headed up stairs to the dining room. I was hungry as hell. Epic, Quan and I had smoked so much in the past hour it was time to get down with this good ass cooking. Mrs. Savannah and Epic's grandma could cook so I know it was about to go down.

When we got upstairs everyone was taking their seats. "Hey Barb, I didn't know you were here," Ms. Joyce said to Nena's mom.

"I guess not. You walked up in here like you owned the place and went straight to the liquor. I was in the kitchen if you must know," Barb rolled her eyes.

"Oh, okay but watch your damn mouth. You're probably three days clean trying to get tough with me," I couldn't believe Ms. Joyce said that.

"Wow, and you probably fucked this ugly nigga in the first three minutes you met him. Don't come for me, Joyce," Barb warned squinting her eyes at Ms. Joyce.

It took everything in me not to laugh. Nena's mom was a beast with her mouth. She didn't give a fuck what came out of it. If she wasn't into taking drugs I would recruit her to be a part of our team.

"Okay now we are not doing that tonight, everybody take your seats please," Harley asked.

"Yeah yawl heard what my baby said," Epic said pulling the seat back for Harley. This nigga was whipped. I ain't never seen him pull a chair out for any chick.

Sundae came and set next to me while EJ sat on the other side of her. She was trying to ignore me. I knew she was still mad, but it was nothing for me to get back in with her. She was still staying at Harley's parents' house and I was respecting her space.

I noticed her phone chime, she smiled as she responded to the text. That shit was making me mad. I was trying not to blow up because we were in front of too many people but in a minute, I was about to go straight savage on her ass.

"I want Grandma," EJ said trying to climb out the high chair before Sundae could unhook him.

"Come here baby, you can sit with Grandma," Ms. Joyce said pulling her seat back.

EJ ran past her chair and put his hand out for Mrs. Savannah to pick him up.

"See this is the shit I'm talking about Sundae! Why is he calling this bitch Grandma!" Ms. Joyce said slamming her hand on the table. Everyone in the room stopped what they were doing.

"Excuse me Joyce, what the hell did you just call me? Yeah, he calls me Grandma because I am. What the hell have you done for him lately you, sorry excuse for a mother?" Mrs. Savannah yelled I didn't know she had it in her.

"You better watch your mouth before I jump over this table and slap your bougie ass!" Ms. Joyce threatened.

"Try it and see how far you get!" Mrs. Savannah's sister stood up.

Shit was about to get ugly in here. I had my money on Mrs. Savannah, she was the quite one.

"You can call me bougie, but I will whip you ass in here!"

Sundae stood up. "Mom what the hell is wrong with you? Why are you being so disrespectful? Didn't I tell you not to come in here starting shit?" she yelled.

"Don't curse at me! Go ahead and take her side, you wish she was your mother anyway don't you? Just say it!" she yelled in Sundae's face.

I got up and stood between the two of them, it was time for Ms. Joyce to go.

"Yo, I can't have you in here talking to Mrs. Savannah like that Joyce, you're going to have to get up out of here," Epic said.

"Huh? Young blood can I get a to go box?" June bug asked.

"Fuck this food June bug, let's go. Sundae you don't have to worry about me anymore, I can't believe you're doing this to me!" she walked out of the dining room with Sundae following her.

Nana got up and started putting food on a plate for June bug. Ms. Joyce was screaming for him to come but he told her to wait and when Nana handed him the plate he told everyone Happy Thanksgiving and rushed to grab his coat.

"Young Blood!" he yelled calling for Epic. Epic came towards the front door.

"Can I have that bottle of Gin youngin?" he asked.

I tilted my head to the side. He was serious as a heart attack.

Epic shook his head and went into the kitchen. He came back with the Gin and handed it to June bug. He thanked Epic and ran out the door because Ms. Joyce was blowing her horn and wouldn't let up until he walked out the door.

Once she pulled off the three of us went back in the house. Sundae apologized for her mom's behavior and we all sat back down to eat in peace.

Sundae barely ate her food, I know she was mad her mom acted a fool, but this was their relationship once things cooled off they would be cool again.

I leaned over and kissed her cheek, I was surprised she didn't push me away. "Don't worry about that alright? You know I got you," I told her. She smiled and went back to eating her food.

When dinner was over everyone was starting to leave. Epic said his Nana and Mr. Fred were going to spend the night so they said their goodnights and went to bed. If you ask me Mr. Fred was ready to go to bed when he got here. He couldn't keep his eyes open the whole day.

About an hour later all of Mrs. Savannah's family left. She packed a bag and said she was spending the night at her sister's house.

Ms. Barb was on the couch knocked out snoring under the blanket Harley was sleeping under all day. I noticed she kept scratching her arms as she slept.

Quan and Nena were sitting on the couch together. This nigga was rubbing her stomach while she scrolled through her phone. I felt bad for my nigga. He had expressed to Epic and I that he was into Nena but the way she switched up on him with her mood swings he wasn't with it.

I told him it was her damn hormones because Sundae couldn't stand me when she was pregnant with EJ. I told him to give it some time. Now he was stressing about what to do with Ebony. I laughed thinking about how he said he wished he never told Ebony he wanted a relationship. I had warned him when he told me she was pressuring him for a title, but his young ass wouldn't listen.

I looked over at Sundae and she was texting on her phone. I don't know who it was, but she was making me mad and I was about to blowup.

"Yo, who the fuck you keep texting on your phone?" I asked.

She sucked her teeth. "Alright yawl, I'm going to get ready to get out of here. He about to start tripping and I don't have time for it," she said getting up gathering EJ's things.

"What the fuck you mean? I only asked you a question. You can't answer me?" I grabbed her arm.

"Hey, hey, Eric, not tonight. Come on now, it's getting late anyway, let her leave if she's ready," Harley said.

"Man fuck that, she is going to answer my damn question. Are you talking to a nigga?" I gripped her arm tighter.

"Eric my arm is starting to hurt, stop. It's late and EJ is tired."

"EJ, is good, he can stay here tonight, Epic already told your ass that earlier, and if you don't answer my question I'm not letting you go," I told her.

"Oh, yes the fuck you are letting her go, Eric don't get dragged up in here," Nena threatened.

Epic gave me a look and I let her go. It was his house, so I was going to respect it. I watched as she packed EJ's bag and grabbed their coats. She was making me even more mad because she was ignoring me.

Once she gathered all their stuff she helped EJ put his coat on she walked to the door with me on her heels.

"Sundae I swear if you don't tell me who the hell you been texting it's going to be a problem," I said.

"I'm not telling you shit, you lost all rights to ask me anything motherfucker when you gave me an STD scare so move out my way!" she yelled.

Sundae thought I was playing with her. I think she forgot who the hell I was. "Okay that's how you want to play? I already said sorry about that shit and I showed you my papers that I'm clear and you showed me yours. What else do you want from me, damn?" she had me on one hundred.

She started walking down the steps to her car that was in the driveway. I took my gun out and shot all four of her tires, she wasn't going anywhere.

"Oh my gosh, are you crazy!" she yelled and EJ got upset and started screaming. I didn't mean to upset my son. I tried to grab him out of her arms, but she moved back.

Epic's door opened, and everyone came out. "Eric what you do now? I thought I asked you to leave her alone," Epic said walking down the steps to approach us.

"She thinks she can fucking talk to some nigga in front of me, she knows better!" I yelled.

"I know better? You not my damn daddy and I'm tired of saying that to you!" she stomped her feet. I saw Quan take EJ out her arms and pass him to Nena as she walked back in the house.

Harley stood beside Sundae trying to calm her down. "I just want to talk to her that's all," I told Epic. Sundae kept shaking her head no as she cried. I had fucked up.

After we all calmed down, Sundae decided she was going to take the ride home with Quan. Epic helped her load Quan's car. When everything was packed in, Quan came out and they got in the car.

Nena and her mom left shortly after. Nena didn't say shit to me when she walked out the door, but I didn't give a fuck.

Harley went upstairs as soon as Nena left. I knew her ass was mad too, but it was cool. I didn't have anything to say to either of them because I bet they knew who Sundae had been texting all day.

I laid my head on the couch and went to sleep. I couldn't drive because of the liquor but as soon as it wore off I was going to get in my car and drive the fuck home. Whoever Sundae was talking to I was going to eventually find out and whoever it was he was a dead man, every nigga in Philly knew she was off limits.

Chapter Twenty "Jamal"

"Nigga how much you going to pay? Don't have us come all the way to Philly and you throw us a few hundred dollars for killing these niggas," my cousin said.

"That's real fucked up man. This nigga killed my mom, your aunt and you worried about money?" I shook my head.

I was still fucked up that Epic killed my damn momma. I could still hear her screaming in my ear as she begged for him not to kill her. I knew that nigga was going to strike but I didn't think he would go for my mom.

She had been good to him when we were young boys. I remember my mom would always let both Epic and Eric spend the night at my crib. She taught us how to smoke weed, gave us our first shots of liquor and told us how not to trust these bitches.

Epic didn't have a mother growing up, the only thing he had was his grandma and she wasn't teaching him the streets like my momma taught him. He didn't have free range to bring bitches in the house and have them chill up in his bedroom.

My mom didn't care about none of that shit, when we started getting girls she would let him entertain in the basement. She threw us condoms and said wash the sheets when we were done.

So, I was fucked up that his get back was with her, but he was going to pay. I had tried to get at Nana and kill her old ass, it was nothing personal towards her, but that nigga killed my mom.

Epic had so many people watching her making it hard for me to get her, so I did the next best thing and that was set my old trap house on fire. I was going to get him where his pockets would feel it.

My first thought was to try robbing it again to get some more cocaine, but I wasn't dumb enough to try the same shit twice. I was running low off the kilo's I stole from Rock, so I had to think of something fast.

"Listen I'm going to pay yawl once we rob these niggas and take all the drugs, just be patient alright?" I assured them.

"Okay well you've been up here for a week nigga talking the same shit snorting all this damn coke. When are we going to do this? Let's kidnap one of their bitches or something." my cousin said, and his two friends laughed.

I can't lie about that either, I was thinking about putting that plan in motion. When I thought about taking Kayla I scratched that from my list. Epic didn't give a fuck about her pretty ass anymore. Last I heard he was checking for Harley. I followed her a few times, but this nigga had people watching her too.

Sundae was going to be the closet person for me to get at, it was nothing personal towards her, but she was going to be next on my list if I couldn't get at them niggas. She was cool and all, but that nigga took my mom.

I was hoping my cousin and his crew could help me pull this off, he wasn't a street nigga, but I didn't care. I needed muscle to get at them. I was about to go hard. Those niggas had a whole team and it was four of us. I have to think this through, but in the meantime, I'll have to lay low here.

I wasn't worried about them finding me up here. They had already come here looking for me at my cousin house, so I couldn't go there. I copped me this little apartment to hold me over for a few months, well until my money runs out anyway.

"So, are you going to share that coke or are you going to keep that shit for yourself it looks A one my nigga," my cousin said admiring how white this shit was. Rock always had the best product in the city.

I heard my phone ring when I looked down it was Strawberry. This bitch had been getting on my nerves lately. I told her not to call me, I would talk to her when I'm heading back to the city, but she was hard headed as fuck.

I liked her, but she had more of an addiction than I did with this white stuff. Most times I felt like I was in competition with her to see who can snort the most shit.

It seemed like when I did snort with her my nose bled more but when I did it by myself I was able do chill take my time and let it do what it do.

My phone started ringing again so I decided to answer before she blew my high. "What's up man? Why you keep calling?" I said into the phone.

"Really Jamal? That's how you do me when I've been letting you lay low at my house? I cook for you fuck you and wash your funky clothes. You left and took all the cocaine with you that's not right!" she yelled.

I wasn't trying to hear what she was saying. At the end of the day I was using her and after I killed these niggas and take over the streets I was going to dismiss her. If she kept talking shit she was going to be next.

"Strawberry man chill. I'll be back in the city soon I'm up here working out my plan and you're distracting me real talk."

"I hear you baby and I'm sorry, but I need some more blow. Is there anyway you can have one of your people drop some off to me before I leave for work?" she asked.

I looked at the phone and hung up. She was a greedy bitch and I was tired of sharing with her.

I snorted another line and laid my head back. I had to put my plan in motion because there couldn't be any mistakes this time around, it was time I came for blood.

21

Chapter Twenty One "Harley"

a **few weeks later**
        I was in a good mood today. I had just reenrolled in my two classes that I had to drop when my dad passed away. I had also told my supervisor at the hospital that I was ready to come back, but she insisted that I take a few more weeks.

I was okay with that because I had some personal issues I needed to work out. I was a little tight with Epic. Now that he was devoting more time to his new position and looking for Jamal I felt like he was ignoring what Jay had done to me.

Jay kept texting me how sorry he was then he would tell me he was going to kill me. This nigga was so sick in the head and I was tired of the threats.

I thought about telling Epic but decided against it. I was getting to the point where I wanted to handle this on my own. Epic obviously had more important things to attend to.

My phone rung and when I saw that it was my boo, I pushed the talk button.

"Hey baby, just checking in with you. What are your plans for today?" he asked as he turned his music down.

"The girls and I are going to the mall in a little bit to shop for

Christmas that's all. I was going to ask if you cannot have me followed today?" I knew what his answer was going to be, but I figured I'd ask him anyway.

"I'm not sure about that Harley. You know this nigga is out there somewhere. I don't feel safe with you riding around with no protection," I could hear the stress in his voice.

The line was quiet. I guess he was contemplating giving me my way which was hard for him not to do. Epic's cold heart was melting at least when it came to me.

"Alright man, just this one time but call me as soon as you get to the mall, leave the mall all that shit," he demanded.

I smiled. I loved this man. He was my everything and I was glad to finally call him mine with no drama attached. I rubbed my belly, I couldn't wait to become a mother and raise my baby with Epic.

I grabbed my things and headed out locking the door behind me. The cold air hit me as soon as I came outside. I couldn't wait until winter was over, I was over the cold.

I got into my car and smiled to myself. I was going to have this car forever because this was the last gift from my dad.

I was on my way to the shop to meet up with Sundae and Nena, so we could take one car.

Sorry by Beyoncé was playing on the radio. I turned the music up and pulled out my parking spot singing at the top of my lungs.

Quan had texted me earlier asking if I wanted to meet up later. I told him to come past the house. He sounded like he was stressing, and I know it had everything to do with what he and Nena were going through.

Nena had been venting about their situation for the last few days. Quan had her head all messed up with his mixed messages, but I can say my girl was holding it down by not giving in to him when it came to sex. She was strictly about the baby and I respected that.

I knew it was hard for her to ignore him, but Quan needed to decide Nena or Ebony and it was as simple as that.

I laughed when I thought about Thanksgiving and how Ebony called herself stepping to me when Nena went upstairs. She called me fake for telling her that Nena and Quan were family that night at the club.

I had forgotten about that but that explained the dirty looks she was giving me from the second she arrived at Epic's house in Delaware. I had to hold Sundae back from breaking her foot off in her ass.

I kindly told Quan if he didn't get her up out of our shit then I was going to toss her out myself. I told her I had no idea what was going no with Quan and Nena not that I had to explain myself to her, but I was far from fake.

No matter what went down I would always have Nena's back. I wasn't about to get into this shit with her and Quan. Harley was minding her business. I was going to let Quan clean up his own mess.

He had no problems telling me he was a *grown man* and to basically stay out of his business so that's what I was going to do. I laughed to myself just thinking about how he wanted to come over later, so I can help him with his little love triangle.

An hour later I pulled up to the salon and found a parking spot. When I walked in it was packed. Jade was a huge fan of Aaliyah so *Age Ain't Nothing, but a Number* was playing, and everyone was vibing. You could tell it was a Friday afternoon and everyone was getting ready for the weekend.

"Hey Boo!" Jade yelled from his station. "Umm I hear Mr. Epic knocked you up!" he clapped.

I narrowed my eyes at him, Jade was always loud. How the hell did he know I wanted everyone in here to know my business?

"Damn Jade tell the whole damn neighborhood why don't you?" Sundae rolled her eyes. "I'll be done soon girl, just finishing up," she shook her head while she chewed her gum.

"That's cool where is Nena?" I asked.

Just then Nena walked out the bathroom looking like her feet hurt.

"Girl I need you to hurry up and have this damn baby. I'm so tired of seeing you walk around waddling all the time!" Jade said throwing his hands up in defeat.

"Fuck you Jade," Nena laughed.

I was with Jade, I wanted Nena to have the baby. It felt like she had been pregnant forever and I was so excited to see my niece. I was just hoping her ass don't go in labor on Christmas.

When Jade's client got out the chair, I told him I needed my eyebrows touched up, so we went to the back, so he could touch me up.

By the time I was done Sundae was cleaning off her station. When she was ready the three of us gathered our things, so we could hit the mall.

A few hours later

We had been walking through the mall for a little while. It seems like forever because Nena didn't move at her normal pace, but my girl was keeping up.

She was hungry, so we decided to sit and eat before we continued our journey. I had gotten Epic some shirts and a new watch, I'm hoping he likes it. He had everything, so I was unsure of what to get him.

"So, what's up with you Ms. Sundae?" Nena said. "I see you smiling and texting on your phone and we know it's not Eric," Nena raised her eyebrow.

"Girl it's Truth. He's in town and wants me to come by his house tomorrow," she shrugged her shoulders as she bit her slice of pizza.

Nena and I looked at each other. "So, are you not going?" I questioned.

"I mean I don't know. This nigga got me all jumpy," she shook her head smiling. Sundae was feeling him.

"What, you afraid you're going to give him some booty too soon?" Nena laughed.

"I got control bitch. I think," we all laughed. "I don't know yawl, I just feel like I'm liking him a little too fast and I'm coming out of this long relationship with Eric. I just don't know. I can't lie and say I don't miss Eric because I do and I'm still hot he blew my tires, but I just can't turn my feelings off." She looked so confused.

I pouted my lips looking at her I felt bad for her situation. "I hear you Sun, but nobody is asking you to marry Truth. Just live in the moment and get to know him. There is nothing wrong with having a friend and we all know you love Eric's crazy ass." I rolled my eyes. "But maybe some time apart from him is what you need," I suggested.

"But what if we don't find our way back?" she said as the tears fell from her eyes. Nena handed her a tissue.

"Well if that's the case, you guys had a good run," I gave her a weak smile.

She didn't say anything she just sipped her drink and continued to eat. I know Sundae wants to be with Eric. Stevie Wonder could see that, but it was time to move on. Eric was never going to change, simple as that and if he did it was going to take a miracle.

"Girl Harley is telling you some real shit. I mean look at me Sun I said fuck Quan and I've been doing good," she said biting her veggie burger.

"Nena shut up, it's been like what two weeks," Sundae laughed.

We changed the subject and ate our food. By the time we finished Sundae was herself again. We had even convinced her to meet up with Truth tomorrow. Nena continued to complain about my brother, but I wasn't getting into their drama.

Our friendship was going to be different going forward. I had talked to my mom about this she told me to stay out of anything that had to do with them if I wanted our relationship to remain the same.

Sundae was going to be her listening ear when it came to their issues. The same thing applied to Quan. They wanted to keep their fling going on after their one-night stand so that was on them.

"Come on, let's see what Bloomingdales has before we leave. My damn feet are starting to hurt," she complained trying to get out the seat.

I laughed to myself. I was not looking forward to the end of my pregnancy. Just watching her struggle to get around had me dreading getting bigger.

When we walked into Bloomingdales we headed straight to the shoe section. We were laughing at Nena because every shoe she asked the sales lady to bring out she couldn't fit she was mad and that made it funnier.

"Well what do we have here, TLC is in the building," Kayla said. She looked at her friend and they both started laughing. "Girl I told you that looked like Sundae's car that we parked next to. I figured it was your car with all that weave hair on the seat. They laughed again.

I was starting to think she was following me. "Bitch don't get smacked up in here alright?" I warned.

"Oh, my, I'm scared! Girl please you don't want it with me," she looked me up and down.

"Harley calm down bitch you're pregnant. Epic will go off if you smack this hoe. You know he is protective of that belly now," Sundae said with a smirk on her face.

I looked up at Kayla and her eyes looked like they were going to pop out of her head. I saw her trying to take a peek at my belly, but it was still flat.

"Yes, pick up your face bitch, she is having your ex nigga's baby, something that he was never going to give you," Nena laughed while she tried slipping her feet in a pair of shoes.

Her friend whiped that smile right off her face and just stood there feeling sorry for Kayla.

"I don't know why this whale is talking to me," she said looking at her friend.

"Oh, I got your whale Kayla. Keep acting like you're tough. I'll put a pen in your ass and deflate that shit," Nena threatened.

Her friend started laughing. Kayla turned to her and gave her an evil eye and she shut up quick.

"Anyway," she slowly turned her head to face me, "Congratulations he ain't going to do nothing but leave you with that bastard child so good luck," she stuck her tongue out.

Sundae walked over to Kayla and the next thing I know she punched her in the face. Kayla went for Sundae's hair and they fell to the floor.

"Jump in if you want and see what happens!" I warned her friend.

Kayla was taller than Sundae she kept trying to get on top of her, but Sundae wasn't having it, she kept screaming for Sundae to get off her. For someone who had a lot of mouth she was getting her ass beat.

Security came over and grabbed them both. Once they were separated Kayla kept trying to get away, but security had a tight hold on her she tried to kick Sundae.

"I'm going to get you bitch! Just wait until I see you on the street!" she yelled at Sundae as security held her back.

"Fix your tracks bitch, whoever put them in need to give you a refund," Sundae said. I noticed she had a scratch under her eye, but she was still good. Kayla was weave less with a busted lip and a knot on her forehead.

"I bet you will keep your mouth shut next time," Nena said laughing as she took a seat in the chair. Shoes were everywhere.

After Kayla was taking out and Sundae had calmed down we were asked to leave the store.

"I can't believe she called your baby a bastard! I'm going to get that bitch again! Watch," Sundae said putting her weave in a ponytail.

"Thanks sis but I was going to get her," I laughed.

"No, you can't be fighting, and I wanted Kayla for a long time so don't worry about it," she smirked.

We walked towards the exit, it was time to go home. When we got to Sundae's car my mouth fell open. Her front window was busted, we instantly knew it had to be Kayla.

"I'm going to kill that bitch! She really busted my window!" Sundae threw her bags down walking over to the car to see the damage.

I was speechless! She couldn't just take her ass whooping and leave, she had to do some real petty shit. I immediately called Epic telling him what happened. He said he was going to send a tow truck driver for the car and for us to wait inside he was on his way.

We went inside and sat at the food court. Nena was eating a sandwich from Subway while I was trying to calm Sundae down. She was sitting here shaking her leg, this shit was going to get ugly real fast and I know if Nena and I wasn't pregnant we would be on our way to her crib right now.

But that wasn't the case, and I had to convince Sundae to let it blow over and we get her later. Sundae had no problem flying solo, but I wasn't letting that happen. She had EJ and her business, that was too much to lose.

Epic called and told me he was outside, so we gathered our things and headed out. When we got to the parking lot he had the meanest look on his face. I'm sure he was ready to dig into Kayla, but that's what she wanted. I didn't need him to say shit to her. Me and my girls were going to handle this.

I walked over to him and gave him a kiss, he took my bags. He told Sundae to hand him the keys to her car. Once she handed them over he passed them to his driver and we all walked over to his car and got in.

Epic wasn't even out the parking lot before Sundae was going off. "Epic where does that bitch live? I'm going to go home, get my other car and go beat her ass!" she yelled. I saw Epic look at her through the rearview mirror with his facial expression never changing, he was mad.

"Sun, I'm not about to give you her address, let me worry about Kayla you know I got your back, but I don't want to have to bail you out. You got EJ to worry about so chill," he told her.

"I'm not trying to hear what the hell you're saying but it's cool. I'll get that bitch address and handle her myself!" she screamed I could tell she was mad at him.

"Do I need to call Eric to meet you at Harley's mom crib? I'm asking you not to go over her house, and I don't ask you for much," he said.

She sucked her teeth and sat back. "I got you Sun, I won't be pregnant much longer. We can get her after I have the baby," Nena said.

Sundae looked at her and shook her head. "Nena shut up, you still need six weeks to heal then seven months for the baby to be on the titty. I'm good sis." The three of us laughed while Epic just shook his head.

We drove back to Sundae's salon. I gave her the keys to my car, so she could drive home. Once they were in their cars Epic and I drove off headed to his condo. My mom called on the drive home. Epic took my hand into his and held it the entire ride.

My mom told me she had found an apartment near Quan and she wanted me to go with her to check it out. I wasn't really listening to her because I was going to have a heart to heart with her, I wanted her to move in with Epic and I.

When we pulled up to the condo I told her I would call her tomorrow, so we can set an appointment, but I wasn't planning on meeting about no apartment. I really had to talk to Quan about this.

Epic turned the car off and put his head back on the headrest. I could tell he had a lot on his mind. "Talk to me," I said facing him.

"It's good, nothing you have to worry about. I have to get used to my position. This shit is work, not that I'm complaining but not having my dad or Rock to talk to about shit is fucking with me.

"Why don't you just make up with your dad? It's really simple," I told him rubbing the back of his head. He looked over at me like I was crazy.

"Naw, shorty negative. That nigga is dead to me on some real shit," he said leaning his head back again.

I unbuttoned my pants and took them off, he looked over at me and started smiling. I smiled back.

Once his pants were down and he released his dick I reached over and grabbed it. It was so beautiful. Epic put his seat back and I climbed over straddling him. We stared at each other for a second then I leaned in for a kiss.

He rubbed my ass then lifted me up. I slid down on his dick as I bit his bottom lip. I can't explain the feeling. I moved up and down, the more I moved the more he was able to put inside of me. But I was a big girl, I was going to take it all.

I moved my hips in a slow motion. He cupped my breast putting them together and licking one nipple at a time.

"Oh baby, it feels so good! I love you so much," I moaned.

"I love you to baby, shit you're so wet," he said biting on my neck.

I knew he was ready to let loose because he gripped my hips making me move faster. I held on to his neck and rode his dick side to side and up and down I wanted to feel all of him. Minutes later we were both cumming together.

Epic kissed me as my body jerked. Once we caught our breath he helped me up and I sat back in the passenger side. "Thank God for these leather seats huh?" I looked at him smiling.

He shook his head and we both started laughing. I was happy to see him smile. I know he has been under a lot of pressure since he took over and I'm not sure what happened between him and his father, but I was going to find out.

The day he came from his visit I could tell something was bothering him but when I asked he said it was nothing. I noticed he didn't get phone calls from his dad anymore. I figured it had a lot to do with Rock getting murdered but that was unfair if his dad was blaming him.

I had Epic's father information thanks to one of my cousins that work at the courthouse she had given me everything I needed to write him. I was holding onto it, I was tempted to reach out to him and ask if he could put me on his visitors list, but I didn't know how Epic would feel.

"Are you ready?" I said after I cleaned myself with the baby wipe and put it in a bag.

"I am but I want to show you something first," he said handing me his used baby wipe and buckling his pants. He reached in the glove compartment and handed me an envelope.

"What is this?" I smile opening it. The documents were for his house in Delaware. "You're putting it up for sale? I asked in shock. I mentioned to Epic about moving to Jersey, but I didn't think he was going to give in.

"Yeah, why are you shocked?" he asked.

"I don't know babe, you love that house, it's your first investment," I told him.

"Well I love you more than that house and I'll do anything to make you happy," he said looking into my eyes.

I started crying. I had been in love with this man since I was a young girl and to be in this space with him having a baby and moving forward was so unreal.

"Why are you crying?" he snickered and wiped my eyes.

"I love you too, with all my heart and I can't wait to raise a family with you," I confessed.

"Yeah because after you have my son, we are at it again. I want them back to back," he laughed.

I hit him in the arm, I wasn't having babies back to back. He could forget that. "So now I can start looking for our house in Jersey?" I clapped.

"Yeah shorty get on that, take your time but we need to be moved in before the baby get's here and this condo will be where we stay when we come to the city," he said.

"I'm with that, but I really want my mom to move in with us, I don't want her to be alone right now. I'm not trying to run her life, but I need her close for now," I said.

Epic shook his head like he understood. "I would feel the same if that was my mom. I think you need to have a conversation with Quan, but I love your mom. Shit she is like a mom to me. She can live with us for as long as she wants to. Just get something big enough so she can have her own space."

"Thanks boo!" I smiled. "Now come on let's go in the house, Quan is coming over, he wants to talk about his situation with Nena," I said grabbing my things.

"Quan is off the chain. That nigga is in love with Nena. I don't know why he just won't admit it. He ain't feeling that other chick like that," he laughed.

"I know you're not talking about their situation, does this story sound familiar?" I laughed referring to how he couldn't decide between Kayla and me.

We got out the car and headed in the house. By the time I took a quick shower and made Epic and I grilled cheese sandwiches, Quan was calling letting me know he was downstairs.

Epic went down to meet him and when they came back I was sitting Epic's food on the coffee table, so he could watch Sports Center while he ate. I swear that's the only thing he watched on television.

I looked at my handsome brother, he looked so stressed. I offered him a sandwich he declined taking his coat off and plopping down on the sofa. Epic started laughing.

"Damn bro, you got it bad man?" Epic laughed.

I went back to the couch and laid in between Epic's legs, I was so tired. "What's going on Quan?" I asked.

He shook his head and rubbed his hands down his face. "Nena is not talking to me man. Everything with her is about the baby and that's it. She ain't got shit to say to me and it's fucking me up," he said looking like a sick puppy.

"Bro, you know I love you so much, but keeping it one hundred with you, that's what the hell you get. You've been playing with my girl feelings for a while now," I told him.

"It's not like that Harley. Nena just so damn bipolar I just don't have the patience to deal with her mood swings. That shit be draining, yawl just don't understand." He shook his head taking a sip of his water.

"I know you and Nena were just having a fling or whatever you call it, but that's not the case anymore. Something sparked between you two and I can see it when I talk to both of you. But Nena has been through so much, so she is not acting the way she does because she wants to be a bitch. Have you ever stopped to ask how her childhood was?" I asked.

He didn't say anything, he just sat there looking at me. Obviously, he wanted to be with her. I was trying to understand why he just didn't tell her how he felt. He was stressing me out, they both were.

"So, let me ask you this my nigga. Are you holding back on being with Nena because of the jawn you're with?" Epic asked.

"I mean not really. Ebony is cool but I'm not feeling her like I am Nena. She is really just something to do. I only agreed to be her man because she kept pushing it." He shook his head. "Nena was on some bullshit talking about she didn't know if she wanted the baby, she kept calling me a little nigga, so I was like fuck it," he shrugged.

That was the dumbest thing I have ever heard. Quan was tripping. "Quan, I need you to stop brother, for real. You need to tell Nena how you really feel and go from there she loves your confused ass," I laughed.

"And don't worry about that bipolar shit when she gets like that just ignore her like I do your bratty sister," he laughed telling Quan.

I leaned up and hit him, I was not a brat. Spoiled yes, brat never.

Quan stayed for a while. He and Epic smoked some weed and had a drink. He had the blues, but he was going to be okay, I can admit I was so against him being with Nena in the beginning, but I was glad they were having a baby. Once they figured their feeling out for each other and stop playing games they were going to be okay.

I laughed to myself wondering what my dad would have said if he knew Quan and Nena were about to be parents.

Two hours later Quan got up to leave. He said he had a few appointments in the morning. I asked how the shop was doing and he said it was coming along. The death of my dad pushed things back, so he paid the rent for the shop he was working at until the new shop was open. The owner at the shop he was currently at was eager to get out of the business, so Quan agreed with the owners of the building to pay a month to month lease at a higher rate of course.

Nena was my girl because even though she was beefing with him he said she was still handing her business at the shop with the designs and that's another reason why he needs to just tell her how he feels.

I did understand what he meant when he said she was treating him like a young nigga. That would frustrate me also, but clearly my brother was way beyond his years and if Nena didn't notice when they first started seeing each other I'm sure she did now.

"I'll talk to yawl tomorrow, let me take my ass home," he said getting up walking towards the door. I followed him to the door and told him to text me when he got home.

"I need to see if I can get me a show. I'm the next Dr. Phil babe," Epic said with a straight face.

I started laughing. That weed was getting to his head. "Yeah okay if you say so but I gave the best advice," I said snuggling up to him under my blanket.

"No, you didn't you were basically co-signing with what I said," we laughed.

"Whatever. Gun range tomorrow morning, right?" I looked up and asked him.

"Hell, yeah. I have to teach you how to shoot, so next time you won't miss," he said kissing me on the forehead. I turned back towards the television and closed my eyes, I was so tired.

22

Chapter Twenty Two "Sundae"

$\mathcal{I}$ was currently sitting in the parking garage of Truth's apartment on Walnut Street in Center City. I was so nervous, I had to talk to Nena the whole way here to keep me calm. She was so evil these days between Quan and her being tired of carrying the baby, she was going through it. Not to mention she said her mom was getting on her nerves, coming in and out the house all times of the night. She wanted so bad to help her, but I couldn't see Ms. Barb wanting the help but that was not my place to tell her that.

I had hung up with her ten minutes ago and I was still sitting here. I laughed to myself because I was a up front chick who didn't let anything scare me, but I was anxious to go into Truths apartment.

I know it had a lot to do with the fact that Eric was the only guy I had ever really dated. I was new to this whole dating thing. I still felt shady for being here because Truth and Eric knew each other and even though they're not friends, I still feel like I'm backstabbing him.

Speaking of Eric, he has been blowing my phone up since Thanksgiving. I had yet to see him because I was still mad at how he acted out when we were at Epic's and Harley house. Niggas were funny, they could cheat on us all day and night sleeping with any hoe they can get their hands on but as soon as we think about another nigga all hell breaks loose.

I was missing him, but I had to stay strong, our connection was our son EJ and that's it. I just wanted Eric to do better and if we found our way back to each other it would be great, like Harley said, if we don't get back together than we had a good run.

I pushed Eric out of my thoughts checked my makeup popped a mint and got out the car. I had on a black sweater dress and some knee boots. I had a bun on the top of my head and soft curls in the back. I whore my charm bracelet and silver earrings. I was hoping I wasn't over dressed, I was only coming over to eat dinner, but I didn't know what to wear.

I took a deep breath grabbed the two bags I was carrying and exited the car. When I got to the door the receptionist called Truth to confirm I was there, he gave her the okay to send me up and I thanked her.

When I got off the elevator I walked down the hall and this nigga was standing in the door with a pair of basketball shorts on and no shirt. I made sure I took a peak and was glad when I saw what he was working with. I was going to have to contain myself, I was so damn horny, but I was not going to give in no matter how sexy he looked with those dreads.

"Why didn't you tell me you had these bags? I would have come down and met you at your car," he said taking them from me and moving to the side, so I could come in.

"It was nothing, they're not too heavy," I said. I was in awe when I walked in his apartment it was amazing. It wasn't huge, but the hardwood floors, cream walls and brown furniture looked beautiful I know a woman had to have designed this for him.

"Beautiful apartment," I said standing by the kitchen island. I smiled at him taking my leather jacket off.

"Thanks, my sister decorated this for me. If it was up to me I would have a bed and a TV," he laughed taking my jacket and hanging it in the closet. I walked over to the table and started taking the food out.

"You look good Ma," Truth said. "But I thought you were going to cook for me" he frowned.

I laughed "I did cook for you in my kitchen. If I cooked for you here I would not look like this," I said taking my hand showing him my outfit.

"That would have been cool, I'll take you any way I can," he winked at me.

I ignored him, he was making me blush. Not to mention him not having on a shirt had me creaming between my legs.

"Anyway, I made some short ribs, cabbage and baked mac and cheese. For desert I made a sweet potato pie," I said putting everything on the table.

Truth had a smile so wide I couldn't help but laugh. This guy was about to make me commit to his ass and we haven't even had a first date.

"Damn you really hooked a nigga up!" he said walking over to me and slipping his hands around my waist, bringing me into him. I looked up into his brown eyes and turned away. He really had me acting all shy.

He leaned down and kissed my lips. I looked up at him and when he noticed I wasn't going to tell him to stop he kissed me again slipping his tongue in my mouth. I put my arms around his neck as our tongues danced.

I felt his hands grab my ass and our kiss became more intense. The more he rubbed the more his dick got hard and was poking me. I wanted so bad to rip my dress off and let him have his way, but I couldn't. Not tonight.

I pulled back and smiled at him. He smiled back and put some space between us. "Respect," he said adjusting his ball shorts.

I didn't say anything, I just went over to the microwave and started heating up the food. We were silent as he sat the table for two switching off containers as they came out the microwave.

When all the food was nice and hot we took a seat at the table to start eating. I was shocked when he grabbed my hand and said he wanted to pray over the food. I had to ask him to reiterate himself to make sure I heard him right.

After we prayed he thanked me again for the meal and dug in. "Yeah, I definitely have to make you mine baby, this food is off the chain," he said

"Well I'm glad you like it, and you better not just be saying that because you like me," I gave him the side eye.

He put his fork down. "Who said I liked you?" he looked confused.

I rolled my eyes. "What you mean? You've been sweating me since you walked into my shop and not to mention your little friend down there," I pointed to his penis. "He told me you liked me a minute ago," we laughed.

"There is nothing little about my friend," he said looking down and back up at me. "But I'm going to let you talk your shit because when I finally get between those legs you're going to be begging me to stop," he said taking a bite of his rib.

"If you say so," I said sipping my wine.

He shook his head and continued to eat. He must have been hungry because he ate so fast and I still had a full plate. I was to nervous to eat anyway. He helped himself to seconds while we made small talk.

"So, Truth, I know you said you have a sister do you have any other siblings?" I set up folding my arms on the table.

"Not that I know of, but I bet my pop got a shit load of kids walking around Philly, New York, Jersey shit the whole tri-state, but I just don't know them. I'm close to my sister and mom." He drank some of his Patron.

I shook my head, I can't lie I wanted to know all I could about this chocolate man that sat in front of me. It scared me that I liked him.

"So, what about you? What's your story? I know you're best friends with Epic's girl but tell me about yourself."

I took a deep breath. I didn't want to get into my childhood that shit made me mad every time I talked about it.

"I mean I'm an only child. I grew up in Frankford. I don't know my father. I have a son little EJ," I smiled just thinking about my son. "I just got out of a long-term relationship with

Eric," I said feeling uncomfortable saying his name and Truth noticed.

He shook his head, "Why you get tense when you speak about Eric? Do you feel bad being here with me?" he asked.

"It's not that, it's just you guys no each other and if you and I continue to see each other this is not going to end well, I can feel it?" I was being honest.

Truth sat back in his chair and crossed his arms. I could tell he was getting his thoughts together before he spoke. He looked so damn good. "I'm saying like I said before, I'm not friends with that nigga. I fucks with Epic and that's it, the last thing I want you to be is uncomfortable. Trust me, we're just kicking it no strings attached. I can't lie and say I'm not hoping shit gets deeper between us because I do, but if you're thinking about going back to him let me know and I can move on. You have a son with him and from what I understand you've been in a relationship for a long time so of course you care but it's a difference between caring and wanting to be with him you feel me?" he raised his eyebrow.

I was ready to curse his ass out, but I had to take a deep breath. He is sitting here acting like I was pursuing him when he was the one stalking me.

"Well Eric and I are done, we're not getting back together," I was more so trying to convince myself and not him. "You don't have to worry about that, I've officially had enough," I shook my head.

"What did he do to make you so mad? I can see the hurt in your eyes," he asked.

I wasn't sure if I wanted to tell him all my business, but then I thought fuck it. I have nothing to hide.

"I mean what hasn't he done? Oh yeah, he never had a kid on me, but he's cheated more time than I care to remember, and the icing on the cake was the fact that he thought he gave me a damn STD," I waited to see if he was going to say anything when he didn't I continued.

"Thank God, the test came back negative, but it was the principal that he could have transmitted something to me. It's one thing to cheat. Shit let's be honest, men cheat we can't stop that and I'm in the hair business not the business of nigga sitting so it is what it is. But if you're going to cheat use a damn condom!" I said throwing my hands up in the air, now I was mad all over again.

"I mean men do cheat. I'm not going to sit here and lie and say we don't because I know I've done some wild shit when it comes to females but, I agree with the protecting yourself but I'm glad he didn't burn you," I could tell he was sincere.

I shook my head, then I asked. "So, your turn, how many chicks do you have?" I wanted to know.

Truth laughed. "I have friends. They're homie lover friends. I don't answer to anyone and when I find that one I want to settle down with all that shit stops," he said looking me in the eyes.

I felt some type of way with his response. He was basically telling me that he had mad bitches, he was tripping.

"I'm just keeping it gucci with you baby that's all. But don't get in your feelings because you may be that one I settle down with," he said shaking his head up and down.

He was right, I had no room to be getting mad at him and who he slept with. He wasn't my man and to be honest I wasn't ready for no damn relationship. I had a baby daddy that was crazy so having Truth as a friend was cool. I wasn't expecting anything from him.

We moved to the couch and continued to get to know each other. The conversation flowed, he lit a blunt and put music on. I took my boots off and laid my feet across his legs, he grabbed my foot and started massaging it.

The weed and the wine had me on one as Lil Wayne spit bars from the surround sound. Being here with him felt weird but I liked it. I wanted to stay the night but that would be a bad idea because I really wanted to have sex with him, but I was going to hold out if I could.

After he smoked the second blunt, I told him I was going to head out. He had moved from massaging my feet to my thigh which meant it was time for me to make my exit. It was damn near one in the morning.

I grabbed my things and we left his apartment. We held hands as we walked to the elevator. When he elevator arrived, we got on and he held me close rubbing on my ass. I wanted him so bad.

I was relieved when the doors opened, and we had to break away from each other to get off, he reached for my hand and we interlocked them as we walked through the garage.

"Are you sure you don't want to stay it's late as fuck?" he said holding me as we stood in front of my car.

I shook my head yeah. I wanted to say *Hell no, I don't want to leave! I want some dick!* "No, I'm sure I have some things to do tomorrow, but I'm fine. I'll make sure I text you when I get in," I said.

He shook his head okay, then leaned down and kissed my lips and again he started rubbing on my booty, he put my hand on his dick, I rubbed it. I was so turned on but the good girl in me told me to pull back.

"Okay let me go," I said turning around to open the door. Truth laughed, once I was in my car, he leaned down and pecked my lips. He moved back so I could pull out and once I headed out the garage I saw him turn to go back in the building.

Lord give me strength, I said turning down the block headed towards the expressway.

———

*T*hirty minutes later I pulled up to Jade's house and texted him letting him know I was outside and to hurry the hell up. Ten minutes later he was coming out the house dressed in all black.

"Damn bitch don't be rushing me! You texted me two hours ago and said you were about to leave," he said making sure his scarf was tied tight on his head.

"I was coming, be quiet, we chilled and smoked a blunt," I said pulling into traffic.

"A blunt? Bitch you know you can't smoke weed, you can't hang," Jade laughed.

I flagged him. "Shut up! You're always trying to play somebody. Do you have the bat and pocket knife?" I asked.

"Yeah, I got it. What the hell were you doing? dreaming of sexy chocolate when I got in the car?" he rolled his eyes. "Of course, I got it bitch! It's in the back seat."

Kayla had me fucked up if she thought I was going to let her bust my damn window and do nothing about it. Epic had gotten my window fixed with no charge because he owned the shop, but I didn't give a fuck. That bitch had violated me.

The best part about doing hair was gossip. That's all women did in the salon. A few girls that came through the shop knew Kayla, so it was nothing for me to get her address. I was still a little tight with Epic for not giving me the information. I felt like he was protecting the bitch, but it was all good I had my own connections.

"Did you tell Harley and Nena that we were on *a bust the windows out your car mission?*" Jade asked. "Yesssss, bitch we're about to send a message to Ms. Barbie!" he yelled all hype. I laughed so hard.

"I'm going to need you to calm down okay? And hell no I didn't tell them what I was doing. What the hell their pregnant asses going to do? I mean I could have let them come along for the ride, but I don't have time to beef with Epic and Quan," I laughed.

"Well you know I got your back to the death so don't worry about nothing," he said. We slapped hands and minutes later I was pulling up on Kayla's block. I spotted her car in front of her apartment. I was happy it was the middle of the night, the block was quiet.

I turned the lights off on my car and got out. Jade went to the back of my car and took my license plate off, we put our ski masks on and walked over to her car, I was about to fuck some shit up. I took the pocket knife out my back pocket and slashed all four of her tires. I took the bat from Jade and hit the shit out of her driver side window, the breaking of the glass was so loud.

Her car alarm started going off, Jade was telling me to come on before one of the neighbors called the cops, I quickly ran around to the passenger side and shattered that window to. Jade was yelling for me to come on when he saw someone lights turn on.

We ran to my car and I jumped in the passenger side as Jade got in and speed off. We laughed all the way back to his house. I wasn't into breaking people's personal property, but Kayla was an exception as soon as she broke my window. I believed in an eye for an eye.

I was hungry from the weed I smoked with Truth earlier, so we stopped at Checkers before I dropped him back off. Once we reached Jade's house I told him I would call him when I got in and drove home.

I texted Truth I was home when I pulled up to Jade's house, so he wouldn't be worrying about if I made it safe.

When I pulled up to Mrs. Savannah house it was almost three in the morning. As I gathered my stuff I thought about my next move. I had to start looking for an apartment. Quan was going to put the house up for sale after the new year.

When I got out the car and walked towards the porch I heard someone slam their car door I immediately reached in my purse to pull out my twenty-two Eric had given me. When I turned around he was standing there.

I let out a deep breath. "Oh my gosh, you scared me, and what are you doing here?" I looked at him in shock then I continued to walk up the porch and unlocked the door.

"Where the fuck you been all dressed up and shit? I came by to talk but I noticed your car wasn't here," he said shutting and locking the door.

"I went out with Jade if you must know, now what you want?" I said sitting down taking my shoes off.

"Yeah okay, where is EJ?" he questioned.

"He is with Mrs. Savannah at Quan's house. She wanted him this weekend," I said getting comfortable. He took a seat at the end of the sectional. I was sleepy, so I wanted him to leave.

"How can I help you Eric? I'm tired so can we make this quick?" I said putting a pillow under my head for support as I looked at him.

"Man, I want you to come home on some real shit, I miss you so much baby, and I'm sorry for your tires and you know I am. I paid to get them fixed," he said.

I was mad that he was sitting her acting like what he did was okay, because he paid to get my tires fixed. As always Eric was tripping.

"It's not about the tires Eric, it's about everything else. I'm still mad that you were out here having unprotected sex and didn't even tell me you slipped up," I sat up saying.

He was quiet. I felt sorry for him, seeing his handsome face all sad but I couldn't give in to him.

"I'm just asking for one more chance, I was changing that night I came in the house and you took me back I was dead ass serious when I said I wasn't going to hurt you, not being with you was fucking me up. I had cut all those bitches off then that hoe said she had a STD, so I had no choice but to tell you, I wasn't going to let you walk around with some hot shit," he confessed.

"Yeah, I understand what you're saying but I just can't do this with you anymore. It's the same shit. We are getting to old for this I can't raise a man and I refuse to. Being with you is like nigga sitting and I'll be damned if I keep doing that." I was so serious.

"Nigga sitting?" he asked with a confused expression on his face.

"Yes. You're a trifling nigga and I'm not your babysitter simple as that," I rolled my eyes.

He chuckled. "Stop fucking playing with me alright? You're talking real reckless right now," he gave me a stern look.

Scooting to the edge of the couch he said, "Sundae let's not act like you don't know my childhood. My fucking daddy used to cheat on my damn mom every chance he got, sometimes taking me with him. You are a product of where you come from and you know my mom wasn't no saint, she did her thing too when my dad wasn't around."

I'm not going to sit here and act like I don't know Eric's childhood, but he always uses that as an excuse. I'm so tired of him saying he is the way he is because of his parents. Yes, his dad was a cheater and his mom did her thing too because his dad was a cheater, but he didn't have to be like them.

I gave Eric all of me. I was never unfaithful to him. I played wifey for a nigga that didn't deserve me.

"I know what you've been through but stop. You're a grown

man. Just because your parents stepped out on each other does not mean you had to do that to me."

He sucked his teeth. I could tell he was losing patience with me, but the door was right there. He was free to leave whenever he was ready.

"Please don't sit here and act like you're some fucking angel Sun, you're not perfect either," he was getting mad.

"What, pause nigga I never said I was, but what I didn't do was step out on you let's not go there because you're a fuck up!" I yelled.

He was messing with my character now. "Maybe it's time for you to go. I'm not doing this with you," I said getting up walking towards the door.

"So, what you're saying is it's over for good?" he asked standing up.

"I'm saying I need a break from us, I want to be by myself. I've been your girlfriend damn near my whole life and I just want time to think," I was being honest.

He got up and grabbed his coat I backed up a little because he was so damn unpredictable.

"Alright, well I'm going to give you time, but you know you're spitting a whole lot of bullshit. I'm going to let you know now you better not be entertaining or giving another nigga the pussy that belongs to me and I'm serious Sundae," he stood there looking into my eyes then he grabbed the knob opening the door and walked out.

I went upstairs to get a shower, so I could get some sleep. I grabbed my phone to put it on the charger and noticed Truth had texted me.

Truth: Damn I can't get no sleep I need you to come lay next to me.
Me: Oh well you never asked so…count sheep.
Truth: Haha, get some sleep beautiful.
Me: Goodnight.

I smiled then got my shower cap and went into the bathroom. Truth was about to get me in trouble.

A **few days later**
I grabbed my car keys and walked out the house locking the door behind me. Truth and I had been talking and texting for the past few days. He had me feeling like I was back in high school the way we stayed up all night talking on the phone.

He had asked me to go to Atlantic City with him overnight just to spend time together. He was going to D.C. to spend Christmas with is daughter. I was a little bummed that I wasn't going to see him until the new year. I loved how he put his daughter first and always wanted to spend time with her. That said a lot about him as a person.

I loved a man that took care of his kids and that's one of the reasons I loved Eric he was a great father to EJ. Sometimes when a man couldn't have the mother he didn't want the kid but no matter what we went through EJ was always his priority.

I was going to enjoy the night because Eric had come to pick EJ up a few hours ago telling me he would keep him for a few days. We were going to spend Christmas together so EJ could be with both of us I was cool with that.

Eric had stopped pressuring me about getting back together he was giving me the space I asked for. He tried to get a quickie when he came over to get EJ, but I shut his ass down real fast.

As I walked down the steps to Truth's truck I smiled when he got out the car and opened the door for me, it was the little shit like that I loved about him.

Once he got in and shut the door he looked over at me. "Okay, I see you thuggin it out today. You got your Tim's on huh?" he said referring to my Timberland boots.

"Hell yeah, I can dress up or down and still look good," I laughed.

"I agree. Let me find out I got a little hitter next to me," he laughed.

I shrugged my shoulders and put my seatbelt on. He pulled into traffic *Views* by Drake played from his Bluetooth.

As we drove down the Atlantic City highway we laughed and

talked about any and everything. I was learning a lot about him and falling for him fast.

His phone rang, and he let out a deep sigh and told me to hold on as he turned the music down. I heard a female in the background sounding ghetto as hell, I figured that was his baby momma.

I was trying to listen. I heard her say something about needing more money and asked when he was coming to D.C. and he must have been in Philly seeing a bitch.

This bitch sound ghetto as hell and if Truth and I took things to the next level I could tell she was going to be a problem, but she could get it too just like any other bitch that steps to me.

When he hung up he was quiet. I took my hand and put it on top of his he grabbed my hand and we interlocked our fingers.

"My bad baby, she just gets under my skin but I'm not letting her ruin the night I have planned for us. I'm good." He looked at me than back at the road.

"Can I ask you a question? I'm not trying to mind your business just curious," I said.

He nodded his head and told me to ask whatever I wanted to ask. So, I was going to do just that. I know he wasn't my man, but I wasn't about to play myself. I was done playing the fool.

"When you go to D.C. do you stay at the same house with her?" I asked.

Truth started laughing. "Hell no, why the fuck do I need to stay with her? Shorty you must not really know who I am. I run D.C. and Baltimore. I'm worth a lot of fucking money I don't need to stay with anybody I got properties all over," he stopped laughing.

"On some real shit Sundae nothing is going on between me and my baby momma everything is about my daughter and that's it, she knows that no matter how much she might throw the pussy I don't want that shit," his tone was serious.

"Alright just asking, I don't know where this is going between us, but I just need to know what I'm getting myself into. I've been in enough drama." I said looking at him.

He shook his head. "No doubt, but I'm not trying to play you and honestly if I wasn't serious about getting to know you I would have hit the first night you were at my apartment." He cut his eye at me.

I laughed and hit him in the arm. "Keep telling yourself that if it makes you happy," I smiled.

The rest of the ride was relaxing. We listened to slow jams, he gave me his phone and I created a playlist on his Apple Music while we made small talk the rest of the ride.

When we finally got to Atlantic City we checked in at the Borgata Hotel and got dinner. After dinner Truth wanted to gamble so I watched him play the tables. When I got bored I walked around then headed to the room.

When I got to the hotel I took a nice hot bath, after I bathed I put lotion on my body and laid across the bed. My phone rung and I noticed it was Nena calling. When I answered she yelled my name into the phone followed by Harley.

"Hey bitch what are you doing?" Harley asked.

"Nothing, how yawl know I wasn't getting fucked? Calling me this time of night," I laughed.

"Whatever, because if you were, you would not be talking to us," Nena laughed.

"Truth is downstairs gambling I can tell his ass loves the casino, so I decided to come upstairs. I was getting tired," I told them.

"I told Harley we shouldn't talk to you. I'm still mad you went on that mission without us hoe," Nena said.

"What were you two supposed to do? Pregnant asses," we laughed.

Nena and Harley had laughed so hard when Jade and I told them about me busting Kayla's windows and flatting her tires. I hadn't heard anything, but I was sure she was going to make some noise soon. She was so thirsty for Epic it was driving her crazy.

We talked for another half hour then hung up. As soon as I disconnected with the girls Truth was walking into the room. He handed me some chips and smiled.

"What is this for?" I asked.

"I just won thirty thousand dollars. It's yours. We can cash the chips in tomorrow before we leave." He took his shoes off and then his shirt heading for the bathroom.

"Well thanks but I can't take your money Truth," I said getting up to put the chips on the table.

"You're not taking it I'm giving it to you, so just chill and buy yourself something nice," He went into the bathroom. Moments later I heard the shower come on. I was tempted to get in with him and suck his dick, but I decided against it.

When Truth finally came out the bathroom he had on nothing but a towel, my middle was throbbing. I don't know if I could get through the night without fucking him.

I scrolled through my phone while he got ready for bed when he was done he pulled the covers back and got in on his side.

I leaned over and put my phone on the charger and turned the light and television off. He pulled me into him and held me. He smelled so good, we laid in the dark for a few minutes without saying a word.

He started rubbing my thigh sending chills up my spine. He kissed the side of my neck and I turned around to face him leaning in for a kiss. As we kissed he pulled my panties down he rolled on top of me as I spread my legs wider inviting him in.

I pulled at his boxers helping him take them off and he helped me out of my tank top. "Shit ma, you're perfect," he said we starred at each other as the New Jersey casino lights and the moon illuminate the room.

I rubbed his big brown arms, Truth was everything that I didn't know I wanted, I didn't know how to feel.

He leaned in and kissed me again then he pulled back looking me in the eyes.

"Why you stop?" I asked opening my eyes while rubbing his dick.

"Sundae I can't front. I feeling you, but I'm letting you know if we about to do this, that shit you got going on with him ends now. I'm not into sharing pussy so if you take this dick there is no turning back." I could tell he was serious.

I shook my head up and down with a sense of urgency. I was

horny as fuck. I wanted the dick and Truth. Shit if he was to ask me to marry him right now I would get on my phone and book us flights to Vegas and make it happen.

"What are you shaking your head for? I need you to say it," he demanded.

"I hear what you're saying Truth. I want to be with you, no games and I told you it's over between him and I." I was being frank.

He leaned over and grabbed the condom off the nightstand and slipped it on. He pecked my lips.

"Open your eyes and look at me," he demanded I did as I was told. I wanted to look away I swear I could see our future in his eyes.

As he pushed his way inside me I gasped, biting my bottom lip and holding on to his ass.

"Shit, baby open up let me in," he said. I spread my legs wider as I relaxed while he worked his way inside slowly trying to fill me up. It felt amazing.

I tried to push back but he grabbed me with a slow deep stroke. When he was all the way in we both let out a deep breath.

"Oh, yessss, Truth oh, right there yessss!" I moaned.

He moved faster. I didn't think my pussy could get wetter than it was already. He leaned down and flicked his tongue over my nipple I leaned my head up and started biting the side of his neck while I rotated my hips.

Truth grabbed my left leg and put it in the air and started fucking me harder. I screamed for dear life it felt so good. He was hitting my G-spot. My body started shaking I came so hard, he kept stroking me as I begged him to stop.

"Turn around," he said leaning up helping me on my stomach. He leaned down and kissed my sweaty back before putting my ass in the air I was tired as hell. He leaned down and bit my ass. I thought I was going to cum again.

He slid his dick inside of me and started off slow. I was a little tense at first but then I relaxed. I started throwing my ass back telling him how good his dick was. He started hitting my spot again and I screamed so loud, I just knew security was coming.

The more he hit my spot the faster I went. Moments later we were cumming together. Truth dropped onto the pillow beside me trying to catch his breath as we starred at each other and laughed.

He got up and went into the bathroom to flush the condom. When he came out I looked over and his dick was still hard.

He opened another condom put it on and got back in bed, leaning over scooping me up putting me on top of him. "Yo, this my pussy now for life," he smiled spreading my ass cheeks as I guided my way down on his hard dick.

This is going to be a long night, I said to myself.

23

Chapter Twenty Three "Epic"

*C*hristmas Eve

I was sitting in my office at my auto shop going through my books for the shop and checking numbers for my main business. Both were doing great, being the head nigga in charge was a lot of work. I had always been on top of my game when it came to this shit but now I had to be more cautious than ever.

It was uncomfortable having police on my side because I still didn't trust those pigs, so I move different when interacting with them. I knew the system was corrupted but the shit I saw was on another level. Having this kind of power was like a gift and a curse.

One thing I do know is this city has a lot of greedy mother-fuckers and the politics of it all is so damn corrupt. Everyone has their hands out when it comes to this money. I was now breaking bread with some of the top dogs in Philly. It was unbelievable.

Truth told me over time I would learn that I'm their boss and if I have them on payroll they would make sure I was good. They're just a bunch of greedy motherfuckers, but like he said the police don't give a fuck about that badge they care about the money.

Truth was my nigga. He was a little older than me and because he had been in the game longer I'm soaking up whatever information he has to offer. Niggas was so disloyal these days I was glad to have him on my team even just to guide me until I get the hang of things.

I didn't know much about being the king of Philly, but I was slowly learning and remembering all the shit my punk ass dad and Rock taught me over the years.

I was a smart nigga and I learned fast, so this shit wasn't about nothing. Eric was on top of his game and even though I was in charge we shared responsibility. The drug business was doing so good and money was coming in hand over fist.

I was in talks of opening another auto shop and a Gentlemen's Club. I hadn't told Harley about the club because I know she may get upset. My baby had trust issues in the past, so I had to think about how I was going to approach this.

I was missing her like crazy. I had been so busy these last few days that I only saw her when she was asleep. I would go into our room and she would be sound asleep with the trashcan by the bed which was normal. I loved staring at her pretty face, while she slept I always made sure to kiss her belly.

I thought about how each night she would cook for me and have my dinner in the microwave. A note was always taped to the microwave door letting me know she loved and missed me.

This is the shit I always dreamed about, a woman who was secure in her relationship who wasn't selfish and took care of her man. I know Harley is having a hard time adjusting to this lifestyle no matter how many times she told me she didn't mind me coming in late or not at all when I had some important shit to do, but the fact that she never complained spoke volumes.

My days were always long when we got a new shipment and she knew this. We talked on and off during the day and texted, but I missed just being around her. Harley was riding for a nigga and I appreciated her so much.

I never wanted a long-term relationship. I could never see

myself with a women long term, but Harley had changed all that. I couldn't imagine my life without her.

She was doing her thing and I was proud of her, loosing her dad had taken a toll on her but she fought through it and I know the motivation was the love she had for our unborn child. Harley was keeping busy, she was taking her last two classes online and soon she would be done. I couldn't wait for us to take a vacation just the two of us.

I had convinced her to wait to go back to work until we moved to Jersey because of the drive and hopefully she could find a job in Jersey instead of traveling back and forth to Philly. We had been staying at the condo for the past few weeks off and on, but tonight we were going to Delaware.

Harley had decorated the house for Christmas. She had put so much work into our first Christmas I wanted to make sure that's where we were, so I had one of our bodyguards follow her to the house.

We were hosting Christmas. I was hoping everybody was on their best behavior this time because if not I was just going to start shooting niggas.

I had promised her that me being in the game was not going to be long term, I know she worried about me.

Things had moved so fast when Jamal bitch ass killed Rock I was still digesting everything. Promising myself that this will not be forever, Harley and I were about to be parents and I want to be around to raise my kids, so I had to make the right business moves to make sure we're set for life. My mission once everything settled down was to start grooming some of my workers, the ones I saw the most potential in, so they could step up and run shit, I won't have to do nothing but sit back and collect my percentage.

I heard some commotion on the floor before I could get up, Jesus, one of my workers came knocking on the door opening it.

"Boss your girl is out here screaming that she wants to see you, but Big Bang said she can't come back here," he said holding his hands up in surrender.

I was confused like hell I had just got off the phone with Harley and she was on the road to Delaware. I got up to see who the hell he was talking about and to make sure I wasn't tripping when I got close I heard Kyla's loud mouth. I let out a deep sigh, I was in a good mood. I didn't feel like her shit today.

"Yo, what the fuck are you doing here and drawing a lot of fucking attention?" I said to her when I reached the front door where Big Bang was blocking her.

"I need to talk to you Epic and now so tell this big nigga to let me pass!" she tried pushing my body guard. I told Bang to let her in. I felt like I was going to choke this bitch.

She fixed her shirt and hair before yelling at me. I just stood there looking at her. I told her to follow me to my office. I didn't need these niggas in my business, but I was going to make sure to tell them she wasn't my bitch anymore.

Once we were in my office I shut the door and headed back to sit in my office chair while she stood there all mad. "What the hell are you doing here Kayla? You know I don't play that coming to my workplace," I gave her a stern look.

"I'm here because I've been trying to call you, but you blocked me, so this is the only place I can catch you at so here I am nigga!" she whipped her neck. I was hoping the shit fell off.

"Okay, you're here so again what the fuck you want man? I have shit to do so I can get home. So, what?" I was getting pissed.

"You need to tell those three ugly bitches to watch their back. I know Sundae fucked my car up and she is going to pay for that shit. I swear if she doesn't give me the money I used to fix my car I'm fucking her up!" she threatened.

I didn't know what the hell she was talking about. I hadn't had the chance to really talk to Sundae and Harley didn't tell me that Sundae fucked her car up, but I didn't give a fuck. I had more important things to think about than some girl fight.

"You like talking shit, don't you? Didn't my sister already beat your ass but be my guest if you want to run up on her again. You fucked her car up first so what the hell did you expect?" I shrugged.

Kayla's eyes got wide. "She didn't beat my ass I slipped on a shoe, so whatever she told you is a lie but make sure you tell her to watch her fucking back," she warned.

I heard a big boom outside my office, so I went to see what it was and to tell Big Bang to come stand outside my door because I was about to put her ass out. Everything Kayla was talking about had nothing to do with me.

When I came back in my office this bitch was sitting in my chair like this was her office. "Kayla get the fuck up stop playing with me," I grabbed her arm and pulled her out my seat.

"Ouch that hurt," she whined walking back around to the other side of my desk. "I can't believe you left me for her, Epic and I heard you got her pregnant. I have been asking you to give me a baby for a while. Hell, you even moved her into your condo!" she stomped her feet.

"Well get over it, you stayed with me when I told you I didn't want the same things that you did so that's on you," I got up and grabbed her arm moving her toward the door. I was done listening to her bitch and keep crying about the same shit.

"Well evidently you did want those things nigga because you are doing them with her! I hate you!" she tried pulling away from me. "Fuck you! That bitch and that bastard baby yawl having!" she yelled

When she said it, I could tell she regretted that shit. I pushed her so hard up against the wall she hit her head and grimaced in pain.

"What the fuck you say about my baby bitch, huh?" I said pushing her against the wall again. She started crying.

"I'm sorry Epic, I'm sorry. I didn't mean to talk about the baby," she cried.

"You and I both know why I haven't killed your ass yet, but you're pushing me to my limit. Keep fucking playing," I grabbed her neck and squeezed.

"Boss let her go, you said if it got too carried away to stop you, and if you don't let go she is going to die," Bang said. I ignored what he said then I snapped out of it and let her go. Kayla fell to the floor crying.

Bang helped her up and walked her loud crying ass out the

shop. I sat back in my chair to catch my breath. Kayla was really testing me.

I drank some of my Red Bull and got back to work. I had one more stop to make after I handle my business then I was heading home to Harley.

After two more hours of going over all my numbers shit looked good. I hadn't realized it was this late until Eric called to see where I was. I wrapped up everything locked my office door and headed out.

I had been so busy I hadn't even noticed the guys had left. I had some of the best Puerto Ricans and blacks in the city working at my shop, we did everything from body work to custom work and repair.

I laughed because my dad had schooled me on making investments that I could use to clean my drug money my shit was legit. Business was growing so fast I had to start making moves on the second shop. I was just unsure of the location right now.

I got in my car and texted Harley to see if she was still awake she texted back and said she was baking Christmas cookies for me. I laughed. I could tell this was her favorite holiday, so I was going to make sure nobody fucked it up.

I loved our family but that shit that happened Thanksgiving was crazy. I made sure Sundae's mom wasn't on the list of guests, Ms. Joyce was crazy as hell. I see why Sundae didn't bother with her much. Eric had warned me that she was rough around the edges but seeing is believing.

Forty-five minutes later I pulled up to my condo and texted Eric that I was outside. He had managed to get a condo for himself in the same building. I shook my head thinking about how that nigga just didn't want to go to the house in Jersey because Sundae wasn't there.

Eric came to the car and got in. "What up my nigga?" We shook hands. Eric was looking like he lost his best friend and I knew he was fucked up because Sundae had broken it off with him, but I hate to say I told you so.

"You good bro?" I asked.

Shaking his head, he said, "Man, Sundae got my head all fucked up. I've been giving her space like she asked trying to get on her good side but I'm starting to think she is fucking with somebody," he ran his hands over his face.

I was thinking about what he just said and was hoping Sundae wasn't messing around with Truth. It makes sense if I think about it because he had asked about her and Eric's situation, but I never gave him any info on her, so I wasn't sure if she was dealing with him how he made it happen. But I was minding my business on this one.

"Just chill she'll come around just go ahead and give her some space," I told him. He gave me this look that said yeah okay.

"Yeah I don't know about that and nigga don't sit here and act like you gave Harley space when she told you to leave her ass alone," he said.

We both laughed, and he was right. I wasn't trying to hear none of what Harley was saying when she told me to leave her alone.

"Well did you handle that other thing with Vanessa is she really pregnant?" I asked.

"Man, I don't know I don't trust none of these bitches she claims she is but I'm telling you E, that's not my baby I know I can be impulsive, but I didn't nut in that bitch. I'm kicking myself for even hitting it raw." He shook his head.

"I mean you're right, you never know so just be prepared if it is. Sundae will kill you," I laughed but he didn't find the shit funny. I changed the subject.

"But on some real shit I'm getting tired of this Jamal shit, this nigga should have been dead. I don't understand why the fuck it's taking so long. Shit has been so crazy. Have you had time to get at those little niggas to see what's up?"

"I did we just have to move smart on this, the jawn Strawberry hasn't been at work but we on it don't worry about it. We went pass her crib, but the house was empty looks like she moved out," he assured me.

"Well Quan's homies came through, so I got an eye on that nigga Jay. I was going to send someone out there to get at him, but I decided against it. This shit is personal, and I want to take care of him myself. As long as he's in Texas he can't hurt Harley, but I'm going to get at that nigga as soon as I get a chance.

"That's cool, so say the word when you're ready and we out there," he gave me a pound.

Eric asked about my dad, but I told him I haven't heard from him. But I wasn't stupid he was planning on getting at me, one thing about my dad, when he makes promises he keeps them.

I always watch my back so whenever that nigga was ready to strike I was going to be ready for his old ass.

My Nana had asked if I'd been to see him and I told her yeah, both of us were faking letting her believe that our relationship is good, but I was hoping I didn't have to kill him. The last thing I want to do is cause her more pain but to protect my family I would.

We sat and smoked a blunt. Eric talked about Sundae the whole time, but I just let him go ahead and vent. We were both stressed the fuck out. Me because I needed to kill Jamal and that bitch ass nigga Jay. I didn't know what to do with my dad, he was my blood. He helped give me life, but he was blaming me for something that I had no control over, but it was all good.

"Alright nigga I'm high as fuck. We've been talking so much I forgot what the hell I came for," I laughed.

Eric reached in his pocket and handed me the three-karat princess cut ring I had purchased. Yeah, I was going to ask Harley to marry me and a nigga was nervous.

"So, you really going to do this man?" Eric asked as I looked at the ring, he broke my train of thought.

"Yeah, man. I ain't no bitch or nothing but I never thought I would say this but I'm in love," I confessed.

Eric laughed. "That's what's up my nigga, I'm happy for you, and Harley is a good girl," he shook his head.

"So is Sundae man, it's going to work out," I told him.

"Alright let me take my ass in the house so you can get home. I'll see you tomorrow," he said getting out the car.

"Yo, don't start no shit tomorrow because if you do I'm going to shoot your ass," I laughed.

"Not if I shoot you first," we laughed.

I pulled out of the parking lot and prepared myself for the ride home. I was hoping Harley was up when I got in. I started to call her, but it was late as hell. I decided to call the car service to confirm all the pickups for tomorrow.

———

*W*hen I pulled up into the driveway the house was lit with Christmas lights everywhere. Santa and his elves were on top of the roof, the company Harley had hired to do the lights had done a good job. I chuckled to myself. I had this house for so many years and this was the first time it looked like someone lived here.

I walked into the house and looked around. My shorty had out done herself. She had the fire place lit, lights were hanging, she even had the Christmas village and baby Jesus off in the corner.

The Christmas tree was lit with presents under it. I went over and took the presents out the bag that I was holding and put them under the tree. I grabbed one of the cookies off the table and bit it. I was high as fuck, so I stood there and ate five more then went into the kitchen to get some juice to wash them down.

I went upstairs when I reached the bedroom I saw the bathroom door open. I walked up to the door and saw my baby relaxing in a bubble bath with her Christmas music playing softly in the background.

She had the TV on mute that was located on the wall in front of the bathtub. She was watching *This Christmas.* "Hi Baby!" she yelled smiling. I could tell she was happy to see me.

"Hey baby, you're over here looking relaxed," I said bending down kissing her lips.

"You want to join me?" she gave me a devilish grin.

"I would love to join you, but not right now. It's after midnight so I want to give you one of your presents."

"Oh really! I love presents boo, so give me a minute and I'll be out." She smiled.

I told her okay and left the room. I know if I would have joined her in the hot tub I would have to wait to give her the ring and a nigga was anxious to give it to her now.

I went into one of the other bathrooms and took a hot shower. I was so fucking stressed right now and couldn't wait to dead the niggas that was causing it, but I was going to let all that shit go and enjoy the holiday.

When I got out the shower I brushed and flossed then put my sweats on and went into the bedroom. Harley was just coming out the bathroom. I watched her grab her body lotion and start putting the lotion on her body, my dick jumped when she let her towel hit the floor.

I waited until she was done after she slipped one of my wife beaters over her small frame she walked over to me. Harley had so many sets of pajamas, but she loved wearing my tee shirts to bed. I didn't know why but the shit was funny to me.

"You look like you have a lot on your mind boo, something wrong?" she asked looking concerned.

"No, everything is good." I stood up and put my arms around her waist and kissed her. "Harley I just want to say this. I want you to know that I never thought I could love any women besides my mom and Nana, but you changed that. I love the shit out of you. I can't even explain." I looked away for a second.

She took the back of her hand and rubbed the side of my face. Looking into her eyes told me everything. I wanted to love her for the rest of our lives. I wanted to protect her. My mind drifted to that bitch nigga Jay and how he kidnapped and beat her.

My heart rate started speeding up. I had to calm myself down and continue. "You know a nigga got a fucked-up past but none of that shit mean anything to me anymore. I want to thank you for being patient with me. I know I'm not perfect and I know all of this is new to you, but you stand by a nigga and that means so much to me."

I want to thank you for carrying my seed. I never really thought about having kids but I'm so happy that you're going to have my baby. Soon you will be giving me the best gift I could ask for."

"With that being said baby, I want to ask you to marry me." I took the ring out my sweatpants and opened it.

Harley stepped back a little bit and put her hands over her mouth in shock, tears instantly started falling from her face.

"I know we haven't been official that long but fuck it, you're mine until death. I want you to be my wife, so are you going to marry a nigga?" I smiled at her.

She started shaking her head up and down. She tired to find the words to speak but she couldn't. I laughed and grabbed her hand, slipping the ring on. "Merry Christmas," I said.

"I love you so much Epic," she finally said jumping in my arms and kissing me. I walked us over to the bed and gently laid her down. She sat up and took her shirt off and crawled over pulling my pants down freeing my dick.

She looked up at me smiling then kissed the head of my dick. She took her tongue and ran it down the shaft and back up to the tip circling the head with her tongue before covering it with her mouth.

Harley moved slow at first taking as much in her mouth as she could. When her mouth was nice and wet she begun to move faster. "Fuck," I said closing my eyes.

I grabbed a hand full of her braids and moved her head a little faster. The slurping noises made my dick harder. I was trying to hold off, but I couldn't when my dick swelled up. I tried to pull back, but Harley wouldn't let me, she continued to bob her head. Minutes later I was cumming all in her mouth. I smiled at her and pushed her back on the bed.

I kissed her lips and palmed her breast, I took them in my mouth one at a time. Her nipples stood at attention. I lightly bit one and she pulled back. "They're really sensitive baby," she warned.

I traveled down to her belly button kissing it. I pushed her legs open wide and bit the inside of her thigh before opening her pussy and sucking on her clit. Harley had a beautiful pussy that smelled and tasted so good. I teased her at first like she did me.

"Stop Epic, eat my pussy. Come on," she sounded frustrated.

I laughed then stuck my tongue deep inside. I grabbed her ass lifting it up a little and continued feasting until she begged me to stop. Her pussy started squirting I watched as her juices flowed.

She was exhausted, but I was just getting started. I looked over at the fireplace where she had a blanket on the floor. I picked her up and carried her over. We laid down and I got on top of her.

"I fucking love you," I said entering her as she moaned. It sounded so good coming from her mouth as I deep stroked her. Harley took both her hands, putting them on the sides of my face. We looked at each other. She had my heart. I'm not sure if she understood the love I had for her.

"It's me and you okay?" I said as I moved faster. "Don't let anyone try to come between us. I promise I will never hurt you," I said stroking her. Harley continued to moan. She started screaming as I hit her G-spot.

"Promise you won't ever let anybody come between us," I went faster.

"I promise! I won't oh my gosh, baby don't stop!" she cried.

I fucked her harder as she screamed, matching my speed. Minutes later we were both coming as our bodies jerked.

I laid beside her and she put her head on my chest. We both stared into the fire place. Harley leaned up and looked at me. "This is the best Christmas ever, Merry Christmas baby!" she smiled and kissed my lips then laid back down on my chest.

I can't wait to make her my wife.

24

Chapter Twenty Four "Quan"

"*I* can't believe you're just going to drop my gift off and leave," Ebony shook her head sitting on the couch next to me with her face balled up.

"Come on with that. You already know I'm spending time with my family at my sister's house. Stop acting like this is the first time you're hearing this. I don't have time for this dumb shit," I said looking at her.

I was at Ebony's house and I made sure to come by early this morning to spend Christmas morning with her because I was going to Delaware today to spend time with the family. If she wouldn't have gotten into it with Nena at Thanksgiving and basically called Harley a liar maybe I would have let her come along. The more I think about it I still would have left her in Philly.

I was really pissed off that Nena still wasn't fucking with me. I only saw her when she had doctor's appointments which were weekly now. She had refused to let me drive her to her appointment last week, so we just met there, when the visit was over we went our separate ways.

A part of me don't blame her for treating me the way she does. I have been playing both sides, but I've been trying to tell her how I feel, and she just don't want nothing to do with me and it's fucking me up. I was surprised when she called yesterday to see if she could catch a ride to Harley's. Epic had ordered her a car but because she was due any day she didn't want to ride by herself.

"I'm just saying you could spend the day with me and spend tomorrow with them," she rolled her eyes.

I looked at her like she lost her damn mind. "Why the fuck would I do that? This is the first Christmas without my dad. You think I'm supposed to let my mom and sister spend it by themselves to make you feel secure?" I stood up.

"Where are you going? I thought you said you were staying until noon?" she walked behind me.

I turned around. "I'm not about to do this with you, as a matter of fact this shit is over, I'm done. I'll bring your stuff pass when I get a chance, whatever you left at my crib," I said.

I could see the tears in her eyes, but I didn't care. I was tired of pretending she was the girl I wanted in my life.

I blame myself for leading her on this long. I knew what I wanted the whole time but because the shit with me and Nena was always on the fence I committed to Ebony. Which looking back on it was a big mistake.

"So, it's like that you're just going to break up with me? Be honest you just want to leave and go be with her. I'm not stupid Quan, like how do you know that baby is yours anyway?" she asked.

"What the fuck you just say?" I chuckled. "I'm going to get up out of here before I say or do something I can't take back." I turned around and walked out.

Ebony was calling my name. She ran outside behind me, but I told her to get the fuck away from my car. I wasn't going to let that shit get to me I looked up at her as she stood near my door she let the tears run down her face the shit didn't faze me at all. I pulled out the parking spot and speed off heading for Nena's house.

When I got there, I parked up and told her I was outside. Normally I would go in, but I wasn't feeling her mom. I know she was just using Nena. I could see it all over her face, Nena had been trying to help her, but she refused. She just wanted to get as much money from her daughter as she could and as soon as Nena stopped supporting her drug habit she was going to disappear.

Nena and I had gotten into many arguments before she stopped speaking to me about her. She kept defending Ms. Barb, so I was just going to stay out of it and worry about my seed.

When I saw her open the door to the duplex I got out the car to help her. I hadn't seen her in a few days. My little shorty was going to be big looking at Nena's stomach. She had three big bags full of presents. She looked like she was struggling with them but her stubborn ass wasn't going to ask for help. I walked up the steps. We didn't speak, I just grabbed the presents and helped her down the steps and into the car.

After putting everything in the trunk I got in and we pulled off. "How you feel?" I asked looking at her then back at the road. I put my hand on her stomach. I don't give a fuck how mad I made Nena she would always let me connect with my daughter.

"I'm not feeling too good, but I'll be okay," she looked over at me.

"Are you sure? We can just chill at my crib today and I'll cook for us," I suggested.

Nena frowned her face up, rolled her eyes and looked out the window. "No thank you," she said without looking at me.

I shook my head. This was going to be a long ride. I started to tell her about Ebony and me, but I decided to wait until later. She wasn't fucking with me and I know she would just make some smart-ass comment.

I turned up the radio when Meek Mill featuring Tory Lanez *Litty* came on. I zoned out as we hit the highway. Ten minutes into the drive Nena reached over and turned the music off. I looked over at her, she had a look of worry on her face.

"You good?" I asked.

She looked down and shook her head no, "I think my water just broke!"

I started speeding up to get off the highway at the next exit, I was scared. When we finally got off the expressway I pulled over jumping out the car and running over to her side to check.

"It hurts Quan!" she cried looking at me like she was afraid.

"I know baby I got you okay? Look at me, this is what we've been waiting for I'm going to grab a towel from the trunk to put under you then I'm going to get you to the hospital."

"Noooo! Please Quan don't leave me please," she whined.

She was fucking me up. I knew she was scared but we had to get going. I pulled my hand out of hers running to the back I opened my trunk. I took two towels out my gym bag and rushed back to the front. She managed to lift herself up, so I could slide it under her and I gave her one to hold. I jumped back in the car and speed off to the hospital.

I held her hand the whole time and managed to call my mom she said she was waiting for the car to pick her up so she could head to Harley's house. I was thanking God she was still in the city. I told her Nena was in labor and to meet us at the hospital she told me she would call Harley and Sundae and we hung up.

"I'm so sorry I've been acting like a bitch Quan I'm so sorry!" she cried. It seemed like her contractions were coming fast and she was in so much pain.

"Nena I'm not thinking about that shit baby, we are almost there." I sped down Broad Street.

"I know but I just have to say this, I was acting out because I love you Quan like I really love you. I'm in love with you and have been for a long time, oh my gosh!" she screamed and squeeze my hand as another contraction hit her like a city bus.

I told her to keep calm, she put the towel over her face and cried for the rest of the ride. I wasn't about to get into talks about our issues right now. I wanted to get her to the hospital and I wanted my daughter to get here safe.

Nena's phone rung and she looked at it. She hit the talk button and started crying harder. I heard Harley's and Sundae's voice come through the phone telling her they were on the road and would be here soon.

Harley told me my mom was already there and waiting for us. Ten minutes later we pulled up. I jumped out and called for help. Two guys came out one with a wheel chair helping her out the front seat. Once Nena was out the car I went to valet parking and handed the guy my keys.

I called my mom and we met up, once Nena was checked into the hospital we went upstairs so she could be admitted for delivery.

I sat there while the nurses asked her questions and my mom helped her undress and get comfortable. We were told by her doctor that she was already eight centimeters and it wouldn't be long before the baby arrived.

———

"*P*ush Nena come on baby you got this!" My mom cheered her on as she held her leg. Nena had been pushing for about thirty minutes.

"I can't Mrs. Savannah, it hurts so bad!" she cried.

"Look at me Nena!" I told her. She turned her head facing me as she cried. "I was going to wait until our baby got here but I'm going to tell you now, I love you okay? I love you so fucking much, no games," I said wiping her forehead with my hand.

Before she could respond another contraction came and she started pushing like her life depended on it, the next thing I heard was cries. My baby girl was finally here.

I stood there frozen as the doctor asked me if I wanted to cut the umbilical cord. I reached over and grabbed the scissors. After I cut it they took her over to this little bed and cleaned her off.

I watched as the nurses did their thing cleaning her up taking her temperature and washing her off, they kept saying she looks good and healthy.

"You did good baby!" I said kissing Nena on the lips. Moments later the nurse brought our baby over and handed her to Nena. She instantly started crying.

"She is perfect!" Nena said looking at her. She looked over at my mom and they both were crying.

I couldn't believe, I was a father and my daughter was so beautiful.

"She is perfect, Nena," my mom said wiping her eyes. She looked over at me and smiled.

When it was time for Nena to get cleaned up, the nurse put the baby in my arms and I fell more in love with her. I couldn't tell who she looked like because right now she didn't look like anyone.

I started thinking about my dad and how I wish he was here to meet his granddaughter but I learned from the best, my baby girl was good I never in my wildest thoughts believed I could love someone so much that's only been here less than an hour.

My mom came over and kissed my forehead. "I'm so happy for you baby," she smiled.

"Thanks mom she is so beautiful. Thanks for being here to help Nena through this," I said looking up at her.

"I wouldn't have missed it for the world, and Nena did a great job." She looked over at Nena who was fast asleep.

I gave the baby to my mom, so she could bond with her. Nena was in and out of sleep, about a half hour later the nurses came to take the baby to the nursery and transport Nena to her room.

I wasn't feeling them taking my baby, so I went with the nurse to see where she was going to be while my mom followed Nena to her room.

I stood outside the nursery just staring at my baby. I wasn't sure how long I had been standing here until my phone started ringing. I looked at it and hit the talk button. It was Harley.

"Quan, Sundae and I just parked come down and meet us and hurry up!" she yelled into the phone like I was deaf. I told her I would be right there and hung up.

When I reached the lobby, they were coming out the gift shop with balloons, teddy bears flowers and candy.

"Why the hell did yawl buy all this shit man?" I said taking some of the stuff from them.

"Congratulations Quan!" they said in unison.

Harley hugged me first then Sundae. "I'm so happy for the both of you! Mommy sent me a picture she is beautiful!" Harley said, she kept smiling.

"She really is, I can't wait to spoil my goddaughter!" Sundae said with excitement.

I shook my head at them both as we headed to the elevator, they asked how the delivery went and I told them Nena was a true soldier. She delivered our daughter with no medicine. That shit looked like it hurt. A few times I got light headed thinking I was going to faint.

When we got into the room Nena was holding the baby and talking to my mom who sat right beside the bed. Nena looked so beautiful if I wasn't sure before today I was sure now I wanted to be with Nena and Nena only.

She looked up when she saw us she said, "You guys made it! Come meet our new edition Nalani Quinna Smith," Nena smiled.

I stood by the door and just watched all the women love over my daughter. This had to be the happiest day of my life.

"Yo, I'm going to go pass your house now Nena and get your overnight hospital bag and the bag you packed for the baby, what do you want me to tell your mom unless you're letting her stay there alone while you're here?" I asked.

"Yes, all the bags are in my closet in my room, umm I tried calling her on the cellphone I got her, but she's not answering. I left her a message letting her know to call me, so I can get her a hotel room, I don't feel comfortable leaving her alone in my house for two days," she confessed.

"Just make sure you lock the door back when you leave, and make sure the windows are locked please. She doesn't have a key to my house, so she just won't be able to get in if she tried," she said.

"I'll ride with you, so you can drop me off at your place. I'm tired and need a nap she leaned over and kissed Nena on her forehead.

"You did a great job baby, thanks for this wonderful Christmas gift and just to let you know, you spoiled the baby shower, we were mixing that in with Christmas she laughed.

"Oh my gosh! Sorry guys," she laughed.

"Don't worry, I'll make sure to bring everything to you when you and baby Nalani comes home," my sister said.

I told Nena I would be back as soon as I can, and my mom and I left the hospital.

"She is so beautiful Quan, if your daddy were here he would be spoiling her right now day one," she laughed.

"I know mom," I looked over at her grabbing her hand.

"I just want you to do right by Nena and the baby okay? I'm not asking you to be with her if that's not what you want but do right by her and if that little girlfriend of yours don't accept the baby then you have a decision to make," she said.

"Mom let me just say this nobody is coming between me and my baby girl okay? And don't worry about Ebony I broke it off with her, so you don't have to worry about that," I assured her.

"Good, I didn't like her little ass anyway. I can tell how jealous she would have been of my grandbaby." She shook here head. I didn't comment on that because I didn't know how she would have acted but it didn't matter anymore.

I dropped my mom off at my house then went to Nena's to get the stuff to take back to the hospital. I made sure everything was in order before I left. I also made sure all the windows were locked so her smoker ass mom couldn't get in then I headed back to the hospital to spend time with them.

When I made it to her room it was almost eight which meant visiting hours were over, so Harley and Sundae had left. I had stopped at Salad Works for Nena and got her some food. She was laying down on her side watching the baby sleep in the little bassinet the hospital provided.

"Hey," she said slowly sitting up taking the food from me.

"I started to bring you some pasta or fried chicken, so I'm glad you called," I laughed.

"No, those days are over for a while. I have to get my body back together. Nalani had me putting on way too much weight," she laughed opening the salad and putting some in her mouth.

"I'll take you no matter what your body looks like," I was dead ass serious.

Nena didn't say anything she just shook her head and rolled her eyes at me. The room got quiet she ate her food and watched television.

I went into the bathroom and washed my hands and when I came out I took my hoody off grabbed the blanket putting it over me and slowly picked Nalani up out the bassinet. I placed her on my chest taking a seat in the chair.

I noticed Nena was acting a little weird, not looking at me. She kept her eyes on the show she was watching and when she was done she drank her water and started playing with her phone.

"Yo, you good?" I asked looking at her with a strange look on my face.

She finally turned around and looked at me and said "Yes, I'm good why?"

"Nena come on now, you acting all weird and shit talk to me," I urged.

She took a deep breath. "Did you mean what you said when I was giving birth to the baby? I remember you saying you loved me and all. Was that just to motivate me to push?" she asked.

I was quiet for a second just taking in her beauty. I was mad at myself for ever playing this game with her and putting her through the dumb shit I put her though.

"Nena, I meant everything I said baby, I love the shit out of you and I'm tired of playing games. I was mad because you kept playing me like a young nigga and I apologize alright?" I got up and put the baby back in the bassinet.

"I'm sorry for everything I did too, especially being bipolar as you would say," we both laughed.

I leaned down and kissed her lips. "Thank you for having my baby. You the shit ma alright?" she laughed, and I kissed her again.

I stayed at the hospital until the nurses came and got the baby she took her back to the nursery once Nena fell asleep I left so I could go home and get some rest.

A **few days later**
"Baby turn that rap music off, Nalani don't need to hear all that cursing," Nena said to me shaking her head.

"What? She is not even a week old and so what she is going to love rap music," we both laughed.

I turned down the radio, so Nena could stop bitching as we drove to her duplex. We had fought yesterday about where she was going after she was discharged.

Even though we were on the same page now about our feeling for each other Nena wanted to take things slow and I was going to respect that.

I know she thought I was feeding her a bunch of bullshit and wasn't done with Ebony, but I was going to let her see that for herself.

We both decided our focus right now was learning how to be parents, we wanted all our attention to be on Nalani.

When we pulled up to Nena's house I got out and helped her out the car. I opened the back door and put the blanket over my daughter face. It was cold as shit out here.

When we got inside the building Nena went to open the door, but it was cracked. I handed her the baby car seat and went in first. The shit looked like it had been ransacked.

"Yo what the fuck?" I said walking through the house. Nena followed me to the back where her room was placing the baby car seat on the floor.

"Quan I can't breathe!" she said holding her chest as tears rolled down her face. I stood there looking at her bedroom. The bed was turned over and her dresser drawers were on the floor.

Nena ran over to her jewelry box and everything in it was gone. "She took my auntie ring, the one she gave me before she died." She hit the floor and cried.

I'm not even sure how the fuck her mom got in here. I had made sure to put the locks on the door and secure the windows, so this shit had me tripping.

I went over to Nena and got on the floor with her and held her while she cried. She just kept repeating *why* as I held her tight.

I waited until she got herself together then we looked through the rest of the apartment. This bitch even took the stuff out the baby nursery.

Nena had put so much work in the design for the room and the furniture now her dope fiend mom done came in here and took all the baby's shit.

"She took everything we brought for Naleni, my expensive shoes jewelry and how the fuck did she get my living room set out?" she picked up the vase that was on the floor and threw it, it shattered everywhere.

The baby started crying Nena ran over and rocked the car seat. "Mommy is sorry baby. Shhh," she said wiping her eyes.

"I locked the damn door so how the fuck did she get in here?" I asked

"I don't know Quan I never gave her my keys. Oh my gosh," Nena said putting her hand over her mouth.

"I did, last week. I sent her to the store to get me some snacks. It took her ass about an hour to come back. She must have stopped off and made a copy, fuck!" she said staring into space.

"Well listen, let's go. One of my homies is a locksmith. I'll have him come and change the locks. I know you said you want to take things slow, but you can't stay here I don't feel safe with yawl here." She shook her head okay and got up off the floor.

"Let me go pack some clothes, we're going to have to go get the baby a crib," she said.

"I know. We can drop her off to my mom and if you don't feel up to it, I'll have Sundae go with me," I told her.

While Nena packed her things, I called my homie and gave him the address. He said he would be here in an hour to change the locks.

Once Nena had all her things we headed out to my apartment. So many things were going through my head. I wanted to smack the shit out of her mom for hurting her and taking all her shit. Woman or not, she needed her ass whipped.

I wasn't worried about the little shit she took or even what she took from the baby all that shit was replaceable, but I know how much that ring meant to Nena. She wore it all the time and for her mom to come in and steal her dead sister's ring that was given to her daughter was fucked up.

When we got in the house Nena and I briefly told my mom what had happened, she couldn't believe the shit either.

"She is sick Nena that's all, I'm so sorry," she said hugging her.

Nena and my mom talked for a few minutes and Nena said she wanted to lay down for a few minutes. We left the baby with my mom and went into my bedroom closing the door.

She took off her clothes. I handed her a tee shirt and she got in bed. "I texted Sundae while we were in the car she said she would go with you to get the stuff the baby needs. I'm not up to it," she said looking at me as she adjusted the pillow under her head.

"Alright baby. Don't worry about none of this shit, I got you okay?" I told her.

"I trust you Quan, I just can't believe she would take all my shit and the only thing I wanted to do was help her. I swear when I see her I'm fucking her up, mom or not," she said closing her eyes then looking up at the ceiling.

I rubbed her leg and leaned over and kissed her lips. "Get some rest and when I come back we can set Naleni's crib up," I told her.

I kissed her again. "Alright I'll be back later." I got up to leave.

When I got in the car I texted Sundae and told her I was on my way. I looked at the phone and saw a few text messages from Ebony. I ignored that shit and pulled off.

I wasn't about to reply to her, I had other shit to focus on like making this money and taking care of my family. My daughter was finally here, and a nigga was happy.

25

Chapter Twenty Five "Harley"

*N*ew Year's Eve

"*B*aby where are you? It's almost nine o'clock," I whined into the phone talking to Epic.

"I'm getting in the car right now I promise. I'll be there. You got my shit laid out?" he asked. I could here him getting into the car and starting it.

"Epic I put my all into this birthday party for you. Please give me one-night baby, please!" I was getting a little annoyed feeling like I had to beg to celebrate his birthday.

"I swear I'm on my way. I do a lot of shit, but have I ever stood you up for anything Harley?" I could hear the seriousness in his voice.

I took a deep breath. "No you haven't please just hurry and you know we have to pick up Sundae," I reminded him.

We said our goodbyes and hung up. I got in the shower, so I could be almost ready when he got here.

I was so excited because at midnight it would be Epic's birthday.

I was undecided about what to do and decided last minute to throw him a party at a club.

Sundae had helped me with getting the word out and finding the right space. I had hired the best security courtesy of Rock's wife Keshia.

I had taken a liking to Keshia after Rock's passing, she helped keep me sane when I was missing Epic when he had to go on business trips or just the day to day of him being the boss.

She kept it one hundred with me about being a hustler's wife and the bullshit that came along with it. The cops the killings and especially the bitches. I wasn't stupid. I knew women came for Epic, I just had to learn to trust him and believe that he won't step out on me.

No matter how much I love him I wasn't ever going to play the fool so if it ever came out that he was stepping out on me I would be out the door so fast.

I got out the shower and brushed my teeth, I went into our room and put lotion all over my body. I went over to my jewelry box and picked up my engagement ring. It was so beautiful. I still can't believe Epic proposed to me.

I heard the front door to the condo open. Moments later Epic appeared in the doorway. I looked up and he was smiling at me with those hazel eyes, my baby was so fine.

"What are you smiling at?" I rolled my eyes.

"I told you I was on my way," he walked over and kissed my lips.

"You better had been, now can you get in the shower, so we can get ready? Sundae is already cursing me out. You know how she is about time," I laughed.

"I'm not scared of Sundae." He leaned over and pulled on my towel and it fell open.

"Nooooo," I laughed as he picked me up and carried me to the bathroom I wrapped my legs around his waist.

"I just showered Epic, stop," I was laughing so hard.

"You know I don't like showering alone," he laughed sitting me on the sink as he got undressed. I bit my bottom lip when he dropped his pants and his dick stood at attention. My baby had the most beautiful penis I had ever seen.

After he turned the water on he picked me up and walked into the shower. "Don't drop me Epic," I said as he kissed me.

"Have I ever dropped you before baby?" he said sliding me down on his dick. I closed my eyes and started moving up and down as the water hit us in the face.

"Damn baby this my pussy right?" he asked as he palmed my ass.

"Yes, it's yours forever," I moaned.

I held on to his neck as I rode him faster, holding my head back letting the hot water beat on my face.

"I love you! Oh my gosh!" I yelled as we came together.

Epic slowly put me down. He kissed me again then we helped wash each other. When we were done we got out the shower and walked into the room, so we could finally get ready for the party.

"We're going to be late messing around with you nasty," I said texting Sundae letting her know we were leaving soon.

"Chill out, it's only nine thirty," he laughed as he buttoned his shirt.

I went over to the mirror to check myself out. I had on a black cat suit that covered my breasts, the sides were cut out showing bare skin and most of my stomach the only thing that was covered was my belly button , the fabric connected to the bottom half of my cat suit. The legs were skinny, and I wore a pair of stilettos.

"Where the hell you think you're going with that on Harley?" Epic said turning around looking at me.

"What do you mean? My outfit is just right for the club," I said spinning around.

"No, fuck that. Take that off, you not gong out looking like that pregnant with my baby." He shook his head.

"Epic don't be like that! It's your birthday, it's New Year's Eve. I look fine," I said walking over to him putting my arms around his waist. He leaned down and kissed my lips.

"Change your clothes Harley or we stay in tonight," he said kissing me again.

I sucked my teeth and let him go. He slapped me on the ass. "I love you baby," he said as he snickered.

"Whatever Epic." I walked into the closet to pull out the second outfit I brought. A part of me knew he was going to tell me to change my clothes.

Shortly after I was coming out the closet dressed in a button up black dress. I accented it with a gold belt and some black thigh high boots my faux lock braids were up in a bun. I put my jewelry on sprayed my perfume and grabbed my clutch purse.

When I walked into the living room Epic was on the phone with his Nana. I heard her singing to him. I smiled and grabbed our house keys.

"Alright Nana, I promise I'll be safe tonight. No Harley is not coming. Yes, I know she can't go to parties while she's pregnant with your great grand baby." He looked up at me shaking his head likes she could see him.

He got quiet for a second and I wonder what she was saying then he said, "Yes, I'm planning to visit him next week, I've been busy," he said.

He told her he loved her and hung up. I noticed his whole mood changed and it had something to do with his father.

"Are you okay baby?" I asked.

"Yeah, I'm good let's go because Sundae called and cursed me out before my Nana called," he chuckled but I could tell he was bothered about something.

I had to remember what Keshia told me, she said don't ask too many questions about the game and if Epic wanted me to know certain things he would tell me and if not, it was for my protection.

"Alright let's go celebrate your birth!" I smiled.

Epic locked the door and we headed downstairs to the car.

Big Bang was sitting in the car waiting for us as he sang along with the Temptations.

"Bang my nigga you need to turn this old shit off man," Epic and I laughed.

"Boss, you are way too young to know what good music sounds

like. I have to school you later, right Ms. Harley?" He looked at me and I laughed agreeing with him.

"Yeah, okay old head," Epic said as Bang turned the music down and drove out the parking lot.

I laid on Epic's chest as we drove to get Sundae. Epic was on his phone. My baby never had a night off. I dozed off on his chest. I didn't want to admit it, but I was so damn tired. The baby was draining me, but I wouldn't miss celebrating Epic's birthday for anyone.

"Babe wake up we're here," Epic gently shook me.

I sat up and stretched when I looked out the window Sundae was walking down the steps of my parent's house.

My bestie looked so pretty, she had on a barely their olive color dress with no bra. Sundae's beast stood up at attention, she had surgery after EJ. They were natural, but she had them lifted a few years back, so the dress was perfect, she wore nipple covers and the dress barely covered her ass. She had on knee boots, her hair was in a side bun she was showing off for sure and I was loving it.

"Hi family," she cooed as she got in and air kissed me.

Epic looked at us and shook his head. "Where the fuck is you going dressed like this and why is your coat in your hand? It's cold as shit out here. You want Eric to go to jail tonight," he shook his head.

Sundae rolled her eyes. "Do I look like I'm concerned about Eric these days? Nope, we broke up Epic you know that," she took her mirror out her purse to check her hair.

"That space shit doesn't mean nothing. Yawl better not start no shit tonight man," he said shaking his head.

I didn't tell Epic about Sundae and Truth because she made me promise not to. She told me she slept with him and he told her he wanted her to be his, but niggas always said slick shit like that when they were inside you, so she wasn't taking what he said seriously. I could tell she was feeling him but only time would tell how all this would play out and I'm hoping Epic don't get blamed for any of this.

"I'm mad as hell Nena is not coming out tonight, I need my partner in crime," Sundae sucked her teeth.

"I know my mom said she is over there spoiling the baby. Shit, they both are and EJ swears up and down that Nalani belongs to him," we laughed.

"I know, he couldn't wait until I dropped him off earlier. He ran right in there and over to her crib," Sundae said.

"Your brother is coming right? He told me he was," Epic asked.

"Yeah he is. He said he's already there. I told him he better be on his best behavior," Sundae and I laughed.

"Right, Nena already told me to keep a close eye on him," she said checking her lip stick.

Twenty minutes later we were pulling up to the club. Big Bang let us out and just like Eric's party months ago, niggas were lined up to get in.

We walked into the club and it was packed. I did notice a lot of chicks were in attendance. At first, I was feeling some type of way, but I wanted all these hoes to know I was here to stay.

"Give it up for the Birthday boy! My Nigga Epic is in the building Happy Birthday!" the DJ said, and the spotlight was turned on us. Epic leaned down and kissed the side of my cheek and put his hand up showing love to everyone that came out.

He grabbed my hand and we headed to the bar. I laughed to myself as all these thirsty females gave me a nasty look.

Work by Rihanna blasted through the speakers. I started dancing on Epic and running my hand over his dick. I turned around and started twerking on him, he was enjoying it I leaned up against his chest my back to him and ran my hand down his neck.

I turned around and kissed his lips then we headed towards the bar, the whole crew was in the building shaking Epic's hand as we placed our order.

"Happy Birthday Epic," Kayla came walking up towards us. I rolled my eyes.

"What the fuck do you want bitch? I know the dick is A one but there are rehabs for bitches like you," I laughed as I sipped my water.

Kayla rolled her eyes and turned her attention to Epic "Anyway, I was just coming to say Happy Birthday," she smiled.

Epic just looked at her and give her a stern look. "Get the fuck away from me Kayla, you know better," he said and turned his attention back to me.

She smiled and kept going. That bitch was up to something and as soon as I drop this load I'm going to beat her ass for calling my baby a bastard.

Epic ran his mouth across my ear. "My dick is still hard from that little dance you just did so since you wanted to put on a show you need to handle my man down there," he put my hand on his dick.

I laughed and grabbed his hand as we headed to the back to find the bathroom. I was never into public sex but just thinking about it made me horny.

26

Chapter Twenty Six "Sundae"

J grabbed my drink from the bar and stood off to the side taking in my surroundings. It was hot as hell in here and niggas were everywhere. I was a little irritated because I was missing Truth like crazy.

I hadn't seen him since the morning he dropped me off after our night in Atlantic City. We talked and texted every day, we were even having phone sex. I giggled to myself as I thought about how he had me cumming so damn hard just from me playing with myself.

"Hey Sis," Quan said walking up and hugging me.

"Hey Daddy!" I smiled.

"Yeah a nigga got a little shorty now."

Quan was going to be a great father. I was so happy for him and how he was stepping up trying to be there for Nena after her mom robbed her for all her shit.

"I was looking for Harley and Epic, but I don't know where they went. I'm about to get up out of here. It's almost midnight and I told Nena I would be home to bring in the New Year with her so tell my nigga I said Happy Birthday," he kissed my cheek.

"I see you Quan, a family man now," I said as he walked away he shook his head smiling and headed towards the exit.

I looked toward the V.I.P section and saw Vanessa all up in Eric's face he was looking annoyed like he didn't want to be bothered, the whole scene looked suspicious to me and I was about to see what the fuck was going on.

I made my way through the crowd when they saw me Vanessa backed up. "Hey baby I was just looking for you," Eric said coming over grabbing me by the waist and kissing my cheek as I starred at Vanessa.

"Hey Sundae, you're wearing that dress girl," she smiled this bitch was fake as fuck.

"She is. My baby is the shit," Eric tried kissing me on the lips, but I moved my head.

Vanessa moved past us and went down the five steps leading to the main floor. I turned my attention back to Eric.

"What the fuck was that all about before I walked over here?" I yelled.

"It was nothing man she a thirst bucket," he waved me off.

"I swear if you're fucking that bitch Eric I'm going to fuck the both of yawl up," I threatened.

"Man stop with all that shit, I'm not fucking that hoe," he said hugging me.

"You heard what I said," I pointed at him.

"Are you coming home with me man? I can't take this shit anymore baby. I haven't fucked any of these hoes since you left me that night. I miss you. I'm trying so hard to prove to you that I'm ready," he confessed.

I admired his handsome face and for once I didn't know what to say, I was torn. I heard someone calling him from across the room he turned around to see two of his workers waving for him to come over.

"Give me a second baby, I'll be back," he kissed my lips and walked off.

I sat down at the table and ordered me a drink. While I waited I texted Truth to let him know I was thinking about him, but he didn't reply.

The waitress brought my drink over. I sipped it as I danced in my seat to *For Free* by DJ Khaled and Drake.

I felt someone come up behind me and bite my neck, the smell was so familiar I turned around and Truth was standing there. I was happy, shocked and nervous at the same time.

I got up and he pulled me into him kissing my lips, it felt so right. When we pulled back he had a smile so wide across his face.

"Damn are you happy to see a nigga? Why you looking like you saw a ghost baby?" he said rubbing my ass.

"Of course, I'm happy to see you. I'm just shocked that's all, you said you weren't coming back for another week," I said.

"I wanted to surprise you, I couldn't spend Christmas with you, so I wanted to bring in the new year with you," he leaned down and kissed me again.

"I just saw Epic and Harley at the bar. That nigga is fucked up. She said she was about to come over here as soon as she can pull him away from the bar, and what the fuck you got on? You look good. I can't wait to take this shit off you tonight," he kissed me again.

"Hey brother why you didn't tell me you were coming?" I heard a female say but the voice sounded to familiar.

I turned around and my eyes got wide "Brother!" I said I was so confused.

"Yes, hoe this is my brother, and why are you over here hugged up with her?" Kayla said folding her arms looking between me and Truth.

"Yo, Kayla watch you damn mouth, yawl no each other?" he asked.

"I can't believe this shit, yeah I know her and call me another hoe Kayla and see what happens. I'm saying are you two like blood sister and brother?" I was hoping they were like neighbors that grew up together that claimed to be family.

"Yeah we share the same damn parents and you need to pay me

my money for fucking up my car," she had her hand out like I was about to put money in it. She couldn't be serious.

"Wait, this is who fucked your car up?" Truth looked shocked.

"Yeah, I fucked her car up because she fucked mine up after I beat her ass at the mall!"

"You didn't beat my ass I slipped on a shoe, and why the hell you over here hugged up with her Truth? Do you know her man is Eric?" she said.

She was calling herself telling on me. I couldn't stand this bitch. I saw Harley walking towards us she came up the steps and stood between us.

"What the fuck is going on over here Sundae? Kayla back the fuck up," she said.

"Everything is good over here Harley we're just talking. My sister Kayla was just leaving right?" he gave her a look.

"Sister?" Harley had a confused look on her face. "Like blood siblings?" she looked at me.

I shook my head yeah. I couldn't believe this was the sister he kept talking about. Truth never mentioned a name and I didn't care to ask.

"Okay, I'm going to leave but yawl better watch your backs because this shit is not over," she threatened.

"You don't want no smoke barbie get your fake ass out of here!" I yelled.

Truth grabbed my arm turning me towards him telling me to stop the bullshit. I heard Eric calling my name and I jumped. I almost forgot he was here.

"Oh shit!" I heard Harley say as she stepped back while Eric walked towards us.

"What the fuck is going on over here? Why you got your hands on my girl my nigga?" Eric asked. I could see the fire in his eyes. I was regretting coming to this party tonight.

"Your girl? Sundae you didn't tell Eric?" he smiled down at me, but I could tell he was mad.

I wanted to die. I just stood there looking between the two of them. For once in my life I had nothing to say.

"What the fuck is he talking about Sundae? I swear on my fucking momma you better start talking. Are you fucking this nigga?" he asked looking down in my eyes.

I just stood there I looked over at Truth and he was waiting for me to answer Eric. He looked so mad I could tell he thought I was full of shit.

I shook my head yeah as I looked at the ground. Eric reached pass me and tried to hit Truth, but I was standing between them, so he didn't connect with his face like he planned.

I screamed, and members of the crew jumped up to try and stop them as I pushed Eric back.

"Move bitch, I should break your fucking neck!" he gripped me up by my dress. "You just stood in my face and said you fucking this nigga! I have a bullet with your name on it Sundae! I'll raise EJ by my damn self!" Spit was flying out of his mouth. He was zoned out.

Epic walked up I heard him tell Harley to get out the V.I.P. He got between us. He had to tell Eric a few times to let me go he finally listened.

I heard some of the crew telling Truth to chill because he kept telling Eric to get out my face. This whole scene was ugly.

I saw Vanessa come up behind Eric and grab his arm. He looked at her like she was crazy and pulled away.

"Don't worry about her Eric she doesn't deserve you, we can start our own family. I'm the one carrying your baby," she said.

The room started spinning. In my mind everything was muted around me the music had stopped playing and the yelling had ceased. the only thing I heard was carrying your baby. I moved past Eric and Epic and hit the shit out this bitch.

She was on the step so when I hit her she fell back, and I started beating her ass trying to bash her head into the ground I wanted blood. I felt someone pick me up off her and I kicked her as I was pulled away.

"Calm the fuck down," Truth whispered in my ear as he squeezed me walking me to the exit. I saw Harley following behind us.

When we got outside Truth put me down. I tried to get pass him to go back inside, I was going to kill them both. I put that on my son.

"What the fuck are you doing?" Truth pushed me away from the club.

"He slept with that bitch that I party with. They stabbed me in the fucking back!" I cried.

"Why the fuck you even care?" he yelled in my face his fist was balled up.

"I don't care it's the fucking principle!" I yelled back at him trying to get pass, so I could go back in he kept pushing me further away from the entrance.

He stood there looking down the street before turning his attention back to me. "Fuck you Sundae! This nigga fucked around on you for years and almost gave you an STD and you're in there fighting one of his bitches like a fucking teenager? You got me out here arguing with you about a nigga? You know what? Go be with his ass, I'm over this shit," he said trying to walk pass me.

My heart rate sped up. We were just getting started and the thought of Truth not being apart of my life scared me. I ran after him grabbing his arm.

"No, Truth I'm sorry don't leave. I don't want Eric where are you going?" I pushed him in the chest.

"I told you when we were in AC what it was, you said you were ready, but you still got feeling for the nigga and it's all good ma," he was still trying to get pass me. I kept pushing him in the chest.

"Harley come get your friend I wouldn't put my hands on her, but you need to come get her out my face, so I can take my ass back to Baltimore," he said to Harley as she walked over.

"No, Truth please don't go back I said I'm sorry!" I cried.

"You're right ma you are sorry. Chasing after a nigga that don't know your worth. Grow the fuck up, only young girls fight over niggas. You're all up in the club with your ass out fighting. You still on that young girl shit. I'm cool, now move so I can get the fuck out of here."

That shit hurt. I stopped and looked at him. He moved pass me. I watched him get in his car and pull off down the street. He was going so fast a few people had to run across the street to avoid getting hit.

Harley stood in front of me with a sad look on her face. I could tell she was feeling sorry for me she wiped my eyes. I hugged her and cried in her arms.

Epic came out the club and walked over to us. "What the fuck was that, Sundae? When the hell did you start fucking with Truth?" I could tell he was mad.

"Not now babe, she's upset we need to just leave," Harley said.

I heard the people in the club count down from ten to one then everyone screamed Happy New Year. I felt awful.

"Bang took Eric out the back door to take him home. That nigga tried to pull his strap out on Vanessa, she all fucked up. Let's go. I had to threaten her. She was trying to call the cops. I got Eric's car keys. I'm dropping you off and we're going home. Yawl blew my fucking high," he said as we walked to the car.

"Happy Birthday baby," Harley said grabbing onto his arm.

"I'm sorry Epic and Happy Birthday," I said.

When we got in the car I tried to call Truth, but he kept forwarding me to voicemail. I told Epic I didn't want to go home, so he took me back to their condo.

I could tell he was mad at me, but I didn't care. He knew the only thing Eric did was cheat on me. So what I was seeing Truth, it's my business not anyone else's. I didn't owe Eric anything but an ass whipping.

The walk to the condo was quiet. I was hoping Epic wasn't taking his anger out on Harley because it was obvious she knew.

We walked in the house and Epic's phone started ringing. I figured it was Eric because he went into their bedroom and closed the door.

Harley gave me some pajamas and toiletries, so I could shower. I had a headache and my body was sore from beating Vanessa's hoe ass.

"It's going to be okay alright," Harley assured me as she hugged me.

"I fucked up Harley, now Truth is done with me forever," I shook my head.

"No, he's not Sun. I can tell he is really into you. His eyes lit up when I pointed to the VIP and he saw you vibing by yourself," she smiled.

I didn't respond to what she said. "Before you leave, where the hell were you? I was looking for you. You just left me hanging," I said remembering that I hadn't seen her since we were at the bar when we first got there.

"In one of the bathrooms being nasty," she laughed.

I threw the pillow at her she picked it up laughing as she threw it back at me.

"Yawl are some nasty freaks," I gave her the stink face.

"Oh well, and Kayla is your sister in law," we both laughed.

"I can't believe Kayla is Truth's sister, that just makes this shit more complicated," I said, and Harley shook her head in agreement.

Harley made sure I was okay then she kissed my cheek and told me goodnight. After she left I went into the bathroom and started the shower. I tried calling Truth one more time and his phone was off going straight to voicemail.

I had really fucked up, I thought. I got in the shower and cried as I washed my body until the water got cold.

27

Chapter Twenty Eight "Eric"

$\mathcal{D}$**ays later**

I was sitting in my mom's living room watching television, she needed me to come over early this morning to let the cable man in to fix her box. I must have fallen asleep after he left because when I woke up I had a shit load of missed calls and messages.

I looked at the text messages first and I had a few from Sundae I opened the thread and shook my head she was ready to fuck me up.

Sundae: When I see you Eric on everything I love we are going to fight

Sundae: You really sleep with Nena's co-worker? You are a nasty nigga. I'm guessing she is the one that had the STD?

Sundae: I hope you choke on a chicken bone low life!

I threw my phone on the couch and headed to the kitchen to get something to drink. I've been avoiding Sundae since Epic's party.

She had been calling me since that night talking about she was going to kick my ass for sleeping with Vanessa and I wasn't ready to face her yet. I had fucked up yet again by fucking another bitch.

I had to pick EJ up last weekend, but I wasn't trying to see Sundae. I had asked Nena or Harley to help me out and drop him off to me, but they weren't fucking with me either, so I had to get

Epic to bring him to me and pick him up when it was time for him to go back.

I hadn't said much to Epic about what happened that night, but I was going to. I was wondering if he knew Nena was fucking with Truth and if he did that would be fucked up and as far as friendship goes I wouldn't be sure at this point.

That's another reason I'm avoiding Sundae because I want to choke the shit out of her ass. This would be the second time she did some dumb shit, the first would be killing my baby the thought of her fucking Truth is making me want to put a bullet in both of them

I was going to see Truth when he comes to town and I can't guarantee the outcome. He is a sneaky nigga because he knew Sundae was my girl and for him to push up on her got my blood boiling.

The more I think about it I wonder how they even met and all fingers point to Epic, the two of them have never crossed paths before.

To my knowledge the first time they met was at Rock's funeral, but no words were spoken. Sundae was with me the whole time.

There were times Truth and Epic were together when I wasn't with him, so it had to be one of those times, but I was going to get to the bottom of this shit.

I would never let a bitch come between me and Epic, but Sundae was different she was damn near my wife so if Epic crossed me by hooking them up then shit was going to get ugly.

I heard the front door open and my mom walked in as I was coming out the kitchen. "Hey son, what are you still doing here? She asked putting her bags down.

"I fell asleep after the cable man left so I figured I'd stay until you got home from work to check on you," I kissed her check and took a seat on the couch.

"Well I'm happy to see you. How are you doing? Has Sundae moved back home?" She looked sympathetic.

"No, Sundae on some other shit right now. I don't know what is going on with us," I shook my head.

"Well she must be really mad at you because I've tried to call her a few times, but she has not picked up or returned my calls," she shrugged her shoulders.

"Don't sweat that shit ma," I said.

"Oh, I'm not this is not the first time she has blamed me for your actions. I know both of you guys need to get your shit together. My main concern is my grandson. Yawl go through this shit and have been since you were teenagers," she flagged her hand at me and got up.

"Are you staying for dinner? I'm going to change my clothes and start cooking," she got up and headed upstairs to change out of her work clothes.

"Yeah, I'll stay," I told her.

My phone started ringing and I saw Vanessa's hoe ass calling. I forwarded her to voicemail. I was going to kill this bitch if she didn't stop lying.

After Sundae beat her up at the party she had called and said she had to go to the emergency room because she was having pains, but I didn't give a fuck. If she would have stayed out my fucking way that night she wouldn't have gotten her ass beat.

Bitches were so sneaky. She couldn't wait to let Sundae know I had fucked her. I was still mad at myself for slipping up and fucking her without a glove but that wasn't my damn baby and I wasn't claiming shit.

My phone rang again I saw it was Cecil one of the workers we had looking for Jamal. I hit the green button and put the phone to my ear.

"This shit better be good my nigga what's up?" I said.

"We at Onyx, shorty just walked in what do you want us to do?" he asked.

"Stay right there, I'm on my way," I said hanging up heading for the front door.

I yelled upstairs and told my mom I had to leave. A nigga was happy right now. Today was going to be the day I could feel it and if it wasn't then somebody was going to die.

I got in my car and sped off to Delaware Ave I thought about calling Epic but decided to wait, he was dealing with some business and I didn't want to involve him if this bitch didn't know where he was.

I was shocked that she had finally showed up to work. I had my workers looking for her for a while now.

I pulled up to the club and parked. Niggas were outside waiting to get in that I recognized. I spoke and walked up to the bouncer. He gave me the head nod and let me in.

When I walked in *Privacy* by Chris Brown was playing, there were strippers dancing. I looked around and saw Drew and Cecil sitting in the corner.

"What's up?" I said walking over sitting with them. "Where that bitch at?" I looked around.

"In the back, she just preformed. Bitch looks horrible like she on that shit man," Cecil shook his head.

I ordered a shot and we sat back and watched the entertainment. It was getting dark outside which was perfect. I had plans for this bitch.

An hour later Drew tapped me nodding his head to the door the strippers come out of. I was assuming that was Strawberry.

"There she is man. What you want us to do?" he asked.

"Nothing, we going to watch this bitch and when she leaves we follow her," I said.

Moments later she came over and asked if we wanted a lap dance, she smiled at me looking high as shit.

"Hey Daddy, you're Eric, right?" she pointed at me.

"Why the fuck is you asking?" I questioned.

"Every bitch in here knows who you are, you want to have some fun? I'll even give you a discount," she smiled again.

Shorty looked like she used to be pretty, but you could tell she was on that shit. I was even shocked she was still working here looking like this. Onyx had nothing but pretty bitches working in here so why Strawberry was getting a check was crazy to me.

"Yeah, I do want to have some fun," I looked over at Drew and Cecil they both shook their head.

"Okay good do you want to go to the back?" she pointed.

"No, go get your shit and come with us," I told her.

"I'm with that, give me ten minutes," she said.

I grabbed her arm and told her to meet us outside. She shook her head and rushed to the back. I picked my glass up and drank my shot taking money out my pocket and throwing it on the table.

When we got outside the parking lot was full of cars but there was barely anyone outside, I saw Strawberry come out looking around the parking lot. I flashed my high beams letting her know what car I was in and she damn near ran over to the car.

She jumped her happy ass in and closed the door. Cecil sat behind her seat and Drew followed us in their car.

"I just want you to know Eric, I'm honored to be in this car with you, I can't believe I'm the chosen one," she said putting her hand on my leg. My dick didn't even get hard this bitch looked nasty.

"Yo, calm the fuck down and sit back. Get you had off me," I moved my leg letting her know to move her hand.

Her smile faded, and she sat back looking at me and then at Cecil. I drove for a while and then pulled over to a little ass block with abandoned houses.

I turned the engine off and then looked at her. She looked like she was about to shit herself. I looked down and she had peed.

"Bitch, why the fuck did you just pee on yourself in my damn car?" I said.

Cecil started laughing. I looked at him with a straight face, I was about to hit him upside his head with his own gun. He wiped that smile right off his face.

"I know who you are Eric and I know you don't play any games, I'm not sure what I did but I'm sorry," she was shaking.

"Shorty you didn't do anything and if you do as I say and don't be on no bullshit I won't hurt you. Understand?" I said looking into her eyes.

She shook her head up and down. I was trying not to be pissed that she just peed all over my leather seat.

"I know you've been kicking it with Jamal, and I need to know where he is," I said.

"He is at his mom's house. He came into town the other day from Pittsburg. I'm not sure what he went up there for," she said.

I grabbed her by the neck and started choking her dusty ass. She was trying to play me, and I was not in the mood.

"Bitch stop playing with me, you know what the fuck he went to Pittsburg for and you know he got beef with us, so stop playing with me. Now where the fuck is this nigga and I swear if you try to lie to me I'm going to crack your neck," I said through clenched teeth.

"Okay, I'm sorry he is at his mom's house we were staying at my house in Sharon Hill, but I lost my house. I swear I'm telling you the truth," she cried.

When she said Pittsburg, I knew exactly why I couldn't find that nigga and why he was in Pittsburg, but I wanted to see just how much she knew.

"So, tell me why he was in Pittsburg?" I asked sitting back in my seat.

"He said he needed more man power to get at you and Epic, so he went up there to get his cousins to help take yawl down," she wiped her nose.

"Okay so where is this crew? Did he come back with anybody?" I asked.

"No, because he said they wanted a down payment before they get involved so he came back to get up some money. He tried to rob the traps but apparently you guys switched things up and moved around so he couldn't find out any information. He needed me to get up the money, so I begged my boss to give me my job back, so I could get up enough money to help him," she cried.

I sat back in my seat trying to figure out how I was going to approach this. Jamal was dumb as shit if he thought his lame ass cousins were going to be able to bring our crew down. Like this nigga was really plotting on killing us with his clumsy ass.

I didn't know what I wanted to do with Strawberry. She was a fucking crackhead that Jamal done fucked up, but she was also plotting against us. I reached behind me taking my gun out my waist. She screamed no, I knocked her over the head and she hit her head on the window.

"Man, it's starting to smell really bad in here boss that's some strong ass Pee," Cecil said.

"I know I should shoot her ass just because she did that shit," I shook my head.

I had Cecil go get Drew out their car and put Strawberry ass in the trunk and take her to the warehouse and tie her up.

I called a few of my young hitters to watch her ass while I went to the office to get Epic to tell him the good news. Once we rounded the workers up we were going to get Jamal and take him to the warehouse to kill him, I wasn't sure what I wanted to do with pissy ass Strawberry yet.

28

Chapter Twenty Nine "Harley"

---

*E*arlier that day

"*S*o, what are your plans for today?" Epic said as he sprayed on his cologne. We had spent yesterday together which was a treat for me.

No matter what he had to do he always made sure he was at all my doctors' appointments, just like he was yesterday.

The doctor said the baby and I were doing great. After leaving the doctor's office we went out for dinner and a movie, of course I fell asleep halfway through the movie which was not surprising because that's all I did these days.

"I'm going over to Quan's to see the baby and I wanted to talk to my mom about her moving with us for a while since the house in Delaware is finally up for sale," I said as I laid across the bed watching him.

"Okay, just stop worrying, she's going to say yes," he leaned over and kissed me then headed towards the door.

"Hey babe what's up with Jay? Have you found him?" I asked.

"Harley what I tell you? Didn't I say I'm going to handle him?" he said. I could tell he was annoyed.

"I heard you Epic, but it's been months and you haven't made not one move. I'm still having a hard time with the fact that I didn't get to say goodbye to my dad," I said.

"I'm not doing this with you Harley. I know what that nigga did to you and I would never let him get away with the shit, stop acting like you don't know who I am. I said I got this, stop worrying alright?" he softened up his tone.

I didn't say anything we stood there staring at each other, when he didn't get a response he shook his head and told me to call him when I got to Quan's house.

I picked up my phone and looked at the last text from Jay, he texted me three times yesterday.

Jay: I miss you Harley and I swear if I have to I will come back to Philly. I'm ripping that baby out your fucking stomach, so I suggest you bring your ass back to Houston!"

This was the last time he was going to threaten me. Epic was taking way to long to handle this, so I was just going to take care of him myself.

I grabbed my phone and booked the last flight out of Philly to Houston. I got up and packed an overnight bag and proceeded to start my day.

I got dressed, ate breakfast and took my prenatal vitamins I rubbed my stomach and smiled when I felt the flutters in my stomach. My belly was growing but it was still small.

I grabbed my things and put them in my trunk, my plan was to visit with my mom, Nena and the baby then head to the airport.

When I got to Quan's house I used the spare key he gave me to get in, my mom was sitting on the couch holding the baby she smiled when she saw me.

"Mom you're going to spoil her rotten just like you did with EJ," I laughed going into the kitchen to wash my hands.

"So, what? I'm going to do the same with the one growing inside your belly too," she laughed.

I took a seat on the couch and she handed the baby to me, I heard the shower running and assumed Nena was in there.

"How is she doing?" I asked my mom.

"She is doing okay. Thank God for baby Nalani because she would be stuck in a depression. I can't believe Barb did that to her," my mom said shaking her head.

Nena had cried her eyes out to me over the phone when she found her apartment tore up and her most important things taken. I was shocked that Barb would play Nena like that, it's sad because she was plotting the whole time waiting for Nena to go into labor to rob her.

My girl was going to be cool, she had us and that was all that mattered.

"Mom I came to talk to you about your plans. I know you keep saying you want to get a house and all and live by yourself. I'm just not comfortable with that right now. I know you miss daddy and it's going to take some time, but I was wondering if you can just move in with Epic and I until after the baby gets here?" I asked.

"Harley, I don't want to be in your personal space. You are about to have your own family, you do not need your mom living with you," she laughed. I could see the hurt in her eyes.

"Epic and I want you to please?" I begged.

She took a deep breath. "Alright I'll move in with you guys for a while, until you get a handle on being a mother and then I'll move out Harley and I mean it," My mom said.

I smiled so wide leaning over and giving her a hug, I told her the house would be big enough and told her she would have her own space.

"Hey Harley!" Nena smiled.

"Hey mommy!" I cooed.

She came over and took a seat. Nena looked good the weight was coming off faster than she thought it was and she looked happy.

I wasn't sure if she and Quan was official yet because neither one of them had said anything, but I was glad she was here with him and they were both able to spend time with the baby.

"You talk to Sundae?" I asked.

"I did last night. My girl is so stressed out, you know she still hasn't heard from Truth and Eric is still to scared to be around her?" she shook her head.

"Yeah, the whole thing was messy, and I promise you we are not having any more parties in any club," we both laughed my mom just shook her head.

"I just wish I was there, but I'm going to see Vanessa so don't worry about that," Nena said.

We changed the subject because even though my mom knew some of what happened we didn't want to say to much. We ordered wings and watched television I kept watching the time, so I could head to the airport.

I texted Epic that I would probably spend the night over here because I didn't feel like driving and I was tired. He said he would pick me up when he was done handling his business.

I was trying to throw him off, but I know Epic and I know he wouldn't be here to pick me up until after midnight and I was going to be boarding the plane at that time.

*T*he present
I was sitting at the airport waiting for my plane to start boarding I dialed Nena's phone number and took a deep breath. When she said hello I contemplated hanging up, but I had to tell someone what my plan was.

"Hello?" Nena said in a raspy voice.

"Hey Ne, wake up I have to tell you something," I said.

"What's wrong Harley I'm up you okay?" she asked concerned.

"I'm about to tell you something and I need you to promise you will not tell anyone only if I call for help," I said.

"Okay I won't, now what is going on?" she said.

"I'm on my way to Houston to get at Jay for what he did to me. You can not tell Epic and I'm only telling you in case I don't make it back or I call for help."

"Bitch are you crazy? Harley you are pregnant first of all and second Jay's ass is crazy. You need to let Epic handle it," she whispered.

"Epic is taking way to long he is so worried about finding Jamal, and this nigga is still texting me," I confessed.

"Okay Harley well you need to tell your man. Epic has not forgotten what Jay did to you, so you need to get your ass home and tell him what is going on sis," she begged.

"Nena you promised you wasn't going to say anything and I promise you I will call you as soon as I land," I hung up.

I looked at my phone the plane would be boarding soon so I decided to go to the bathroom.

I was nervous as hell for what I was about to do, but it had to be done. I had faith I would come out alive.

29

Chapter Thirty "Epic"

J was back at the shop. The shipment had come in three days ago and business was looking good. The product that we were selling was so pure and the dope heads were loving it.

The connect loved what he saw and as promised if I get rid of everything I had he agreed to increase our product, so shit was looking good for Eric and me.

I noticed Eric had been short with me these last few days and I know it had to be about that shit that happened at my party but that was their business.

I didn't even know Sundae was fucking with Truth, so I was just as shocked as he was. I asked Harley why she didn't tell me, and she said she had made a promise to Sundae and I could respect that.

I couldn't think about the shit because it was none of my business and if Eric didn't let that affect our friendship and business none of that shit mattered to me.

I didn't have any beef with Truth, he was a grown man too and whatever he and Sundae were doing was between them but a part of me knew shit was going to get ugly.

I texted Harley that I would be to get her in about an hour and she texted back that she would be ready.

I had been thinking about our last conversation all day. I was still mad at her for thinking I wasn't going to deal with Jay. I had eyes on him and had plans on flying out to take care of him next week since no one could find Jamal's bitch ass or the jawn Strawberry he was fucking with.

I wasn't about to tell Harley what my plan was until I came back home, and the shit was taken care of. She didn't need to know my plan, I liked to keep that shit separated from our personal life.

She knew the shit I got into, but I would never sit, and pillow talk with her about it because that side of me lived in the street. She only needed to know the one part of Epic and I was going to keep it that way.

I heard a knock at the door and looked up to see Eric walking in. This nigga was smiling hard as hell making me wonder why he was here.

"What are you doing here smiling and shit?" I laughed.

"Tonight, is about to be the best night of our fucking lives, I got the drop on Jamal the workers got him from his mom house and they're taking that nigga to the warehouse as we speak," he smiled.

I stood up and went into my safe to grab my strap. Eric stood up we looked at each other dabbed and headed for the car.

While we drove to the warehouse Eric filled me in on what happened. I laughed at the thought of Jamal thinking his cousins were tough enough to get at us. That shit just made me even more mad because they all were a bunch of bitches.

We pulled up to the warehouse and I turned the engine off. We didn't say anything as we got out the car and headed inside.

Some of the workers were outside surrounding the building like always when we brought someone here to kill.

When we walked in I saw the bitch Strawberry tied up to the chair with a big ass knot on her head and blood on her forehead, when she saw me her eyes got wide. I could see the fear in her eyes.

I walked pass her and over to where Jamal was hanging from chains. He had on nothing but his boxers, he was knocked out and his face was all fucked up.

It looked like he put up a good fight when those niggas went to get him. Too bad for him he couldn't get away.

I walked over to him and smacked the shit out of him and he opened his eyes. When he saw Eric and I standing there he started smiling.

"What the fuck are you laughing for nigga?" I took my gun out and shot him in the knee the only thing that could be heard was his screams.

Eric took his gun out and shot him in the other knee, he continued to scream that did nothing but give me a rush.

"Oh, nigga you screaming now? What is all that shit you were talking when you were going behind our back robbing us and when you killed my fucking cousin?" I yelled shooting his ass in the shoulder.

"Lower that nigga!" I yelled to one of my workers.

Once Jamal was lowered I hit him in the head with the gun repeatedly until my damn hand got tired and blood covered my hand. I couldn't get the image of Rock lying on the floor dead out my head, because this bitch couldn't control his drug habit.

I backed away trying to catch my breath. I looked over at Eric. He nodded his head to me, letting me know it was time to end this shit.

I looked at Jamal and his bloody body. I was sick to my stomach at the fact that I trusted him once upon a time. I was sick because I made it easy for him to steal from us and get at my cousin because I was a loyal nigga.

One of the workers handed me a wash cloth with ammonia on it and put it under his nose. He opened his eyes and shut them I could tell he was in pain and I was loving every bit of it.

"Look at me!" I screamed.

Jamal lifted his head up and it dropped he did this a few more times before he was able to focus in on me.

"You killed my fucking mom, man!" Jamal whined.

"You killed Rock first! You trippin my nigga! None of this would have happened if you would have listened to us, I had your back man!" I yelled.

"No, you didn't yawl were trying to cut me out. I heard you was looking to replace me!" he cried in pain.

"No, we weren't Mal. I wanted you to get clean and then we were going to bring you back in," I got in his face.

"I'm sorry man, please let me down. Don't kill me E, we go back to first grade! I'm sorry I really am! I don't want to die!" he cried.

I couldn't believe he was in front of me crying after all the shit he started. All this shit could have been avoided if he would have just kept his weak ass away from the product.

I stepped back and look at him. He was a nut ass nigga. Jamal was like my damn brother I couldn't believe we were really here.

"Stop crying like a little bitch. Take this shit like a man. I'll see you in hell," I pointed my gun at him. He begged harder I let off two shots to his head.

I stood there looking at his lifeless body. I thought I was going to feel better once this nigga was dead, but I didn't feel shit.

"Yo, it's over," Eric said taking my gun, I shook my head and walked away.

I went into the bathroom located in the corner and took my shirt off. I washed my face and hands. When I came out the bathroom I handed my shirt to one of the workers, so he could burn it.

The clean-up crew was already here cleaning up Jamal. I saw Eric off to the side standing in front of Jamal's girl.

"Why the fuck this bitch still breathing?" I asked.

"Man, I'm just going to let her ass go, she over her with the shakes and shit. She need a hit, she ain't worried about us," Eric said.

I looked at him like he was crazy. Was this nigga serious? We never leave witnesses and we weren't going to start leaving them now.

"I don't give a fuck! This bitch just saw us commit a fucking murder, and she was plotting against us with that nigga. Are you fucking crazy? You're letting this shit with Sundae cloud your judgment. You know the rules, now do her ass or I will and hurry up, I have to pick Harley up," I said walking towards the door.

I heard Strawberry scream then the gun went off. "Yo, yawl let me know when this shit is all cleaned up alright?" he instructed, then caught up with me.

When we got in the car I peeled off. Eric lit a blunt and we smoked until we got back to my shop. I pulled over and handed him the blunt. We hadn't said a word the whole ride back.

"I know what just happened won't bring Rock back my nigga, but he can rest knowing we got Jamal alright?" Eric said.

I looked over and shook my head. We dabbed each other up, and he got out.

"I'll see you in the morning and don't be late," I said to him. He laughed and got in his car.

My phone rang just as I was about to drive off. I looked at it and saw Nena calling.

Eric beeped his horn as he rode pass me.

"Hello? What's up Nena? Everything good?" I asked.

"Epic I just got off the phone with Harley. She is at the airport, she said she is going to handle Jay herself. She made me promise not to say anything, but I think she is in way over her head," she said.

"What did you just say? She is about to do what?" I had to make sure I was hearing her right.

"She booked a flight to Houston. I think her flight is taken off soon."

"Fuck!" I hit the steering wheel. "Alright Nena I got this, I'm on my way to the airport keep this to yourself alright? Quan don't need to know I'm going to get her," I told her. She begged me to call her when I found Harley and we hung up.

My hand started shaking as I dialed Harley's phone number. I pulled into the street and drove as I waited for her to answer.

"Hey baby," she said like shit was good.

"Harley what the fuck are you doing? Where the hell are you?" I said.

"I'm at the house, getting ready for bed," she lied.

She was fucking me up right now. Harley never lied to me and for her to be lying right now was making me mad.

"Harley my patience is running thin right now. I just talked to

Nena you're at the airport on your way to Houston trying to play a game you know nothing about!" I yelled.

"I'm doing something you refuse to do! You're so focused on work, I'll handle this myself!" she said.

I chuckled, she was pissing me off. "Harley I'm on my way to the airport. I'll call you when I get there. Have your ass outside because you're tripping right now. Did you forget you're pregnant?" I yelled.

I heard the announcement on the speaker say that the flight to Houston was boarding. Harley was really at the fucking airport on a mission like she was Angelina Jolie in the movie *Salt* or some shit.

"I can't do that. I have to handle this myself. I'll see you when I get back. I love you, bye," she said before hanging up.

I looked at the phone and the call ended. I tried calling her back, but it went straight to voicemail.

I stopped at the light and dialed Eric, a car pulled up beside me and when I looked up I saw a gun and the next thing I heard was the sound of the gun going off and my window shattering.

Pop! Pop! Pop! Boom!

"Yeah! Nigga what!"

To Be Continued...